"Touching you is a pleasure all its own."

Ty dropped the brush and stroked her hair with his hands. "A crowning glory," he whispered, feeling the way the silken strands clung to his fingers in a soft caress deep inside him.

Dixie reached back and caught hold of one of his hands. She drew it forward with her fingers curled within his, and pressed a kiss on his palm.

"Thank you, Ty."

"The pleasure, as I said, is all mine."

Dixie felt the heat of the sun disappear from her face. Her eyes drifted open to find Ty leaning over her. Dark and dangerous, he appeared both a dark angel and a tempting devil.

Gently rubbing his knuckles from her cheekbone to her chin, he eased her head back until his breath blended with hers.

"You know you're safe with me, Dixie. As safe as you want to be...!"

Dear Reader,

This month, we are very proud to bring you *Once a Maverick*, the first in a new Western series by Theresa Michaels featuring a trio of brothers, the infamous Kincaids. The first story is about a young woman bent on revenge and the ex-gunslinger who comes to her aid. We hope you enjoy *Once a Maverick*, and keep an eye out for the next title in the series, *Once an Outlaw*, in December. And don't miss Theresa Michaels in our August short-story collection, RENEGADES, featuring *New York Times* bestselling author Heather Graham Pozzessere, and our own Merline Lovelace.

And speaking of Ms. Lovelace, she also has a new book out this month, *His Lady's Ransom*, a sweeping medieval tale of a nobleman who sets out to discourage his brother's infatuation with a notorious woman, only to find himself under the captivating spell of Lady Madeline.

Also this month are a new title from the author of *Across Time*, Nina Beaumont, *Tapestry of Dreams*, a passionate tale of danger and desire, and a new Western from author DeLoras Scott, *Addie's Lament,* the heartwarming love story of a young woman determined to make a better life for herself and the man who seems to always want to get in her way.

Whatever your taste in historical reading, we hope you'll enjoy all four titles, available wherever Harlequin Historicals are sold.

Sincerely,

Tracy Farrell

Please address questions and book requests to:
Harlequin Reader Service
U.S.: 3010 Walden Ave., P.O. Box 1325, Buffalo, NY 14269
Canadian: P.O. Box 609, Fort Erie, Ont. L2A 5X3

THERESA MICHAELS

Once a Maverick

Harlequin Books

TORONTO • NEW YORK • LONDON
AMSTERDAM • PARIS • SYDNEY • HAMBURG
STOCKHOLM • ATHENS • TOKYO • MILAN
MADRID • WARSAW • BUDAPEST • AUCKLAND

ISBN 0-373-28876-X

ONCE A MAVERICK

Copyright © 1995 by Theresa DiBenedetto.

This edition published by arrangement with Harlequin Enterprises B.V.

® and TM are trademarks of the publisher. Trademarks indicated with ® are registered in the United States Patent and Trademark Office, the Canadian Trade Marks Office and in other countries.

Printed in U.S.A.

Books by Theresa Michaels

Harlequin Historicals

A Corner of Heaven #104
Gifts of Love #145
Fire and Sword #243
Once a Maverick #276

THERESA MICHAELS

is a former New Yorker who resides in South Florida with her husband and daughter—the last of eight children—and three "rescued" cats. Her avid interest in history and her belief in the power of love are combined in her writing. She has received the *Romantic Times* Reviewer's Choice Award for Best Civil War Romance, the National Readers' Choice Award for Best Series Historical and the B. Dalton Bookseller Award for Bestselling Series Historical. When not writing, she enjoys traveling, adding to her collection of Victorian perfume bottles and searching for the elf to master her computer.

For Susan, a friend who endows me with her wit and wisdom, joy and laughter...WRITE ON!

Chapter One

Warm. Wet. Woman.

Tyrel Kincaid listed his needs in that order. He was standing at the end of the planked bar of a miner's saloon in a back-of-nowhere camp, losing the chill of the drizzle that had started hours ago. He was too far from the potbellied stove to feel its heat, but the pack of bodies warmed him. The single room was smoky, stinging his eyes.

The rotgut was wet and he relished the liquor's bite as it wiped the dust from his throat when he tossed back his second drink.

And the woman...well, she was here, not that anyone else would think of her in that term, though.

There were those who drifted through the Arizona Territory who claimed that Ty had maverick's luck. If asked, Ty offered a cocky grin in answer.

Luck was not how he described what followed him.

Trouble was the word.

And trouble was what he smelled brewing after his horse broke his leg and Ty was forced to shoot him.

Hauling his saddle gear through the drizzle had done little to ease the flutters of tension that trouble sent walking up his spine.

On intimate terms with trouble, Ty named the types that he sensed. Sometimes it was as elusive a scent as water in the desert. Other times, trouble smelled like a storm gathering, wicked and wild, striking out of nowhere. Or trouble drifted in on the fragrance of a woman.

This night, Ty had all three aromas warning him. This was a special kind of trouble. The kind bred in a miners' saloon that was as cheap and plentiful as the whiskey he ordered to help him mourn the death of a damn fine horse. With his third drink, a quick scan of the smoke-filled room brought his gaze to rest on the most powerful potential source of trouble. The woman.

Dixie Rawlins.

He knew that angel's smile beneath the shadowed brim of a hat as battered as any miner's. He had sat across a poker table from her a few times in the past year or so, and pondered that smile of hers as she raked in a winning pot. The woman had no mercy when gold was in the kitty. Twice now, she had cleaned him out of a fresh stake.

Since he had time on his hands, Ty recalled that Dixie never stayed around. She'd pick up her winnings after a game, refuse to have a drink with any who offered to buy, refuse to buy a round herself.

Just like she refused to admit the sparks that flared between them each time they met.

Nursing his drink, Ty watched her. She wasn't hard on the eyes despite the rough garb. But then he had another memory of how Dixie looked, and right now that image was what he was seeing.

It didn't take him long to realize that Dixie had an animal-like awareness of everything that was going on. Each rise and fall of men's voices brought a quick, sharp gaze around the room, as did the comings and goings of the miners. Her gaze touched upon him, briefly, hotly, but without a hint of acknowledgment that she was aware of him.

Ty was aware. Too damn aware.

He topped off his glass, feeling the tightened pull of the tension that rode his lean body. He was stuck here until he could buy another horse. If the drunk at what had passed for a livery was to be believed, he might have that opportunity tomorrow. The thought crossed his mind that the owner could name a price that would beggar him. It wasn't unheard-of to charge triple the going price for decent horseflesh this far from what passed for civilization in the territory.

The table where Dixie sat dealing out a fresh hand began to have an irresistible appeal despite his own warning. Ty couldn't help but think of the other times he had crossed trails with her.

What drove a woman to follow the strikes from camp to camp? He had never thought about her reasons before, but then a strange mood was on him tonight. Dixie wasn't just moving from camp to camp gambling for a night or two, then drifting on. She hung around long enough to ask questions about a man.

Something about a scar.... He dug deep in his memory to recall what it was.

When the description escaped him, he shrugged and sipped his drink. If Dixie had once asked his advice, he would have told her to stop wasting her time.

The territory offered plenty of places to remain hidden until a man wanted to be found. Unwritten law in the lands opened to settlers and drifters alike said that no one questioned a man about where he came from, where he was going, or what he was doing in a place. If a man volunteered the information, even his name, smart folks kept their curiosity under lock and key.

But Dixie puzzled him. The more he thought about her, the more he understood that, like him, she was a loner. He had to respect that.

Just as he owed a little respect to the promise he had made himself never to gamble with her again. Her fingers moved like quicksilver, shuffling then dealing the cards. But he couldn't deny that watching her delicately shaped hands was a pleasure as she made those cards do all she wanted but sit up and sing for her.

He rather fancied those hands of hers, and from the looks on other men's faces he was not alone. He found himself annoyed that others might speculate, as he did, on how she would use those hands on a man.

Like tinder to dry brush, his memory supplied a very womanly image of Dixie sitting by her camp fire, brushing out a wealth of long, thick brown hair. He didn't even close his eyes to bring the image into sharp focus. He could see the glint of golden strands melding into shadows where the fire's light hadn't reached.

Each brush stroke had pulled taut the man-style shirt she wore, revealing sweet feminine curves that she kept hidden.

He had almost hailed her that night, almost ridden up to ask to share her fire, but she had turned as if she sensed someone near and he had seen the sparkle of tears. Ty had few rules that he lived by, but one was steering clear of crying women. And everyone had a right to privacy.

He lit out. But he was left with the haunting image, and the odd moment of wondering what would have happened if he had stayed. The night was going to be long and lonely. He was warm. His thirst had been quenched. Now, he needed a woman.

But Ty wasn't about to be careless. Dixie knew which end was the business end of a gun.

Dixie Rawlins didn't like to cheat. She had broken her own rule and stayed in Wobe camp for two nights now. She knew the value of the gold pokes she had already won, knew how much more she needed to move on, for information was as scarce as the aces the men she gambled with were counting on. There wouldn't be any dealt to them this hand. Dixie already held three of them.

She had little need to watch as she dealt. Her gaze constantly roamed the room, searching for the man with the scar.

The past eighteen months of hunting had taken their toll on her. She had accepted as truth that if a man wanted to hide in the territory even the shadow he cast could be lost.

Gone were the feminine trappings she had taken pride in wearing. Her long hair was the only female vanity she allowed herself. And even that had become a danger to her.

She still had a small skinned patch on her scalp where a big Irishman had wrapped her hair around his fist and yanked when she refused his offer to share his tent. Lights had exploded behind her eyes as he used his grip on her hair to bring her to her knees. But Dixie had sworn a vow never to be helpless with a man again. The Irishman had learned to take no for an answer.

But the night had cost her, not only in pain and fear, but in being cold and filthy.

Dixie hated being dirty. She hated wearing clothes that reeked of weeks spent on the trail. She had been forced to cultivate the knack of breathing through her mouth so she couldn't smell herself, or the men she often gambled with. She would do anything to get the men who sat at a table with her, the men she questioned and sometimes paid for information, to forget that she was a woman. A delicate shudder slithered over her slender frame as she recalled some of the close brushes she had had when her ruse hadn't worked.

Like any animal scenting danger, Dixie looked up and saw that Kincaid watched her. It was not the first time. Nor was it the first time she had experienced a strange hitch to her breathing when he was around.

She knew Ty Kincaid's reputation. Men and women in the territory said his word was as binding as a hangman's knot, and that he was a man to ride the rivers with anytime. Not that anyone dared to call him soft.

His eyes could easily chill a fresh-skinned side of beef, and some claimed he could slice a body with words. Hard as a whetstone, there would be no angel's wings waiting for Ty. The devil was more likely to roll out a welcome party to have his own back home.

Dixie took a poke to her arm from a miner, and met the last raise. Like worrying a sore tooth, she couldn't seem to get her thoughts away from Kincaid.

There was a sense of strength about him that called to her. Ty wasn't quite six feet tall—he lost out by a good two-inch measure—but there was a lethal quality to his lean frame that forced a comparison to the gun she wore to protect herself. A quality reinforced when her gaze clashed, over the miners' heads, with his dark gunmetal blue eyes.

He had watched her with those same eyes a few times before tonight, eyes framed with black lashes so thick a woman would have to be dead not to envy them.

Tonight there was something different about the way he looked at her. Ty Kincaid made her aware that, despite the mud streaks on her face, despite the filthy clothes, he knew she was a woman.

The thought was both exciting and a warning of danger.

Dixie concentrated on her cards, dismissing it. She had no time for a man to clutter up her life, even if there were times she wished to have a man like Kincaid riding by her side. But she had learned a brutal lesson in the past months; men didn't get involved in someone else's trouble. All her thoughts, all her efforts were directed toward revenge.

The mission she had set for herself at times seemed impossible, but she was committed to see it through to the end. Nothing and no one could be allowed to interfere.

Drawn by some inexplicable force, Dixie looked up at Kincaid again. The moment their gazes met, she was alerted to the warning in his eyes.

She suddenly became aware of the tension at her table. And the silence. Dixie slowly glanced down at her cards. The cards she had unknowingly fanned out to reveal the four aces she held.

Her breath caught as each of the four men at the table began to shove their chairs back and stand. She sat frozen in place when their cards were spread on the table for all to see. And one by one, each man called out his hand.

"King high flush."

"Four of a kind. Eights all."

"Seven over nines." George McGurth hitched up his pants. "Elroy's got three ladies and two knaves. Another full house. Every one a winning hand in an honest game."

"That's right." Elroy nodded, then pointed around the table. "Hands like these only happen when a deck is marked."

Dixie was no stranger to tight spots. She did not cheat often, but her trail was cold and she needed gold, a lot of gold to buy information.

The ensuing silence was fraught with tension. The kind that could get a person killed. If she needed any confirmation that she wasn't getting out of this saloon easily, the glaring, murderous looks each of the miners cast her way made sure she understood.

Before anyone made a move, she scooped up her winnings and saddlebags, stood and kicked out the chair from behind her. Backing up against the wall, she drew her gun.

There were too many men between her and the door.

As odds went, she didn't have any.

Kincaid. His name whispered through her mind, but Dixie couldn't spare a glance his way. She hadn't asked for help when she started her hunt, and couldn't start now.

Ty sized up the odds against Dixie. Steal a man's horse and you deserved hanging. Cheat a man at cards and get caught, there was a rope or a bullet waiting, or you were run out, depending on the crowd's mood. The fact that Dixie was a woman complicated matters.

He set his drink down and thought about another of the rules he tried to live by: don't get involved in someone else's fight.

He caught the flash of panic in Dixie's eyes before it was replaced by a calm acceptance as she too realized her chances of walking out were not the best.

The very fact that she stood facing them, brazening it out, had Ty moving before he thought about what he was doing.

"Hey, Rawlins," Ty called out, taking it as his due that men stepped aside for him. "Finally caught up with you. The boys here won't mind if I collect my winnings first. You welshed and that gives me first claim."

His reputation cleared the path for him. The underlying cold threat in his voice kept it cleared until he stood in front of Dixie. Ty ignored the mutterings about hanging her. He yanked the gold pokes she had snatched up from her hand and tossed them back onto the table.

"What'd she lose, Kincaid?" someone called out.

"A ride." Ty looked over his shoulder at the men loosely clustered behind him. His grin invited laughter. His gaze demanded it. "A long ride."

Snickers and loud guffaws filled the room.

"Takes a desperate man to bed a mud toad."

Ty didn't turn around this time. But he answered. "Hey, a bet's a bet." He looked at Dixie. "Right?"

Dixie thought herself hardened by months on the trail. But she felt heat steal into her cheeks, a melding of fury and embarrassment as Kincaid clamped his hand over her wrist.

"Come quietly an' maybe we'll both keep our skins." He caught her looking at the pokes on the table. "Don't even dream about it—" Ty would have added to that warning, but he heard the whisper of metal sliding against leather. He slipped off the short rawhide thong that held his gun nestled in its handmade holster. With one hand locked around Dixie's wrist and the other hand on the canted butt of his gun, he turned very slowly.

"Not so fast, Kincaid." George reached for the rifle leaning against his chair. "There's the winnings she took from us last night to divvy up. An' I ain't so sure she's gonna walk without answerin' for cheatin' us."

Ty smiled. It wasn't a smile to invite one back. "Then get sure. Get real sure before you touch that rifle."

"Kincaid!"

The shout from the doorway distracted everyone. They all turned to view the newcomer. Ty didn't allow his gaze to pick out who'd called his name until George turned his back on him. The barely dry-behind-the-ears kid wasn't alone. Two other men crowded the doorway behind him. Rain dripped from their oilskin slickers and hat brims, but Ty sensed the kid was the one he had to watch. Trouble. It was dogging him tonight like a bitch wolf in heat and was of the same variety—mean.

"I've been looking for you, Kincaid."

Tense and edgy, the kid's voice rang out in the silent room.

"Can't figure why," Ty answered. "Don't know you. Like to keep it that way."

"Yella, Kincaid?"

Ty thought about kicking the kid's rump so far it would take a hound six weeks to find his scent. The aggressive stance, the cocky look as he tossed his hat aside, even the continual fingers-spreading-and-closing motion he made with his right hand warned Ty the kid was looking for another scallop on his gun. It didn't take any courage to face a kid like this down, it took no more than a few moments. The low keening sound from Dixie almost made Ty turn around. Almost. But the kid, hungry to boast of taking him down, demanded his attention. Softly then, Ty began to talk.

Dixie was surprised that Kincaid had come to help her. Even more so by his protective move to stand in front of her. She had heard the challenge in the young man's voice and knew neither she nor Kincaid were walking out of here without a fight. But it was the other man, one of them behind the kid, who drew her gaze as he raised one hand to push up his hat brim. Dixie would never forget the scar on that man's hand.

She couldn't forget it. She had put it there with a broken piece of glass when he had attacked her after he had killed her father.

The trail she had followed for eighteen months just got hot, but Ty Kincaid was in her way.

Hands damp, heart thudding with anticipation and fear, Dixie came to with a start. Kincaid's voice held an edge as if his time of reasoning were at an end. She didn't know when he had released his hold on her wrist. Her need for revenge was overpowering all else, but she owed Kincaid for coming to help her when no one else had.

The choice churned through her. With the shuffle of feet indicating that men were backing away, leaving a clear path between Kincaid and the kid, Dixie knew she had to make her decision fast.

Rain suddenly drummed loudly on the tin roof. She lost sight of her quarry in the crowd. She couldn't lose him now! She just couldn't!

"Stop all the jawin', Kincaid," the kid yelled. High-pitched and tense, his taunts rose above the downpour. "You yella? Takin' you is gonna make me. Draw, Kincaid. You're gonna die."

Dixie saw the boy draw. She watched his gun clear the leather holster, and still Kincaid did not move. The boy's eyes held the feral gleam of a hunter, then fear replaced it. She couldn't see Kincaid's face. She was watching the kid so intently that when the shot rang out, it took her a few moments to understand that it was the boy's gun that fell with a thud, that his was the hand that bled, not Kincaid's.

"You bastard! You ruined me!"

"Maybe," Ty answered, then added, "And maybe I just saved your life."

"Who the hell—"

Dixie fired twice over the boy's yelling, her shots deafening, her move to stand back-to-back with Kincaid done without thought.

Gripping her saddlebags with one hand, she held her gun before her and moved as Kincaid did, half circling their way toward the door. Her ears rang with both the echoing sounds of the shots and the pounding rain, but her gaze remained steady and focused on the miners, alert for any sudden moves. The mood was ugly. The tension in the room was as thick as a good steak waiting to be cut.

Dixie faced the bar once more, sensing even before Kincaid took the next step, that he would shift his body so that she could clear the door.

But she needed to see once more the man she had hunted, the man who had killed her father and stolen everything of value to her. There had been times in the months past when she doubted he was real.

Her hesitation made her stumble. She looked up in time to see the gleam of a knife blade raised for throwing, just as her gaze settled on her target. The man didn't show a sign of recognizing her. Why should he? She was not the same innocent who couldn't pick up a gun and shoot him when she had the chance. But he wasn't the one holding the knife. It was the other man who had come in with him who held the blade, waiting for Kincaid to turn.

"No!"

Chapter Two

Dixie didn't realize that the screamed warning was hers. This time she was not helpless. She didn't have to watch another man die. She raised her gun just as Kincaid turned.

The knife found its mark. Kincaid's sudden grunt, the slight rocking motion of his body against hers told her she was right. She felt the impact as if her own flesh had been pierced by that wicked-looking blade. Kincaid was hurt. No longer a threat. The growls of the men closest to them confirmed it. She couldn't even look to see where he had taken the knife. She couldn't take her eyes from the men starting to move toward them.

She fired into the floor, sending dust and splinters flying to keep them back.

"Go! Damn it, move!" Ty yelled.

She found herself shoved through the doorway, instantly soaked by the pelting rain. The wind rose, tearing off her battered felt hat. There was no time to run after it. Ty pushed her toward the four horses hitched by the rail. He wasn't giving her a choice. She had to run with him.

She moved as he did, ripping the reins free, slinging her saddlebags over leather, barely able to mount the prancing horse. The stirrups were too long for her. Dixie squeezed her legs tight and angled her boots beneath the horse's belly, using the reins as a whip. She had no idea how Kincaid was able to ride, and the slashing rain and darkness made visibility nearly impossible.

Chilled to the bone, she rode out into the night with a man she didn't know, hunted as she had once hunted. She had little control over her mount for, like her, the horse blindly followed the one that Kincaid rode.

With the cold rain came a numbness, but her thoughts could not be stilled. She had come within seconds of shooting her father's murderer. And she had passed up her chance in order to protect Kincaid's life. She couldn't stop herself from reliving those minutes back in the miners' saloon, the minutes when she could have ended this quest for revenge. Now she ran from being called a card cheat and a horse thief. One was enough to get her hung, two left no doubt about it.

She glanced repeatedly at the shadowy figure riding slightly ahead of her. How was Kincaid managing to stay in the saddle? Everything had happened so fast back at the saloon that Dixie couldn't recall if he had pulled out the knife. She wasn't even sure where he had been hit. His wound wanted tending immediately if he wasn't to bleed to death, but she knew that he wouldn't be stopping anytime soon.

The rain continued its unrelenting beating, stinging her eyes. Useless though the move was, Dixie lifted one hand to wipe her face. There was no point in bemoaning the loss of her hat, for they were riding into the storm, and the hat wouldn't have kept the rain from adding to the frightening sense of blindness.

She had no idea where Kincaid was heading, or even if he knew where they could find shelter. There was no question that they would be followed. Men didn't take kindly to having their horses stolen and there was still the matter of the gold she had won from the miners the night before. How had everything turned from bad to worse for her?

They were cresting a small rise, Dixie holding on to both saddle and reins as the horse beneath her struggled for footing in the treacherous mud. Her voice rose to a scream, asking Kincaid where he was heading, but rain and wind tore the words from her and it was too late, for he was already plunging down the slope. Dixie had no choice but to follow.

They were on a flat now, running full out, a pace she didn't think they or the horses could maintain for long. But it was putting distance between them and the men sure to pursue, so she forced herself to find a reserve of strength to keep up with him.

She had not been able to trust anyone for so long that it came as something of a shock that she was trusting Kincaid with her life.

Ty knew he couldn't keep up this pace much longer. He had always admired courage, and Dixie had a fair share. She rode with him, never once trying to stop him and ask the hundred questions that must be prowling her mind, and for that he was grateful. Truth to tell, he wasn't sure what he could answer her.

He rode for the Tonto Buttes, over foothills covered with fine grass, heading for the spring in Mint Valley. They were in Yavapai County as near as he could figure, somewhere northwest of Prescott. The valley took its name from an early settler named McKee who found the spring and the profusion of wild mint that grew close by. McKee was long gone. Indians had forced him to abandon his ranch about ten years before. Ty just hoped the buildings were still standing. He had to get them and the horses into shelter.

The pain in his shoulder didn't bear thinking about. The chilling slash of the rain had served the purpose of numbing his body to a degree, but he could still feel the warmth of his blood welling up with every bone-jarring step of the hardmouthed mount he had stolen. The horse fought him, and Ty could feel his strength ebbing. What devil had made him get involved with Dixie Rawlins? That too didn't bear close scrutiny.

Ornery and wild was how his family described him. And he guessed the description fit. He was determined to remain unshackled and look where his path took him. For five years he had been drifting through the territories, returning home on occasion, only to get that restless itch and move on after a few days. Ty couldn't explain the restlessness to himself, much less anyone else. The only thing he hated about his years of drifting was a reputation as a fast gun.

It was an unwanted title, for he believed that words could bring most men around to his way of thinking better than a bullet. It was a belief instilled in him and his two older brothers by his father.

Damn that kid! Ty could have told him not to take him on, for despite his belief, he always made sure he was the one that walked away.

"Kincaid!" Dixie shouted, crowding her horse up against his. She reached out to keep him upright in the saddle. "We need to find shelter! Do you even know where we're heading?"

"I know. I always know," he managed to answer.

The rain slackened as they rode into the mouth of the valley. The grass was boot high and the going slow. Ty felt himself slipping sideways in the saddle, and again, Dixie's hand was there to steady him. The creek fed from the spring was running full and he could just about make out the rushing sound of the water over the lessening rain. What he couldn't make out was the darker bulk shape of any buildings left standing.

He knew he was growing weaker and given no choice but to depend upon a woman he didn't know. There was no help for it.

"Head toward the far slope. There's a cave back a ways. If we're lucky, we'll find a 'Pache stash."

"Apache?" Dixie repeated, gripping her reins.

Ty didn't answer her. He scanned the area, angling his horse closer to the boulder-strewn wall of the valley.

"You'll have to get down and find the opening on foot," he ordered her. "Can't see worth a damn."

Dixie did as he bid, groaning at the idea of her boots hitting solid ground. When she slipped taking the first step, she amended her thought. It was a muddy bottom she forced her way through. Keeping a tight grip on the reins to lead her horse, she had to ignore the bone-deep cold that had her shaking.

If it was bad for her, she thought, how much worse was it for Kincaid with his wound?

Feeling the weight of responsibility that his wound was her fault, Dixie forced herself to keep going. It was difficult to see, so she urged her horse closer to the wall and used one hand against the rock face to find the cave's opening.

Be there, she prayed silently, please just be there. The horses were blown, they needed shelter and rest as much as she and Kincaid did.

Dixie staggered when her hand slipped on the wet rock face and touched emptiness. She cried out, fighting to regain her balance as her boots slid out from under her. The horse shied, jerking against her hold, and the leather reins stung her bare palm.

She grabbed with both hands to keep the horse from bolting and found herself yanked forward. Her knee came down on a jagged piece of rock and she could no more stop the tears of pain then she could stop the rain.

"Let go!" Ty shouted. "I've got the horse."

She felt his hand cover hers, his voice a soft murmur calming the horse, and realized that she was sprawled belly down on the ground. She didn't think she could be colder, or wetter, but the rivulets of water running from the rock face proved her wrong.

Dixie heard him urging her to get up. She wanted to. Making her body obey was another matter. *Need you.* She heard him repeat it several times, and thought how long it had been since someone needed her. She managed to get up on her knees, wincing as pain shot from where the rock had cut her.

Ty kept on urging her to get up. She would never know what it cost him to admit that he needed her help. He never asked anyone's help. But he could feel himself swaying on his feet and there was no way he would be able to strip the horses of their gear and secure them.

He fired orders at her once she was standing, hurrying her along, swearing under his breath because he couldn't help her drag the saddles inside the cave. It wasn't deep, but it would serve to get them out of the rain.

"Tie them tight or we'll find ourselves afoot," he snapped.

"Everything's wet. My fingers are numb with cold and I'm doing the best I can, Kincaid."

When she crawled in behind him, Dixie realized just how small the cave was. He had stretched out with his back against his saddle and she had to climb over his long legs to find a place for herself. Her eyes longed to close, her body cried out for rest, but once she caught her breath, she turned to him.

Dixie saw nothing but shadow, so it was by feel that she reached up and searched for his wound. The knife was still embedded in his shoulder. Her cry brought Ty's hand up to cover her mouth.

"No noise. Understand? There was no way to check the back trail to see if they followed us, and I don't know who else might be close."

Dixie nodded, fear snaking through her. The moment he lifted his hand, she leaned close to his ear. "The knife has to come out. I don't know how you rode with it. But I won't lie. I don't know if I can do it."

Breathing in her fear, Ty knew he had to fight off the waves of dizziness that threatened to overcome him. He needed her, much as it galled him to need anyone.

"Straddle my legs," he ordered.

If Dixie thought the cave too confining before, she felt panic at the intimate press of her body to his. But there wasn't room to maneuver, so she settled herself on him. Despite the cold press of rain-soaked clothes, she felt a glimmer of warmth from where they touched.

She steeled herself for what she had to do, trying to unbend fingers numb with cold.

"I can't wait. You'll have to pull it out."

"My h-hands are too c-cold, Kincaid."

Ty ignored the warm weight of her straddling his hips. He needed a distraction from the pain that was spreading through his body, but the unwelcome arousal she caused wasn't it.

"Give me your hands."

Dixie lifted them up and found his ready to hold them. He brought both her hands to his mouth. "What are you going to do?"

Ty didn't waste time answering her. Breathing as deeply as he dared while fighting the pain, he inhaled through his nose and exhaled through his mouth trying to warm her stiff fingers. She was shaking with cold, and he knew unless he got her warm quickly, she wouldn't be of any use to him. It was just his luck that he couldn't find a cave with a stash of dry wood to make a fire. Just his lousy maverick's luck.

Dixie had to bite her lip to keep from making a sound when he drew her thumb into his mouth. Heat blossomed as his tongue bathed her thumb. Heat that slowly spread as he repeated the suckling motion with each of her near-frozen fingers. She understood why he was doing it, but wondered if he knew that he was stirring to life unfamiliar sensations inside her.

The cleft of her thighs cradled his manhood, his very aroused manhood, and the quivers that racked her body were no longer from the cold. She was appalled at the direction of her thoughts. More, because she sensed that he knew.

"I won't apologize, Dixie," Ty said, lifting her other hand to his mouth. "Be foolish to waste the words. Put your hand inside your shirt. Under your arm to keep it warm."

She closed her eyes, wishing away the impersonal, calm tone of his voice and thinking she could close off the feminine stirrings that she believed she had buried.

Ty made a lie of that. He was gentle holding her hand, but there was a difference to the way his tongue bathed her fingers. Dixie didn't want to linger on what exactly was different. It was enough that she felt it.

Trust was not something she gave easily. The glimmer of it died. "Kincaid, I won't pay you for your help with my—"

"I didn't ask for anything more than your help pulling out this knife. Hands warm enough now?"

For an answer Dixie wrapped one hand around the protruding handle of the knife, then gripped her other hand over the first. She nearly jumped when she felt his hands slide up and grip her hips.

"Just helpin' to steady you. You'll need every bit of strength to pull it out. Knife's easy enough goin' in, but the very dickens to pull out. Say when."

"Now." She gritted her teeth and yanked hard. The knife was deeply embedded. She felt as if his flesh didn't want to yield up the blade. Once more she braced herself to pull it free, only this time she felt Ty's good hand come up and cover both of hers.

"Now. Do it now," he whispered. Sweat beaded his body. The pain sent him in and out of darkness. The pressure built to an intense throb. He thought he heard her whisper she had it... It was the last thought he had.

Ty's body was no longer a heated, tense force beneath hers, but slack as a rag doll. Dixie let the wound bleed, it was the only way she could cleanse it. Scrambling in the dark, she found her saddlebags by feel. She drew out her only spare shirt, wishing it was clean. The other saddlebags belonged to the man whose horse Ty had stolen, and foolish as she felt, she reluctantly opened them.

A tin cup, a battered coffeepot and a spare shirt stiff with sweat and grime were all her search yielded. She had intended to replenish her supplies in the morning. Even if they had had a fire, there was nothing to cook on it, not even coffee to boil.

She made a pad of her shirt, tying it in place with her sodden neckerchief. Somehow, she had to find a way to keep Kincaid warm. Sheer force of will was all that kept her going as she went out in the night and dragged back deadfall, hoping that it would be dry enough by morning to light a fire. She checked on the horses, which stood in the drizzle, their heads down as if exhaustion had overtaken them, too. Both horses lipped rain water from a depression in the rock.

The cool mountain air was bracing and helped her dispel the tiredness that made her long to lie down. She had covered Kincaid with the saddle blankets, and spread the sleeping blankets over rocks inside the cave so that they, too, could dry. Beyond offering what little body warmth she had, Dixie had no way to keep him warm.

She knew she needed to rest, but as she settled herself next to Kincaid she didn't think she could sleep. Her body overruled her mind.

Thorne Lasser knew he didn't have a hope in hell of picking up Kincaid's trail. He ignored Peel Hickman's bellyaching about riding the spare horse that knew one gait . . . slow. The mountains into which he had led the kid Cobie and Hickman were rugged. Even with the lessening rain, he knew he was doomed, still he urged his horse to skirt the lower shoulder of a mesa and headed across an open stretch of sandstone that would lead them toward the river.

It was a land he knew well, and he scanned the terrain with flat-lidded eyes, thinking of possible hideouts that two exhausted riders and their mounts would seek.

That girl with Kincaid puzzled him. She had stared at him as if she knew him—knew him and didn't much like what she saw. He would have remembered her. He was sure of that. There weren't many women traipsing around in men's clothes. Women weren't something he forgot. Ever. Thorne rubbed the scar beneath his glove. Pity that he had to leave the wildcat that laid his hand open with a piece of glass. He had been looking forward to taming her, but her attack caught him by surprise. A first, he grudgingly admitted. After spying on her and her pa he'd thought she'd be easy pickings. Most ladies were. It was just too bad he had to lose her.

"Tol' you we ain't gonna find no trail in this rain," Cobie said. He cradled his wounded hand inside his shirt, wishing he had stayed dry back at the miners' camp. "Fool's errand. That's what we're on."

"Cut your whinin', boy. Thorne knows what he's about. Ain't that so, Thorne?"

"That's right, Peel. I'll find them. And when I do they'll pay for stealing our horses."

"An' for shootin' me. Don't forget that, Thorne. Kincaid's mine. Made a fool of me back there. Talking an' talking enough to bore a body to death. Ain't gonna let him get away with it a second time."

"Figure I'd get my knife back. Right fond of that there knife. Took it off some half-breed Mex who claimed he stole it from an Apache escaping from Fort Bowie. 'Course now it all might be true, but don't really matter none. I sure did love that blade. Can peel a skin off a peach that you'd damn near see through. Ever tell you 'bout the time I—"

"Quit jawing, Peel," Thorne ordered, moving out ahead and picking up a fast pace.

Thorne decided to head north where deep-sided canyons ranged. In all of them were seeps from the intermittent streams where a man could find water.

Kincaid was hurt, how bad none of them knew. If he was half the man that rumor claimed, he would be aware of the caches of food to be found that the raiding Apache or others on the run left behind.

But even without a cache, Thorne knew there was plenty of game: bear, elk, deer and birds. A man could hardly find himself a better place to hide. A man would need time and cunning to track another man through this land.

Thorne didn't have time. He wanted his saddlebags. Wanted them before Kincaid or that woman had a chance to examine them and find the trinket he had kept. It was the only link between him, his last job and unfinished business.

Without waiting to see if the other two were following him, Thorne once more set a hard pace. They had to find Kincaid today. And the girl. He couldn't forget about her.

Chapter Three

Dixie found herself snuggling closer to the warmth. For the first time in the long months she had been on the trail, she was warm and safe. She didn't want to be taken from this place of refuge.

Someone was murmuring. It was minutes before she understood that she was the one making the sounds. She fought against awakening, but she wondered who she could have been talking to.

Resenting whatever it was that seemed determined to rouse her, Dixie stirred. A nagging warning was trying to make itself heard. Dixie ignored it. Her body was more than happy to remain as it was, draped on a hard bed where no cold or damp could seep bone deep and leave her feeling as if she awakened with more aches than she had gone to sleep with.

From one breath to the next she was half-awake. Her senses stirred to life. Senses that sent messages she refused to believe.

Suddenly her bed came to life, too.

Her gritty eyelids opened with a snap. She identified the source of warmth. She understood why her senses were awake. Her nose was buried against Ty Kincaid's chest hair.

"Oh, my good Lord!" she groaned, promptly closing her eyes. Dixie prayed that when she looked again, she would find the coarse weave of the saddle blanket in front of her face. She opened her eyes. The Lord was not in a mood to show her mercy this morning.

"Oh, my good Lord!"

"You already said that. Believe me, it didn't bear repeating." Ty heard the edge in his voice, but his patience had been stretched to the limit. Waking up with a warm female body draped over him in pleasurable abandon without his having received a bit of benefit made his mood downright surly.

"You were cold, Kincaid."

"*I* was cold?"

"We both were. All right? I am sorry. I never meant to sleep on you."

"Forget it. Just move. For both our sakes, just move."

Dixie scrambled backward. She instantly realized her mistake. Her warm and very hard bed groaned and it was not in appreciation. With his soft-voiced swearing ringing in her ears, she rolled off to the side and lay there staring up at the cave's ceiling. Kincaid woke up randy as a goat. And with the disposition of one, too. Despite his wound.

Guilt forced her thoughts away from her embarrassment. "How's the arm feeling?"

"Hot and throbbing, Rawlins. Just like the rest of me."

"My knee feels the same way. Maybe it could meet up with what else ails you to give you a new misery to think about."

"Sassy mouthed, ain't you? That the best solution you can come up with?"

Dixie took a deep breath and huffily exhaled it. "No, it's not. The stream's outside. You can be cold and shaking in a moment."

"Not what I had in mind. There are more pleasurable ways to spend what might be my last day on earth."

"Well, it won't be heaven that's welcoming you, for sure, Kincaid."

"Which brings us back to hot places, doesn't it?"

His words were uttered in that same soft voice, but the hard edge of anger was missing. Dixie didn't want to think about what replaced it. She had to disabuse him of any notions that she would do more than take care of his wound.

And then...why, then they could follow separate trails.

"Look, Kincaid," Dixie stated, rolling to her hip so that she faced him. It was disturbing to find that he made the very same move.

"Good morning," he whispered, planting a kiss on her nose. "Guess we were both on the wrong side of this makeshift bed."

His admission and implied apology disarmed her. She could only murmur her agreement but couldn't shake off the question of his sudden mood change.

"Let's try this again, Kincaid."

"Name's Ty. Short for Tyrel."

"And that's just the way I want to keep it." Dixie eyed his shadowed features, wishing the dim morning light had penetrated a little farther into the cave. "I mean it, Kincaid. Our being together will be short. Real short."

"Well, I'm a real pleasin' kind of man. Short it is."

With no more warning than that, he kissed her.

Ty intended the kiss to be sort of a peace offering, a short—as the lady requested—good-morning-aren't-we-lucky-to-be-alive kind of kiss. A let's-try-to-get-along kiss... friendly...

But the small hitch in her breathing, the whimper of shock or surprise that he caught with his lips, and the sweet, momentary yielding of her mouth sent thoughts of friendly out of his mind. Like a kid hitching a ride on a green bronc for the first time, Ty wanted to hold tight and ride the kiss to the end.

Dixie, to his vast disappointment, jerked her head aside, breaking the kiss. She flopped over onto her back, and for long moments the only sounds were those of their breathing, hers panting like a hound after a race, and his none too steady.

She was the first to speak. "Do you know that you are wounded?"

"Yep. Hard to forget."

"You are sane and not fever-riddled?"

"Sane? About as much as you. Fever-riddled? That could be the cause of all this heat steaming up the cave."

"Kincaid, listen to me. We have serious problems to deal with. I will not, cannot, fight off unwanted advances—"

"Dixie, hold it right there." Ty, despite the painful throbbing in his shoulder, levered himself up to a half-reclining position. "Short-term or long, don't ever lie to me. I can't abide a liar. Never could. Never will. You met that kiss halfway, maybe a bit more than that, but it was no unwanted advance. A woman like you would be downright insulted if I hadn't tried."

A woman like you. Dixie repeated the words to herself. It had been so long since she had thought of herself in terms of being a woman, and all that went with it. She had spent so much time hiding the fact that she was female, denying any feminine longings, that his seeing beneath the dirt and rough clothing came as something of a shock. She struggled to rise, unwilling to discuss this, unwilling to admit that he was right. She had met him halfway.

Dixie bolted to a sitting position, clasping her hands around her upraised knee. She started to turn to look at him when a small shower of falling stones outside arrested both their attention.

Kincaid had drawn his gun from one breath to the next. She didn't need him to warn her to silence, and thankfully, he made no attempt to do it. She knew as well as he that they were trapped in here. If anyone was out there, the horses would give them away.

There was no place to hide.

Shoving aside the tangled length of her hair, Dixie was surprised to find that she too had drawn her gun. In all the months she had been on the trail, she had shot it once, when a rattlesnake used her boot for his sleeping quarters. Now, within less than a day's time, she once again prepared to shoot her way out of a tight spot.

Alarm overtook her when she saw Kincaid stand with a swaying notion. The man hadn't the good sense to remember that he was wounded and in no condition to be making another confrontation.

At least he made no move to motion her back when she stood at his side, despite the danger they could face.

She stood listening as intently as he was to hear if the sound was repeated, so that they could locate whatever or whoever was out there. She admired his calm, and strove to match that and the shallow breaths he drew, so shallow she could hardly hear him breathing. What she had heard about him was true; he was a man to ride the rivers with, and her courage level jumped higher because he was with her.

Reaching the entrance of the cave, she saw the mist being burned off the valley floor by a rising sun. The horses stood quiet, right where she had secured them the night before. Beyond their lazily swishing tails the animals showed no sign that the noise had alerted them to danger.

Dixie felt the tension that gripped her ease, but when she glanced over at Kincaid, she knew it was not the same for him. The man was bathed in a cold sweat.

Dark, wet patches stained his shirt, his face was beaded with droplets that brought the swift realization of what even standing there was costing him.

He had to have drawn the same conclusion that she did. There was no immediate danger. But before she could say a word, he made a twisting dive that took him outside the cave and behind the shelter of rocks. She bit her lip to stifle her cry, and tasted blood.

Uncertain of what, if anything, he wanted her to do, Dixie waited for him to either signal her or make the next move. She hated being in a position where she couldn't see anything.

The seconds stretched out into minutes and her nerves were stretched to a breaking point right along with them. Sweat from the fear that was building inside her trickled down her back. Tension returned with a force that was twice what she felt before. Why didn't he move? The thought that he might have hurt himself and was unable to move crossed her mind. But the more she thought about it, the more it made perfect sense that Kincaid had knocked himself out cold.

She had not heard any sounds to indicate that someone, or an animal, had been walking on the slope above the cave. Surely it would be safe for her to step outside now?

Cursing herself seven ways to Sunday for standing there, Dixie gave a last thought to Kincaid's anger if she moved before he was ready to admit that the danger didn't exist. It was simply a chance she had to take.

Picking up a small rock from the cave's floor, she tossed it at the rocks that Kincaid hid behind.

Nothing. Not a sound. She inched her way clear of the cave's opening, keeping close to the rock wall as she stepped out.

"Kincaid," she whispered, searching the area of the rocks, listening for him. Her breath seemed to catch in her throat, her heart was drumming until she heard the pounding in her ears and fear held her frozen in a vise.

She didn't know how long she stood there before she came to with a start. Unable to wait a moment more, Dixie made a dash for the very rocks that Kincaid had disappeared behind.

A scream lodged in her throat. Kincaid wasn't there!

She never knew what made her look up and see him, all lithe darkness against mountain's slope. The moment she met his gunmetal blue gaze, something strange happened to her, something so compelling and blatantly sexual it made her sway where she stood. For one timeless, crazy moment, she swore he was feeling the same startling sensation—that of perfectly attuned mates who have come through danger together unscathed and want to confirm that in the most primitive way possible.

He started down the slope, favoring his left side, without a word being exchanged. All Dixie could do was watch him.

Ty found his inner warning system silent. That sixth sense, finely honed from years spent living alone, was no longer telling him to keep the hell away from Dixie Rawlins.

He couldn't even begin to explain to himself why he felt both protective and possessive about her. One brief kiss did not a lover make, and that was the only reason why he should feel this strong surge of desire.

Danger, which had proven groundless, had sent its own sizzle into his bloodstream. A small animal must have dislodged the stones. He was grateful, for the smoke he spotted warned they might have company. Ty paused a moment before walking the last steps that would take him off the slope and bring him level with her.

What was there about her that caught his attention? Curiosity. There was that. It had never left him since that night he had seen her brushing her hair. The sun caught the gold that was buried in her brown hair. Tangled, her hair added a wildness to her face. Her head was lifted so that she could watch him. The mouth was most certainly kissable, her eyes wary, and he could almost feel the tension that held her still.

His own body echoed her tension. It had not forgotten the soft, warm weight of hers making itself at home on him during the night.

Thing was, he didn't know what, if anything, he wanted to do about it. Dixie Rawlins was a complication he didn't need. Gut feeling said he couldn't bed her and ride away.

As if she had sensed his decision, Dixie made an abrupt turn toward the stream, holstering her gun as she walked away.

Ty knew the moment was lost and felt a momentary regret. Good sense told him it was better this way. No more involvement than necessary.

Dixie suffered a slight chill, feeling his gaze still on her. She knelt by the streambed, scooping up water to splash on her face, trying to understand what had passed between them. For a moment there, when Ty had stood and just watched her, she had had a feeling that she was facing a very determined predator. The moment was gone, but the feeling still lingered.

It was all foolishness, brought upon them by the fact that they were stuck with each other for a while. More pressing than these fanciful thoughts were those of hunger, if her stomach's growling was any indication. If she kept her mind on practical matters, Kincaid would be forced to do the same.

She scooped up a handful of the water to drink and caught the pungent scent of mint. Glancing down, she saw that she had crushed the delicate stems growing close to the water and began gathering the small leaves.

"They won't do you much good unless you fill the coffeepot first," Ty said, holding out the pot to her.

"Make some damn noise, why don't you? Sneaking up on a body can make their heart quit, Kincaid. I'm not your enemy," she finished, snatching the pot from his hand.

"Enemy? No. But you sure are a snapper. No wonder you're always alone."

Dixie paused, counted to ten, took a deep breath and released it before she lifted the filled pot and rose to her feet. She faced him, holding on to a sudden rush of anger.

"Kincaid, you don't know me and I'm for keeping it that way."

Dixie made the mistake of looking at him. His soft voice, no matter what he said, had a dangerous effect on her. Almost as much as his eyes. Those gleaming dark blue eyes were watching her without giving away any hint of what he was thinking. A warning chill made her look away.

"I'll get a fire started. Mint tea for breakfast, then I'll tend to your wound."

Ty waited until she was even with him before he reached out and caught her chin. Lifting her face, he studied the delicate lines of her features. "I don't know you, that's true. But you're prickly as any cactus the moment I try to find out more about you. Why, Dixie? What makes you follow the mining camps, gambling with men that would as soon slit your throat as bed you?"

"That puts you one up on them, doesn't it, Kincaid? You didn't try to slit my throat."

She saw his mouth tighten, almost as if he bit back what he wanted to say. She found herself needing to close her eyes against the intense directness of his gaze. Both defeat and despair seemed to roll over and through her, wiping away months of struggle and bringing her back to the night that began it all. Her hand shook and she let him take the full coffeepot from her.

"I'd really like to know why, Dixie. When you're ready to talk, I'll be ready to listen."

This time she heard him walk away, but she didn't make a move to follow him.

Her thoughts turned to the moments before the miners' confrontation in the saloon. She had wished then that she had a man like Ty Kincaid to help her find her father's killer. Which brought up the question of why he had involved himself last night with her troubles. She couldn't continue to ignore the fact that she had had the man who murdered her father in front of her and her only thought had been to help save Kincaid's life, not end her search for revenge.

She opened her eyes to see that he was awkwardly trying to build a fire with one hand. Practical matters first, she reminded herself. Then she'd make the decision about telling Kincaid what he wanted to know.

Dixie sipped the last of her mint tea, surprised at the way she kept repeating to herself Kincaid's soft-voiced compliment of the nearly smokeless fire she had built. His easy acceptance of her as his equal helped dispel the tension that had become as much a part of her as the gun she wore.

She checked the other coffeepot to see if the water was hot enough to wash his wound and caught his rueful smile.

"Don't tell me I'm going to have trouble with you over cleaning that shoulder, Kincaid."

"I'm not looking forward to it. This makeshift bandage is stuck but good. The skin's hot, but near as I can see there's no cause for alarm."

"Now you're a doctor, too?"

"Man alone learns to be all things if he hankers to survive."

"Not just a man. A woman, too," she added softly, once more withdrawing to her place. Leaning back against the rock at the cave's entrance, Dixie sent a searching glance over the valley. "It's peaceful here. I can understand why someone would want to build a home in this valley. The grass is lush and that stream-bed must run all year."

"McKee must have agreed. He struggled long and hard to hold on to it before he gave up. But not all men think about owning land and settling down."

"You sound like a man who's tried and found it didn't work for you."

"Could be."

Dixie took his words for what he meant them to be—a warning about himself. She set aside her cup and stood up.

"It's time to tend that shoulder."

Removing the pot from the fire, she stuck her finger into the water to test the temperature. "It's just about hot enough."

She eyed him where he sat. "It would help if you would lie down."

"Prone and biddable isn't my favorite position."

"Most men would agree with you, Kincaid. But I guess most women would agree it might be nice to have the boot on the other foot, so move."

He stretched out on the saddle blankets she had dragged from the cave and waited until she was kneeling at his side. "What man tried to make you prone and biddable, Dixie?"

"You. This morning, remember?" she snapped, spreading open his shirt to untie her neckerchief from his shoulder.

"If I remember correctly, you were well on your way to prone. But I'll give you this, the biddable part was going to take a bit of work."

"Just goes to show you, Kincaid, how differently men and women view the same happening. I wasn't prone. I wasn't going to be prone. And I had no intention of becoming biddable then, or ever, for some man."

"Take it easy!" he yelled as she used the soaked cloth to remove her padded shirt from his wound. "You're sour on men for sure, but don't make me pay for all their sins."

Her fingers stilled. She met his direct gaze with her own. "No, Kincaid. I won't ever make that mistake."

Ty found that he needed to keep her talking, for it offered a little distraction from the feel of her hands gently probing his shoulder.

"Why don't you try telling me where you learned to play cards? I watched when I played with you. Figured you could do just about anything with a deck, but make them sit up and sing for you."

Her laugh was soft and husky and went through him like lightning. He wanted to capture the sound, capture the sparkle in her eyes, the smile on her generously shaped mouth.

"Dixie?"

His fingertips grazed her open palm before he curved his fingers over hers, stilling her.

"My father was a gambler. He taught me." She allowed a moment more of resting her hand within the nest of his. Large and warm, his strength was there in the tapered, long fingers, and the thick calluses. She stared down at the minute scars. For a shocking few seconds, she found herself thinking of how his hand would feel on her skin.

Dixie quickly withdrew her hand from his grasp, and buried the wanton thought.

"Gambling's an odd thing for a man to teach his daughter. Most would protect their—"

"My father wasn't most men. He took me everywhere with him after my mother left us. When I was ten, he gave it up and settled down."

Keeping her gaze focused on rinsing out the neckerchief, she gave herself another warning to beware of Kincaid's ease in prying her past from her. True, she had kept to herself for these long months, but talking about her father, or what their life had been like, never came easy for her.

The wound, now that she had cleaned it, was raw looking. "I should stitch it closed, Kincaid," she said, sitting back on her heels.

"You askin' or tellin' me?"

"Asking you. I don't have your experience in dealing with wounds." Not the ones visible to the eye, she added to herself.

"Wish I had my saddlebags. I've a salve that's good for just about anything that ails a body. Works fine on a horse, too."

"No sense bemoaning its loss." Dixie folded up the cloth and set it in place on his shoulder. "You rest easy while I wash out my shirt. At least it will make a clean bandage."

"We can't stay here too much longer," he warned.

"Why?" Dixie rose and looked around at the quiet valley. "We have shelter and water and surely there's game."

"You figurin' on shooting something to eat? 'Cause if you do, you'll bring whoever's huntin' us to the valley."

"Maybe they gave up. The rain had to wash out our trail. And I haven't forgotten how to make a snare. Unless you can come up with a better reason for moving on, I'm for staying right here another day."

Dixie started for the stream, then turned back and went into the cave. She came out carrying the stolen saddlebags. Withdrawing the filthy shirt, she held it up.

"I'll just give this a wash, too. It'll give you something to wear when I wash and mend yours." Tossing the bags down beside him, she added, "I couldn't find much of use in them last night, but it was dark. You might have better luck, Kincaid."

"You told me to rest."

"So I did, but you strike me as a man who needs to be always doing something. Figure that's a good way to keep you busy and out of trouble."

Dixie set the shirts in the fast-running water of the stream with a decent size rock to hold them. Kincaid called her. She turned to look at him. Even with the distance that separated them, she knew from the way his gaze went from her to the object he held, what he had discovered. One of the missing items her father's killer had stolen. The one that she worried over after she had buried her father and lost their ranch. When she found it missing, she felt warned that the man might come back for her.

Very slowly, and very deliberately, she lifted the wet shirts to the bank before standing.

"Want to come here and explain this to me, Rawlins?"

Berating herself for not being more thorough in her search of the saddlebags didn't do a lick of good, so she didn't waste time on it. She settled her gunbelt lower on her slender hips, buying time to gather the courage she needed to do what she must.

"You giving me any choice, Kincaid?"

"Nope. None at all. What the hell is this tintype of you doing in these saddlebags? And it is you, isn't it? A heck of a lot cleaner, and younger looking with your hair down, but you just the same. A real pretty lady. Not the Dixie I see now."

Chapter Four

Dixie briefly closed her eyes against the condemnation she heard in his voice. Bravado was in short supply, but she dug up what she had left and stared at him.

"Figure I was in cahoots with those men?"

"I figure," he said in his soft voice that nonetheless demanded attention as he stood up, "on hearing the truth from you."

Dixie's steps were slow but steady toward him. She knew what her choices were. Tell him or leave. Telling Kincaid the whole story would drag him into it. That unshakable truth settled in her mind and wouldn't be dislodged. He was already wounded. Dare she put his life at risk?

"What makes you think that isn't the truth?"

Ty leveled his hard gaze on her. "Try again. The truth."

She stumbled and quickly straightened, but while she still held his gaze she leveled her gun on him.

"Wrong move, Dixie."

"No. It's the right one. Move over by the horses."
She didn't think he would do what she ordered. Then
for seconds he stared at the tintype of her, tossed it
down and complied.

"Untie the chestnut's reins."

"It's awkward using one hand. Why don't you help
me? I'll give you my word I won't—"

"Stuff thinking I'm a fool into your boots, Kincaid,
and just do it."

"Takes a lot to shoot a man," he noted, working the
leather, which had dried hard and stiff after being
soaked. "Don't think I'm using a delaying tactic here,
the knot's hard."

"So's your head. Stop trying to talk me to death. I'm
not the kid you faced last night. I don't want to shoot
you, Kincaid. Hear that? I don't want to doesn't mean
that I won't do it."

"You're the lady with the gun. Guess that makes you
the boss. For now," he added, finally freeing the knot.
He glanced over his shoulder at her. "Now what?"

"Now you drop your gun belt and take your horse
for a walk down to the other end of the valley."

Dixie refused to look away from his eyes. She knew
she had to watch a man's eyes, a lesson from her father she never forgot, for that is where the clue to a
man's moves would come. Unfortunately, Kincaid
must have had the same lesson. His gaze offered her
nothing.

"Save us both grief by not putting me to the test,
Kincaid. Go for your walk, and I'll be out of here."

"Maybe I don't want to let you go."

"It's not your choice."

Ty heard the underlying note of regret, but he wasn't about to push her. Not now. He took the reins in his right hand and walked away. The lady had secrets. He didn't want to get involved. He was damned if he knew why he had to keep reminding himself of that.

As Dixie watched him approach the stream where he let the horse drink, she suffered an attack of guilt. She'd not spared a thought to caring for the horses this morning. She had broken one of the first and hardest rules she had learned on the trail. You took care of your horse before you saw to your own comfort.

"Cross over to the other side and keep walking, Kincaid," she called out. Not wasting time trying to undo the knot, she holstered her gun and used her pocketknife on the ends of the reins. A quick look showed that Ty was still walking, so she ran into the cave and came out carrying one of the saddles.

Kincaid was still walking in grass that was knee-high.

Dixie made short work of saddling her horse. She snatched up the tintype and her coffeepot and cup, stuffing them into her saddlebags. Tossing the bags behind the cantle, she quickly tied them in place with the rawhide hanging from a fancy silver-worked concha. There was no time to adjust the stirrups to her leg length the proper way, so she just shortened a few notches on the belt and prayed for the best. Swinging herself up onto the saddle, she took one last look at Kincaid's back before she set off at a lope toward the opposite end of the valley.

Ty glanced back and watched her go. With the same leisurely walk that had taken him this far, he set out to return to the cave site. She'd be back.

He was sure of it.

Dixie rode beneath the tall pines that shadowed the rock-strewn entrance to the valley. At the far south, sunlight lay on the peaks like a cloak of golden glory. She drew rein and took a moment to get her bearings. She had gold enough to see her through a few weeks, and the most pressing thing was to get supplies. She was hungry, but she had been hungry before. She couldn't afford any more mistakes like last night. Word would spread about her from one mining camp to another. It might be a good time to lay low for a while, or head south.

But being away from Ty Kincaid allowed her thoughts to return to her missed chance last night. If she left the area, she might not pick up the scarred man's trail again for months.

Letting her horse pick his way at a walk out from the pines, Dixie managed to set Ty Kincaid from her thoughts. She headed south, watching the land as she rode forth. She had ridden less than half a mile when she thought she saw a rider in a rock crease up ahead.

Shading her eyes with one hand and cursing the loss of her hat, Dixie scanned the area. There was no sign of a man and horse. Likely it had been a shadow that had caught her attention and nothing more.

Urging the horse forward, she realized that the trail she followed disappeared beyond the next bend. A strong sense of warning came over her, telling her to go back, but Dixie shrugged it away.

The land was broken and rugged, offering a hundred places where someone could hide. She refused to hug the rocks and forced the horse to the middle of the trail.

On her right, she saw a rattler slither into the shade of an overhanging rock and repressed a shiver. She hated snakes. The horse snorted, and she leaned forward to rub his neck, whispering reassurances.

A shot sprinkled rock in a sudden shower upon her. A second shot peppered the ground and the horse shied. Dixie kept her seat by virtue of hanging on to the animal's mane. She yanked hard on the reins, kicking the horse into a dead run back the way she had come. Two more shots flattened into the rocks behind her.

Running in fear, uncertain of the bay's responsiveness, Dixie tried to think what to do. She had abandoned Kincaid in the valley and might make good her own escape, but whoever was shooting at her was sure to discover him. He was wounded. She couldn't forget that.

If she kept riding, would the shooter follow her? The valley could be a trap, with only one way out. But if they couldn't get out, no one else could get in.

Wishing she had her sweet little mare, bred from hardy mustang stock, beneath her, Dixie demanded more speed from the bay. Wind whipped her hair back from her face in a tangled snarl. Fear had her heart pounding at an alarming rate, and yet an icy chill snaked its way down her spine when a few more shots told her how close her pursuer was.

How long ago had she left the valley? Twenty minutes? Half an hour? Longer? She wasn't sure. Decide, she told herself. Go back or keep riding.

Keeping low in the saddle to make herself as small a target as possible, she felt the start of tears. She was coming to the end of any courage or strength she had.

Don't be a quitter, Dixie. Her father's words rose from memory. Words that were always telling her that she could do whatever it was she set her mind to.

She had to survive. She had to get out of this particular pickle barrel. She was the only one who could make her father's murderer pay for what he'd done.

The shadowed pines up ahead were a welcome sight, for she knew they offered her a few minutes' safety. Urging the bay into the shaded coolness, she faced making her decision now and quickly. Back to the valley and warn Kincaid, or keep riding in the hope of drawing her pursuer away.

Drumming hoofbeats sent her fear up a notch. There was more than one rider chasing her down and closing too fast.

Shots rang out, sending deadfall branches crashing to the ground. They were too damn close to her. Dixie guided the horse in a weaving pattern through the thick pines, thankful that the layers of pine needles deadened the sound of her horse's movement.

But just as the thick carpet offered a measure of safety for her, it also concealed the sounds of her pursuers.

A few moments more and she would be at the mouth of the valley. And Kincaid would be there.

She couldn't question why the thought of him instantly eased her fears. She just accepted that it did, the same way she accepted that her parched throat closed off a scream that wanted to be vented.

A single shot plowed into the trunk of the tree she was passing. Dear Lord! she prayed, and suddenly heard return fire. There, up ahead, with a streak of sunlight glinting off his gun barrel, was Kincaid.

"Keep going!" he shouted when she slowed, coming abreast of him. "Ride the stream through the valley. There's a crease in the rocks. Lead your horse through, and I'll meet you there."

"Kincaid—"

"Go, damn you! I'll hold them off."

The blaze of anger that made his features sharp and predatory stilled all the words she could muster to argue with him. He was right. This wasn't the time to discuss partnerships and equal-share-and-share-alike rights.

Dixie rode into the valley with shots ringing in her ears. He was stronger than she believed, for he had managed to saddle his horse. The fact that he was mounted and clearheaded enough to give her orders told her that her earlier fear for him was groundless.

Flagging her tiring horse, she followed the streambed until she came to the split in the rock wall. She was off her mount and running up the small slope, yanking on the reins to make the horse follow her, when she heard another horse running full out.

Kincaid! And behind him were three horsemen!

Dixie stood at the top of the split, knowing she was a perfect target but unwilling to let Kincaid try to make it through with those riders so close on his tail. She wrapped the reins quickly around one arm to keep her horse from bolting and drew her gun.

Giving him protective fire so that he had a fair chance was small payment for what he had done for her.

"Go on!" Ty yelled, when he saw what she was doing. Damn fool woman couldn't follow an order worth a damn. She'd get them both caught or killed. In his mind he had blocked the pain in his shoulder, but knew he couldn't fire his own gun and ride on. If Dixie didn't get over to the other side so he had clearance, he wasn't going to make it out without taking a bullet somewhere.

"Get clear, Dixie. I'll ride through."

She emptied her gun, firing over the pursuers' heads, and made a scramble for the other side. The horse snorted and tried to rear, and her arm felt as if it were being torn from her shoulder. She couldn't reload and mount at the same time. Kincaid came through the crease and took the decision from her.

"Hit the saddle, Rawlins. We ride."

He led and she followed over a divide peppered with streams. There was no trail to speak of. They were threading their way through a labyrinthian mass of granite boulders whose shapes and giant size were the stuff of nightmares. She had heard of Skull Valley and wondered if that was where Kincaid headed.

Dixie wasn't sure when the sounds of pursuit died away. It didn't come with a sudden realization, but a gradual one that she had not heard the drumming hoofbeats behind them for some time.

Still Kincaid didn't slow the pace. And she had no choice but to keep riding. Broken country. Stream banks covered with dense undergrowth. Sun, like an avenging god, beat down without mercy.

They rode through small untouched valleys where the grass was belly high on the horses and there were no signs of life beyond the game they startled on their way through.

Exhaustion settled in and Dixie tried to find enough moisture to wet her lips to tell Kincaid that she couldn't ride another step. She couldn't talk. And she wasn't at all sure he would have listened. The man had to be made of stone to keep riding the way he was, never looking back to see if she was with him, never offering a chance to stop. He had to be as aware as she was that no one was chasing them now.

But every time she attempted to push her horse closer to his, Kincaid managed to get ahead of her.

He led them upstream, turned up a draw and doubled back. They rode up a hill and crossed the saddle of land into the bed of a dry wash. Still he didn't stop. She grew confused as to where they were, weaving back and forth, until she finally came to understand that he was covering their trail by using every trick he knew.

Dixie wished that she could see past her exhaustion to learn from him, but she had as much chance of doing that as her horse had of learning to fly.

Knowing full well that he could ease their pace, Ty pushed on. He was riding on sheer nerve, and had been for most of the day. Dixie had long ago reached the point of exhaustion, and he had to admire her tenacity for sticking with him. He just wanted to make sure that they were not followed, for they needed to rest themselves and the horses for a day or so.

Following one of the tributaries of the Santa Maria River, Ty thought of the Rutland Rancho, which was close by. Greg Rutland would give them shelter and food, but Ty was going to make damn sure that he brought no trouble to the man or his family.

Greg had a sister—Jessie, he thought her name was—who, if he remembered right, was about Dixie's slender build. Clean clothes went a long way toward making him forget a day like today, and it had to work for a woman, as well. Hot food and a clean bed held the same appeal as finding the sidewinders who had bushwhacked Dixie. His head felt heavy and his shoulder was a gnawing agony.

When he believed he was about two miles from the rancho, Ty found a low place to cross the river. The sun was setting and the wind had picked up, but Ty didn't think it would rain. Before him, the land he had been born and bred in softened with a velvety darkness. The bluffs turned into shades of rust and crimson, reminding him of the colors of the desert in the daylight. A faint twinkle of stars was showing like far-off lamps in the night sky.

He didn't know how long Dixie had been riding by his side, but the moment he looked at her, he knew she had been doing some serious thinking.

He waited while she tried wetting her lips, and drew rein to offer her his canteen. She had been in such an all-fired hurry this morning to leave him that she had never bothered with hers. To his surprise she was smart enough not to gulp too much water, but sipped it slowly before she handed it back to him. Ty satisfied his own thirst, capped the canteen, then slipped its leather over the horn of the saddle.

"You know where we're going, Kincaid?"

"Always. Greg Rutland's place. Hot food, clean beds and the company of women for you, Dixie. We can rest up a day or so before we figure out where to go from here."

We. She didn't want to like the sound of that word. She let it pass for now, too tired to argue with him. But she had questions.

"You were waiting for me in that stand of pines, weren't you? Almost as if you knew that I'd be back. Almost as if you knew I'd be chased there. Want to tell me how you managed that?"

For long moments she didn't think he was going to answer her. They kept the horses to a walk, letting them pick their way over the rocky path leading to the low buildings she could see down the sloping valley before them. The lamplight in the windows spelled a welcome that went a long way to ease the aches and pains of riding for almost ten hours.

"Pull up, Dixie. Best we get this over with here. No sense in giving Greg and his family a colorful earful."

"And who was going to deliver that? You or me?"

"You more'n likely once you hear what I have to say. And I don't want you thinking that I know more about human nature than you. But this morning when I came off that slope, you distracted me. I never got around to telling you what I saw when I was up there. I spotted a camp fire's smoke about three miles beyond the mouth of the valley. Stood to reason, without the brains of a horned lizard, that the camp belonged to whoever had come after us for stealing these horses."

In silence she mulled over what he told her, letting him wait. Then Dixie gently slapped the reins on her mount's neck and moved off at an ambling walk.

"Dixie? Ain't you got nothing to say?"

"Nope."

"I figured you for a skin blasting."

"Well, hate to disappoint you, Kincaid, but when you're right, you're right."

Ty spurred his horse to keep pace with hers. "That's it?"

"That's it."

Shoving his hat back, Ty stared at her shadowed form. "Well, I'll be damned! A woman with sense!"

Dixie smiled in the darkness, knowing he couldn't see her. Let him enjoy his moment. She'd fix his saddle but good.

Chapter Five

At first glance, Dixie decided that Greg Rutland was not a handsome man. He was taller than Ty, big and rawboned, his nose was long and crooked, half of his right earlobe was missing, and his bushy eyebrows grew together in a straight thick shelf above his dark eyes, giving him a perpetual scowl. But his smile was as warm and welcoming as his greeting once Ty hailed him.

Dixie had trouble dismounting. She didn't think her legs would hold her. She hadn't thought about her looks all day. Truth was, she rarely thought about her appearance anymore, but when Greg called his wife from their cabin, she found herself struggling not to cringe from the lamp that Greg held high.

Livia Rutland was as blond as Greg was dark, petite and fine boned as a bisque doll Dixie had once owned. Her apron was white and starched, her hair neatly coiled, and her blue calico gown was trimmed with an edging of lace around the neck. She rushed past Dixie to enfold Ty in a gentle hug, and Dixie caught the faint,

sweet scent of lavender. It was not envy that forced
Dixie to take a few steps back into the shadows as she
listened to Livia's voice, as soft and gentle as her looks
when she saw that Ty was wounded. It was simply the
sharp reminder that she had once prided herself on the
same feminine attributes that brought a gleam of ad-
miration into Ty Kincaid's eyes and a smile to his lips
that she would love to have directed at her.

"Elwin, Gilby, come tend these horses!" Greg
yelled, holding the lamp high once more. "Who's that
with you, Ty?"

"Dixie Rawlins. She helped me out of a tight spot
and I owe her, Greg."

"A woman? Land's sakes, Ty," Livia said, sliding
her arm from around his waist and stepping forward,
"why ever did you keep quiet this long? Poor dear
must be half-dead if your horses are ready to fold."

Dixie couldn't hide any longer. Taking a deep breath,
telling herself it didn't matter what she looked like if
they gave her someplace warm to settle her aching
body, she came forward to meet the Rutlands.

The boys leading the horses off behind the cabin, a
sprite dressed much like her mother, flinging herself at
Ty's legs, and yet another towheaded youngster spill-
ing out of the doorway at a run with a shouted greeting gave Dixie an image of Ty Kincaid that was
different from the one she had formed. Very different.
Despite the pain he had to be feeling, he managed to lift
the little boy in his good arm, and keep from tripping
over the small girl clinging to one of his legs.

He caught the expression on her face as Livia shooed her brood off to give Ty breathing room and grinned at her. "What can I say, some people like me."

"I'm sure that they do, Kincaid." Reaching his side, Dixie leaned close to whisper, "Don't you think you should tell them we're horse thieves on the run?"

"Julia," he said, addressing the little girl, "meet Dixie. She's a horse thief."

"Ty!" Unable to resist either his grin or the child's giggles, Dixie found herself smiling. "All right. You proved your point. Your friends wouldn't care."

"Darn right we wouldn't," Greg said from behind her. "I owe Ty more than I can ever repay. Wouldn't matter what he done, he'd still find a welcome under my roof. An' that goes for anyone he brings with him. You get yourself inside and let my Livia take care of you, Dixie. We'll set down for supper in a shake of a cow's tail."

Warm. It was the one word that Dixie summoned as she stepped inside the Rutlands' cabin. It wasn't only the actual warmth coming from the cheery blaze in the stone fireplace, or the stove whose pots emitted aromas that had her stomach growling, it was the warmth of welcome. Wildflowers sat in a crock in the middle of a rough-hewn table. Quilted curtains dressed the few windows. Colorful rag rugs were scattered over the planked flooring of the large room. Scraps of material spilled from a basket near the rocking chair as if Livia had just risen from her work.

The blanket strung on a rope was pulled back to reveal the homemade bed, and in a basket by the footboard, a cat nursed her litter of kittens. There was an alcove off the cooking area where Dixie could see part of the steps leading up to the sleeping loft.

The crockery on the shelves, the browned biscuits Livia placed on the table and the smiles of the children as they took their places on the long benches on either side, all bespoke of home.

A longing that Dixie thought she had burned from her memory rose within her, and she had to turn away for a moment to fight the start of tears. She didn't know what was the matter with her. Twice today tears had threatened her. They were a feminine weakness she couldn't allow herself. Not until she had her revenge.

"Dixie?"

She looked up to see that Ty was watching her. His eyes were concerned, and she could almost see a question forming on his lips. Quickly shaking her head, she gazed again at the cat.

"Do you like kittens?" Julia asked, sliding off the end of the bench. She took hold of Dixie's hand. "Witchy won't mind if you come to see her new babies. She likes showing them off."

"Julia, love, I think Dixie would like to wash the trail dust off first. After we eat you can show her your cat's litter."

"Yes, Mama."

"You show Dixie where to wash, and, mind you, get a clean cloth for her."

Still holding Dixie's hand, Julia led her into the alcove off the kitchen. Next to the stairway stood a small table with a plain white china washbowl and pitcher.

Livia bustled up behind them carrying a lamp in one hand and a steaming kettle in the other.

"There. Now you can see," Livia said, setting the lamp down. "Little James has gone to fetch your saddlebags. I'll tend to Ty's wound and keep the men away from here until you're done."

Julia remained behind, and after handing Dixie both a washcloth and a towel, the child locked her hands behind her back and stood swinging her body from side to side.

Dixie smiled at her, then looked into the mirror that hung above the table. It would take more than a quick wash to make herself presentable.

A whole lot more, she reminded herself. She added cold water from the pitcher to the hot water Livia had poured into the bowl, so she wouldn't burn herself.

"Are you Ty's lady? He never came to visit with you. Will you marry him and have lots of babies?"

Dixie scooped up water and soap, bending over to scrub her face to avoid answering the child. She heard the thump of her saddlebags deposited on the floor and paid no attention to Julia's giggles. Her skin felt as if it were soaking up every bit of water she splashed on her face.

Momentarily blinded, Dixie groped for the towel, her murmured thanks muffled by the cloth the second it was handed to her. She would give a full gold poke for a real bath in a tub filled with buckets of hot water that she didn't have to lug herself, and milled soap that didn't smell like lye and ashes.

Emerging from behind the towel, she saw that Julia was gone. She found herself meeting Ty's gaze in the mirror. She felt trapped by his night-dark eyes—smoldering and smoky with heat—which seemed to stop time and leave her unable to move.

"I wondered if you're as... hungry as I am."

She noted the pause, knew he had done it deliberately and her thoughts flew back to this morning, when she had awakened in a wanton sprawl on top of him. There was an instant stomach-tightening reaction that she couldn't fight or control, and from the grin that tilted the corner of his mouth, she had a feeling he knew exactly what she was feeling.

Dixie tore her gaze away from the mirror and his disturbing reflection. She bent to her saddlebag to get out her hairbrush, but a quick search revealed it was missing.

Ty came forward then, stopping when he was directly behind her. "This what you're looking for?"

She glanced from the brush—her brush—which he held up to his face. A mixture of excitement and warning filled her with tension. She started to reach for the hairbrush, but he caught her by surprise. From the bristles, he lifted several long strands of her hair, and wound them around his finger.

"I watched you brush your hair one night," he noted softly, tucking the curl he had made into his shirt pocket. "I wanted to come into your camp that night. Wanted you—"

"But you didn't come into my camp, Ty. And if you had, most likely I'd have shot you." She took the brush and noted the strength of will it took for her to turn her back on him.

With his uninjured hand, Ty caught hold of hers, raised to brush her hair. "Don't make me wait too long. I've found that I'm not a patient man."

"Why are you doing this to me, Kincaid?"

"Kincaid, is it? Helps keep you distanced, doesn't it? But I'll be honest. Damned if I know. Last thing I want in my life is a female to complicate matters."

"We agree on something. I don't want you." Dixie turned to face him. "I'll leave in the morning. You can tell your friends whatever you like."

"Are you two gonna stand there jawing while supper gets cold?" Greg asked, looking from one to the other.

Dixie didn't know if she was grateful for his interruption or not. Ty left her and she made short work of unsnarling her hair, deciding that some knots couldn't be brushed out, they could only be cut free. She wasn't sure if Ty Kincaid took her seriously or not. She couldn't let it matter. He didn't want any complications, and she certainly wanted nothing to do with the man.

She delayed as long as she could. Her reasons for avoiding the table had everything to do with hunger—more than what Ty had mentioned, it was the hunger for all she had turned her back on.

Dixie took the seat next to Julia, thankful that Ty was seated on the same bench but at the opposite end. With one of the older boys, whose name she didn't know, James and Julia between them, she didn't have to worry about seeing Ty or touching him as dishes were passed back and forth.

She didn't pay too close attention to what Greg was saying, until she heard anger in the man's voice at some question Ty asked.

"Jessie wouldn't listen a plugged nickel's worth to me. Marrying Harry Winslow was the most pigheaded thing my sister's ever done." Greg, red faced, with his voice rising, banged his hand on the table. "Took her up too damn far away for us to know what's happening to her. Told her he wasn't worth a damn. Man didn't know horn from tail on a cow. Rancher? Hell no. More likely he was gonna get lost in the Superstitions hunting for gold."

"Now, Greg, don't get riled again," Livia warned. "Jessie's a woman grown and able to make up her own mind about the man she wanted."

"Livia, most times I respect your opinion. But you didn't like Harry any more than I did. Go on," Greg urged his wife, "admit it. Tell Ty how you had that bad dream the night before they got hitched."

"No need," Ty said, before she spoke. "If I can, I'll make sure to swing by the junction and find out where his place is. I'll get word to you about Jessie."

"Ma always figured that you and Jessie might get—"

"Elwin, that's enough."

"Aw, Ma, you said it plenty of times. You even tried chasing off Harry that one time—"

"Your ma said that's enough, boy."

"Yes, Pa."

The boy shoveled in a mouthful of stew, but Dixie saw his gaze met his brother's sitting across from him, and the look they exchanged.

Feeling uncomfortable, Dixie tried to find some excuse to leave. But she was still hungry, growing more relaxed and tired by the second, and struggled to remind herself that she didn't care who people paired Ty Kincaid with as long as it wasn't her.

"Been home this past year, Ty?" Greg asked as the tense silence grew around the table.

"No call to. My brothers don't need me there."

"Bet your ma misses you plenty," Livia said, setting down her fork. She sent a quick searching gaze around at everyone's plate, and satisfied that no one needed immediate attention, she spoke again to Ty.

"When Elwin and Gilby helped the Duncans make their gather this spring, I missed them terribly the month that they were gone. Couldn't stand worrying about them, not knowing if they were eating right, keeping warm or even watching out for each other like they promised. Your ma—"

"Livia," Ty interrupted, "no one makes hunter's stew near as good as you. I'd sure like another helping."

"All right. I won't say another word. But you think about what I did say."

Dixie took it all in, fending off the questions that rose about Ty. Why did he drift if he had a home? Lord, it made no sense to her why he would want to sleep in the open when a roof waited and family beneath it. She sipped her now-cooled coffee, but even the pungent brew couldn't keep her awake. Twice she smothered yawns behind her hand until Greg caught her.

"Livia, fix this young woman a bed in the loft. She's about ready to fall face first in her plate."

Protests didn't do Dixie a bit of good. Her suggestion that she could sleep in the stable was refused. Dragging her weary body up the stairs to the loft, she barely managed to murmur good-night and thank Livia before sleep claimed her.

Long after the children had climbed the stairs to the loft and Livia had drawn the blanket across to seek her bed, Ty spoke softly to Greg, telling him what had happened. But his thoughts were with Dixie and how she looked when he had snared her gaze with his in the mirror. For a brief, unguarded moment, he had seen a reflection of the same hunger that prowled his body and left him . . . restless.

There was a softness to her, so at odds with the image that others saw, and he found that he wanted to protect that softness. A strange notion for him to have after he told her that he didn't want a woman to complicate his life.

But he wanted Dixie Rawlins.

Didn't make a lick of sense. He couldn't figure any good reasons for it.

Yet his mind supplied reasons as Greg poured them another drink from his whiskey jug and made a silent toast.

Ty liked her independence. Her mouth was so damn kissable. He could feel himself growing hard just thinking about her mouth and how softly she had yielded to his kiss, how the fit of her body seemed made for his.

"Come on, Ty, have another drink," Greg whispered. "You got a look in your eye like a bull ready to jump the fence. Livia won't take kindly to you joining Dixie in the loft."

"I wasn't . . ." Ty looked up as he held out his cup. "Aw, hell, Greg, she's got me feeling like a green kid."

"Better for you to figure why someone was carrying a picture of her."

"I've been over and over everything that happened in the saloon. And the little, damn little, that Dixie told me. She's been gambling for gold to buy information for some time now. I figure she's hunting someone." Ty closed his eyes, letting images form and suddenly he sat up. "The man with the scarred hand. Of the three men in the saloon he was the only one that held her attention."

"You figure it was his saddlebags you found that tintype in?"

Ty stared into the glowing coals. "She asked if I thought she was in cahoots with them? Could be they had a falling out. I know the picture was of her. Younger, softer, but Dixie just the same. Those hombres were snake mean." He met Greg's concerned look. "Doesn't make any sense, does it?"

"You ever figure she might be hitched to him? Man would carry around a picture of his wife."

"No. I'd stake my life on that. She ain't married."

Greg set his cup down and stretched, yawning widely. "We'll both sleep on it. Morning always makes things clear. Your lady's got some secrets for sure. You bet on that." He disappeared behind the blanket and moments later his boots hit the floor.

The creak of the rope spring told Ty that his friend was in bed. *Your lady...* Ty couldn't help repeating the words. He eyed the jug that Greg left him, but whiskey wasn't what he wanted. Drinking hadn't dulled his need, if anything, the liquor had sharpened it.

Cradling his head with his good arm, Ty lay down on the rug before the dying fire and stared up at the planked ceiling. Secrets. Dixie, from what he had learned today, had plenty and she wasn't going to share them with him anytime soon.

Strange thing was, he was beginning to want her to. *Don't get involved.*

Too late, he answered the small warning voice in his mind. *I am involved. Knee-deep, and sinking fast.*

Fact was, he wanted the lady's secrets. Wanted them as much as he wanted to explore the lady's body. He needed to rid himself of a growing hunger that was prowling deep inside him like a hungry wolf circling prey.

His sigh was deep and tinged with frustration.

Between the throb of his shoulder and the ache in his groin, he didn't think he was going to get much needed sleep.

When he recognized the creak on the stair as more than the settling of the house, he knew he wasn't going to get any sleep at all.

Chapter Six

Ty wasn't surprised to find Dixie creeping through the kitchen to the back door. He waited until she had her hand on the latch before he stepped out from the deep shadows of the doorway.

"Had a bad dream? Or were you thirsty, Dixie?"

She spun around and he heard the slap of leather against the door.

"Disappearing like a thief in the night? Didn't you learn any manners at your father's knee? Ain't polite," he offered, coming toward her, "to run off when folks invite you into their home to spend the night."

Dixie wasn't about to lie to him. She didn't want another confrontation with him, either, but it seemed that lady luck had other wishes.

"I just thought it best for me to leave quietly."

"All this running away you do, Dixie, is getting mighty hard on my constitution."

"Just one more reason . . ." She lost her breath for a few moments when he crowded her against the door. She managed to duck her head before he made another move. "Like I was saying, it's just one more reason for me to move on. No goodbyes, no see you around, just a short day together."

"It was more than that, and you know it."

To her surprise, he reached down and unhooked the latch. She ignored the way his hand skimmed up her hip before he urged her outside in front of him. She shivered in the night cold of the mountains and waited for him to close the door. There was no sense in trying to run now. She had a feeling that wounded or not, Kincaid would only come after her until he had his answers.

"It's too damn cold to stand out here and talk." He grabbed hold of her arm with his right hand and held her beside him. "And make no mistake, we are going to talk. Take the lantern down. The stable should be warm enough."

Dixie found the metal case of wooden matches above the doorframe. She lit the lantern and held it to light their path. Once inside the stable, they both ignored the restless stampings of the horses and the penned orphaned calves. She followed Ty to an empty stall.

"Hay's clean." He released her arm and took hold of the lantern. "Go on in and make yourself comfortable. We both know you're not riding out tonight." He didn't even bother to look at her as he hung the lantern from a protruding nail on the post of the stall. Kicking up some hay against the wooden stall slats, he settled himself prone in the thick, fragrant hay and patted the place next to him.

"Join me. You already proved you can hold your own with me more than once."

Her chin rose a notch, more for the challenge of his look than for his words. She let her gaze roam over him, noting the boxy fit of the shirt he wore. It was the same faded gray as the one Greg had worn at supper. But if he had borrowed the pants, it must have been from one of the older Rutland boys, for the neatly patched material gloved his long legs like a second skin.

Ty grinned and cradled his head with his good arm.

Tossing aside her saddlebags, Dixie refused to acknowledge what else her gaze had taken in, but her body responded with that same strange mixture of excitement and warning that Ty was fully aroused and doing nothing to hide it from her.

She chose to sit across from him. And his grin deepened as if he knew why.

All she could do was level a stare that had kept more than one man away.

Ruefully Dixie admitted that Ty Kincaid was not most men. He wasn't like any man she had met before. The knowledge didn't help her. It left her in a quandary. How was she to deal with him?

Ty's grin disappeared beneath her stare. But the hard level look in her eyes had little to do with it. The light cast by the lantern overhead fell upon her face, and he saw for himself the bruised look of her features, and the deep shadows of exhaustion beneath her eyes. If he pushed her too hard now, he would have the answers he wanted. But he would earn Dixie's hate right along with them.

"You don't give your trust easily, do you?"

Averting her gaze, Dixie shook her head. Is this what he wanted from her? Trust?

"We've been through a lot together in a short time. Yeah, I know," he added when she shot him an accusing look, "that's what you wanted. Short and sweet. But it didn't turn out that way and you're stuck with me."

"Why? You're here with friends. We part company and I'll take care of my own problems."

"Horse stealing is *our* problem. Being shot at happened to both of us. I don't take kindly to folks who shoot at me. Matter of fact, you know I usually shoot back."

Dixie scooted back until she could lean against the side of the stall. Heaving a sigh, she stretched her legs out in front of her. "If I tell you what you want to know, will you let me leave then?"

"You offering me a bargain?"

"Of sorts," she answered, sifting hay through her fingers. Keeping her gaze focused on her hands, she added, "You've got mule in you, Kincaid. I admit, I don't know what to do about you. You saved my life. Twice now. I can't give you more than my thanks. Why you think I need you around is a fool's race to figure out. I don't need you. I don't need anyone."

"You keep repeating that and soon you might start believing it."

"What do you want from me?" Tossing aside the pieces of hay she had toyed with, Dixie closed her eyes. She tilted her head back against the stall and listened to the small rustlings of the animals as they once more settled down. The silence that followed soothed her. She could feel the tension ease from aching muscles. But as her breathing regulated itself to that of Ty's, a new awareness of him forced her to open her eyes and look at him.

"Why did you help me out in the saloon?"

"Didn't like the odds against you."

"I was cheating them, Kincaid."

"I know that. Figure you cheated me a time or two. I'd like to know why you needed the gold."

"I know that you've heard I buy information with the gold I win. Information about a man with a scarred hand." She watched him closely but only found mild interest in his eyes. Clearing her throat, she wondered just how much to tell him.

"You were right to say that I don't trust anyone. There hasn't been anyone for me to trust since my father was killed. Not one of our *good* neighbors wanted to get involved."

Her laugh was soft but filled with bitterness as she once more closed her eyes. Emotion seemed to have been drained from her voice.

"The best advice they all gave me was to marry some man and forget what happened. I couldn't forget. I didn't want to forget. And I lost it all, land, cattle, belongings, just because I was a woman who fought alone."

"A very tired woman," Ty observed, fighting not to take her into his arms, fighting every instinct that shouted a warning over and over for him not to get involved with her. "Tired and about at the end of your rope."

It was not meant to be a question and she let it pass. She couldn't summon an argument. She was indeed at the end of her rope.

"How did you meet Greg?"

Sensing her need to distract him from probing her secrets, Ty figured to bide his time and answered her.

"Greg bought cattle from us and I volunteered to help drive them up here. He offered me a job to stay on and work the place with him. Had no reason to go back home so I stayed through the winter and spring with him and Livia."

"Is that why he said that he owed you?" It was not the question she wanted to ask him. Dixie had a burning curiosity to know why Ty had left home to drift. The flat tone of his voice didn't invite any questioning in that area. But she wished he was more forthcoming.

"It's all in the past. Can't change the way a person thinks. Greg figures he owes me, I don't. End of the matter."

"And his sister Jessie? Wasn't she here, too?"

"Damn!" he muttered, turning to his side, resting his head on his crooked elbow. "You're worse than a barber probing a sore tooth." She merely looked at him, no hint of a smile on her face, just a plea in her eyes that he keep talking.

"Jessie came in the spring after their aunt passed on. And before you ask, I never entertained the notion of her and me getting hitched. Never met a woman yet I wanted to spend more than a night with."

"Then why not let me go, Ty?" she asked softly, once more shutting him out by closing her eyes.

"Told you before, and I'll tell you again. I'll be damned if I know why. Could be I'm curious. Could be you arouse me like a house on fire and I'm hoping to put it out."

"Could be," she added, "you're a liar, too."

"I'll admit I've done my share of lying. But Dixie," he noted in a suddenly husky voice, "I'm not lying to you. And I've answered your questions, so now you answer a few of mine."

There was a telltale tensing of her body, although she didn't move, didn't open her eyes. Ty watched her and he patiently waited.

"If I wanted to, I guess I could piece together all the things you didn't tell me. Who wanted to run your father off his land? What kind of trouble did he make that neighbors didn't help you? Then, if I really wanted to discover all the secrets you're keeping from me, I'd find out where you came from and exactly what happened that night."

With a weary sigh that she didn't even attempt to hide from him, Dixie clasped her hands on her lap and leveled a hard look at him. No matter how he said it, Ty asked her to trust him.

"I let him go," she said after a few minutes.

"Who?"

"The man who murdered my father. He was one of the three men at the saloon. I had him in front of me, but... but I..." She stopped and shrugged. "Lost my chance and I can't go back now."

With relentless force, the hardships she had endured in her quest for revenge slammed into her. The fact that she had let her father's murderer escape was brought back with a renewed fury.

"Dixie?"

He was at her side, cupping her chin to lift her face. She appeared beaten, and he felt a hate for the man who had brought this spirited woman so low. As much as he had wanted answers from her, he didn't want to see her vulnerable. Kneeling beside her, Ty could no more stop his thumb from brushing her cheek than he could have made the night into day.

She heard the whisper of her name on his lips once more, heard it in the hushed intimacy of the enclosed space that locked the world out for a little while. His touch was gentle, and after so long without it, she craved the gentleness.

His thigh brushed hers. Ty felt a hot shaft of desire go through him. He met her startled gaze for a timeless moment. He knew that whatever was happening between them was more than a need for sex. What he was feeling was too powerful, too sudden and too damn confusing.

He caressed the curve of her jaw, tilting her chin up a bit more, his thumb rubbing over the corner of her mouth. He absorbed the warmth of her lips with his touch, heard the sharp intake of her breath that rushed quickly over his hand when she released it. He couldn't hide what he was feeling when his gaze locked with hers.

He wasn't about to even try.

His thumb seemed to have a mind of its own, repeatedly brushing over her lower lip until her mouth parted slightly. Still holding her gaze with his, her eyes filled with a darkness that beckoned him, he lowered his head, stopping just short of joining his mouth to hers.

"I know you're gonna tell me to stop. Gonna tell me that I shouldn't kiss you. That you don't want me to. I know all that," he whispered, sliding his hand beneath the heavy braid of her hair to cup the back of her neck. A half smile creased his lips when he felt the slight tremor of her body caress his.

"I know. And I'm going to do it anyway 'cause it's all I've thought about all day. Kissing—" he breathed the word over her mouth, barely touching his lips to hers "—you." A shudder rose from deep inside her. Dixie found herself leaning toward him, wanting to deepen the breath-stealing contact of his lips touching hers. Her eyes drifted closed, her lids suddenly heavy, but she needed the protection of hiding behind them to dim the blaze of passion that sparked from his.

No man had ever wanted her this way. She could feel the trembling that shook her body transfer itself to his. She knew she had been seduced by the husky, rich intimacy of his voice. Closing her eyes didn't help her deny the exquisite torment of waiting for his kiss.

She reeled with awareness of his very strong, very lean body only a breath away. Her wildly beating pulse warned how dangerous this was. How dangerous he was. She was so close that each labored breath lifted her breasts into his chest. Even through their shirts his chest felt hard and warm. She could feel her nipples tighten in response to the contact, sending fragile threads of pleasure winding downward to flutter deep in her belly.

Dixie was no longer sure about anything but that she wanted more than the mere brushing of his lips against hers. She wanted his mouth on hers. And he wanted it, too.

There was a tension in his every muscle that she could feel. No, that wasn't right. It wasn't tension as much as excitement. For the same excitement was in her, too.

His hand beneath her hair heated the skin on the back of her neck. Excitement coiled, winding tighter and tighter by the second, waiting to be strung or to be banished. One move, one word, that's all it would take to break this breathless anticipation and see them past the brink of danger.

Dixie couldn't draw enough breath to speak. His fingers slid up into her hair, cradling the back of her head, tilting her face more to his. The slight move, the feel of his long, strong fingers holding her still for him, sent a fresh burst of tremors through her.

"Sweet," he murmured, touching his tongue to the curve of her bottom lip, his breath shuddering against her mouth. "Sweet Dixie."

"Yes...oh, please, yes," she murmured, not sure of all that she was answering or asking for, but very sure she wanted to find out.

His fingers tightened an infinite bit, dragging her head back. Ty sucked in a harsh breath. "You know that I want you? How much I want you?"

"Yes," she whispered, nodding.

The slight, spare motion of her head was enough to bring their lips together. Like a pile of dry tinder touched by a match, their kiss exploded. His mouth took hers, ravishing it with a rough, raw splendor. Dixie parted her lips willingly in answer to the fierce demand of his tongue. It moved inside her mouth with strokes that were hot and wet and sweet, sending a shivering heat coursing through her body.

Hay rustled beneath the settling weight of their bodies, releasing the scent of summer sun-dried grasses as his knee wedged itself between her thighs. Dixie had no thought to stop him, no thought to stop herself from touching him. Her arm wound around his neck, holding him closer as their lips clung and tasted, parting the mere fraction needed for them to gulp air only to once again seal their mouths in yet another soul-shattering kiss.

She trembled against his wiry body, refusing to hear the dimming voice that warned her to stop, to think of what she was doing. She was tired of thinking, of being alone. She wanted the feelings he aroused, wanted to savor the new sensations he awakened in her.

There was a joy here with Ty, a joy she thought had been almost stolen from her. The joy of being a woman, one who could desire a man. And every deepening stroke of his tongue, every longer lasting moment of their kisses, chased the memory of cloying breath and grasping hands that had tried to steal what was hers alone to give. Her fingers tightened within his hair, the other hand sliding over his hip to find his back pocket. She slipped her fingers inside, cupping his buttock at the same time he pressed his wounded arm around the small of her back. The move drew her to straddle his knee and she broke the kiss, dizzy with the need for air, afraid that she was losing control.

Ty scattered kisses over her face, some gentle, others hot, openmouthed kisses that once more forced her eyes closed and gave him back the sweet taste of her. He tugged free her braid, sliding his hand through the straight, heavy weight of her hair before he wrapped it around his wrist and hand to hold her still for the unrestrained passion he unleashed.

He coaxed her tongue forward to meet his, stroking eagerly against it, teasing her by plunging and withdrawing until she sought to learn his taste.

Secrets. Dixie had more than she had told him, more than he had discovered now. Hot secrets. Sleek and arousing and he knew he wouldn't let her go until he had learned every one of them.

Her knee pressed against his arousal, sending the ache deeper, the need higher. And he slid his hand from her back to her hip, dragging her closer. Her thighs gloved his leg, and he guided her to ride him, wanting more of the wildness he sensed waiting to be free.

Dixie uttered a small gasp that turned quickly into a moan. The fiery pressure was too much, yet in seconds, wasn't enough.

He cupped her hips with fierce urgency, lifting her into his body, drawing her to match the provocative rocking movements of his hips.

Her head fell back as desire streaked through her. Ty's lips followed the arch of her bared throat, impatiently seeking the pulse point throbbing at the base.

And the tight rein Dixie had kept on her emotions suddenly snapped. She needed too much. Needed Ty far too much. He made her forget. And desire ebbed as fear replaced it.

She cried out, fighting not to let passion sweep away the last remnant of the will to stop him...and stop herself.

Twisting her head from side to side, her whispered denial grew in intensity. She felt the bite of his fingers digging into her shoulders, the rough shakes he gave her before she heard his demand that she look at him.

His hair was in wild disarray from the kneading of her fingers and, despite the deep tremors shaking her body, she wanted to lift her hand and smooth the damp locks from his forehead. She couldn't look at his eyes, but her gaze noted the slight flush that tinted his prominent cheekbones. His breaths, like her own, were labored. Her gaze fell on a drop of sweat that slowly trickled down the browned column of his throat. She was seized by a fierce and unknown desire to catch that drop, to touch her lips to his skin and keep the salty-sweet taste of him on her tongue.

Ty saw the confusion cloud her features, but he had no pity for her. He was raw and aching, battling himself not to stretch her out flat beneath him and take what her every kiss had promised.

"Why, Dixie?"

The words were harsh, sharply bitten off, and she felt the power of his gaze drawing her head up to look at him. When she couldn't summon the will to deny him this, she met his gaze and instantly wished she had not.

The blue color was nearly gone, eclipsed by the dilated black centers that hid nothing of the passion that still held him in its grip. She didn't know she was crying until he spoke.

"Tears? Now? Tell me why. Tell me what I did. Or what I didn't do. Talk to me," he demanded, giving her yet another rough little shake. "I didn't have you pegged for a tease. I told you I wanted—"

"Let me go, Ty. Just let me go."

Soft. Ever so soft her voice washed through him. But far from making him release her, the demand only made his resolve harden.

"Mercy's in short supply. Just tell me why you pulled back now. You were hotter than—"

"Stop it!" She closed her eyes, sagging against his grip and unable to control the tremors that racked her body. "I couldn't stop you before. I couldn't stop myself. I didn't . . . didn't even want to try. Satisfied?"

Her words were mere whispers, and Ty had to lean over her to hear her. He heard part of what he wanted. Far from being satisfied, he still felt a need to punish her for leaving him raw and aching.

"Then why the hell didn't you push me away when I first kissed you? Answer me, Dixie. I'm listening."

She tried to pull free of his hold, but once more he held her tight. Beaten, she didn't attempt to protest again.

"Go on, finish it. I can tell there's more to it."

"Stop badgering me, Ty. I'm exhausted. I only slept for a few hours before a nightmare woke me. All I wanted to do was leave here. Leave you. But you couldn't let it be. Couldn't leave me alone. You had to come after me . . . had to have your damn answers. No more. You hear me? No more," she repeated, raising her hands to wedge a space between them.

"Hell, Dixie! I'm not your enemy." Desire warred with a powerful need to comfort and protect her, even from himself. The mixed feelings left him shaken and he found himself releasing her, hating the way she quickly scampered back to get away from him. Her brown hair hid half her face from him, but he saw the sparkle of tears on her cheek and noted that she made no effort to wipe them away. He lifted his hand, but once again she moved back from him, and Ty let his hand fall to his side.

Staring blindly down at the hay, he found himself clutching a handful, squeezing it tight as he struggled for control. In a useless gesture, he flung the handful across the stall, and watched the bits fall.

"I didn't lie about wanting you, Dixie. But I came after you because I thought you needed comfort. It's not right for a woman to be so damn high-fired independent."

She heard the underlying rawness in his voice. While she longed to quietly lick her own wounds, honesty forced her to answer him.

"I'll admit I wanted comfort, and things just got out of hand. I've been alone for so long, Ty, and you were right saying I'm at the end of my rope. I didn't mean to use you."

He shot her a look still simmering with anger. "Use me? Is that what you call it? I've got a broadside for you, lady, when a woman—"

"Don't. Lord, please don't say any more." She curled herself against the back wall of the stall, huddling her body tight to contain the pain that lashed at her. She had been alone too long in a world that men controlled. But along with the pain came an anger that mixed with fear when she glanced at Ty. The man made her feel. He reminded her that she had once been a woman with dreams.

There were so many she had lost in the past months. Love was something she had hoped to find one day. She wanted a husband, a family and the much-needed security of laying her head upon a pillow each night knowing where she would wake in the morning. There was a need within her to nurture a family as she longed to nurture land, and she desperately wanted a man to love, one who would be strong enough to stand beside her no matter what they had to face.

Dreams. Empty, cast-off dreams.

Things that she wouldn't, couldn't tell Ty about.

Revealing weaknesses to anyone could be her downfall. The only way she could survive and do what she had to was to deny everything that had once mattered to her until she had her revenge.

Ty raked back his hair with one hand and slumped against the slats. "I'll be damned if I know what to make of you. I'll be doubly damned if I'll let you ride out alone with those men after us."

"It's not your fight, Kincaid. Remember, no complications? Your insistence is making one big complication for me. I can't deal with you. I don't want to."

If he hadn't heard the slight tremor in her voice, Ty would have believed her. He would have walked away right then and left her alone. But she chose that moment to look at him, and their gazes met in a clash of wills. Ty understood that in the long, passing moments she was taking his measure as he took hers, weighing strengths and weaknesses. Dixie pushed him away the moment he got too close. Not just body close but when he dug at her emotions. Far from discouraging him, she only intrigued him.

And he had the most ridiculous notion that she was somehow protecting him.

He would have laughed, for she looked weak-kneed as a newborn filly, but the battle light of temper seeped into her eyes and he knew there was a hard core of strength within her. She was vulnerable now, but come morning he'd have a fight on his hands.

"And if I can't let you go, what then, Dixie?"

Chapter Seven

Defeat and despair forced her eyes closed. She shut him out, but his question replayed over and over in her mind. He wasn't really giving her a choice. And while she longed to say "Yes, help me," something refused to allow her to say the words.

"Just as well that you don't answer me," Ty said, his own voice echoing her exhaustion. "Those men are killers, and you can't ride off looking for them alone. End of the discussion. Not a thought more about it. I couldn't call myself a man and live with that."

Dixie came to her knees in a rush, throwing handfuls of hay at him. "I wish I had something harder and heavier to throw at you. Kincaid, you're more than a mule, you're pure rock. I never asked you—"

"On that we agree. You never asked me. But you could."

"Never." She glared at him, watching as he came awkwardly to his feet. He couldn't hide the wince of pain as he used his wounded arm to support himself.

"Go to sleep, Dixie. No sense in disturbing the rest of them for what's left of the night. We settled enough for now."

"Settled? We settled nothing. This has gone far enough. There is no us! I don't know how to make you hear what I'm saying or to make you understand that I don't want a damn thing to do with you, Kincaid!"

He eyed her with a taunting look. "Swearing doesn't sound nice coming from a woman."

"Where are you going?" she demanded as he lifted the lantern off the nail.

"Miss me already?"

"Like hell."

"Well, I'll tell you. I'm heading for the tack room to find us some blankets. We can bed down right here."

"I won't sleep with you."

He turned and offered her a knowing grin. "You've already done it and a hell of a lot closer than I was counting on."

The shadows hid her flaming cheeks. Dixie didn't bother to refute him. The stall was large enough for them to stretch out without touching each other. And morning would be soon enough to deal with the arrogant, pigheaded Ty Kincaid.

All too fast he was back, tossing her two thick wool blankets and spreading one out for himself.

When she saw that he was going to blow out the lantern, she asked him not to.

"Can't leave it lit, Dixie. Wouldn't want to get another fire started, now would we?"

He had mentioned it deliberately, channeling her thoughts back to those minutes when she had lost herself in his arms. Pillowing her head on her hands, Dixie tried to blank out the feel of his body against hers. She licked her lips and found a residue of his taste, or maybe it was just fanciful imagination taking over.

She damned the luck that had crossed her path with his, and in the next breath called herself a fool. She wouldn't have survived that night without his help. But that didn't mean he owned her. Around and around, her mind circled what to do about Ty, and she drifted off to sleep without reaching any conclusion.

Ty knew almost to the minute when restlessness turned to sleep for her. He envied Dixie for a few moments while he wrestled with the trap that waited for him. He had told her the truth. He couldn't call himself a man and leave her alone. She'd have to accept that. He wasn't giving her a choice. But he sure wouldn't make any sucker bets on the outcome when Dixie finally understood that. His daddy didn't raise no fool.

Dixie was dreaming. She had to be dreaming that soft, whispering voice that tickled her ear and announced that coffee was waiting for her. What a lovely dream…someone serving her coffee in bed. She sighed and nestled deeper beneath her blanket. She still craved sleep, her aching body deserved it, so she fought against being awakened.

Seeing the dreamy smile play around her lips, Ty had to restrain himself from waking her the way he would have liked to. If he tried stealing that smile of hers with a kiss she'd more than likely come up spitting and snarling at him. And he didn't want to fight with her.

The early ride he had taken left him assured that he had covered their trail here, and he saw no sign that they had been followed. He needed time to pry the rest of her secrets from her. His shoulder could do with a day of rest, too. Livia had offered to wash his clothes, and he knew that Dixie wouldn't mind the same for hers, as well as have a real bath. It wasn't kindness that prompted his thought. Or so he told himself. Possessions seemed to matter a lot to her. She wouldn't run off without her clothes.

He called to her again, and when she refused to open her eyes, he gently blew on the coffee, then fanned the rising aroma toward her face.

With a moan, Dixie inhaled the rich scent of freshly brewed coffee. A scent so rich she dreamed it had to come from just-ground coffee beans. It had been weeks since she had tasted it. Her stomach reacted with a loud growling, and her mind sent wake-up messages to her body. Messages soon became a demand that she taste this dreamed-of promise.

It took Dixie a little while longer to figure out that she had never dreamed about the aroma of coffee.

Still groggy after a restless night's sleep, she barely managed to open her eyes. Her eyelids felt as if she had pried them open. Since she was curled beneath the blanket, lying on her side, the first thing she saw was a pair of knees.

An all-too-familiar pair of knees and legs tucked Indian-fashion and nearly touching her nose. Those particular knees had figured in a dream or two, whose content lingered too close for comfort and had her clamp her thighs together.

But there was temptation, too. Cradled within long-fingered hands dead center of those spread knees was the cup of coffee she craved.

"Kincaid." She wrinkled her nose as her ripe scent rose and mixed with that of the coffee. She forced herself to look up, and stopped when her gaze found his mouth wearing a grin so taunting she had to call it cocky.

Another moan forced its way past her lips. Dixie turned over to her back. Closing her eyes wasn't enough to shut out the image she retained of him. She flung up one arm as an added shield.

"Go away, Kincaid."

"Is that any way to greet the man who came all the way out here to serve you coffee? Time to rise and shine, sleepyhead, it's past ten. This is a damn good cup of coffee, if I do say so myself."

"You would. You're arrogant enough."

"Ah, a cranky lady upon waking. I'll remember that."

"Don't bother. You won't be around to see it again. And," she added, trying to resist the wafting scent that once more sent her stomach growling, "I am not cranky."

"Whatever the lady says."

Why was he being agreeable? Dixie didn't trust him. She shifted her arm and peered up at him. His hair was damp. He had shaved. A foolish thing to notice—that the beard stubble might be gone, but he looked just as dangerous as he had the night she saw him in the saloon. Her hand came up from under the blanket and touched her cheek then her chin. She wondered if all the kissing they had done had left its mark on her.

"Open up, Dixie."

She felt the soft press of crumbly, still-warm biscuit against her lips. Now that her eyes were adjusted to the bright spill of light in the stable, she lifted her arm over her head and took a bite of the food he offered.

"That's a real fresh egg I fried and put in there."

Dixie licked her lips and wiggled backward before she tried to sit up. "Next you'll be telling me you went out to the henhouse and collected the egg just for me."

Shooting her a wounded expression, Ty offered the cup to her. "Why do you find that so hard to believe? I can be nice. More than nice. I can be—"

"Spare me." She wrapped her hands around the cup and sipped repeatedly. He was still holding out the egg-filled biscuit, but when she reached for it, he pulled his hand back.

"I'll feed you."

Her mouth watered. She set her teeth together and reluctantly shook her head.

"That's not being dependent on someone," he reasoned. The glaring look in her eyes spoke volumes, unfortunately it wasn't what Ty wanted to hear.

"Here," he said, handing the biscuit over, "eat up. You'll need your strength for the busy hours ahead."

Ignoring him, she enjoyed her breakfast, even licking her fingers before she drained the cup. "That was good. Thank you, Ty." She shoved aside the blanket and rose before he did. "You were right about it being late. I'll get saddled up, then say goodbye—"

He came after her so suddenly that Dixie dropped the cup to the hay and found herself crowded against the back of the stall.

"You didn't hear me last night? You're not running off. You think you can hunt a man that doesn't want to be found? Think you have the guts to pull a gun on him, face-to-face and then shoot him cold? Think about it, Dixie. Really think about it hard and long. You're a woman—"

"Stop yelling at me! There's no one else to do it. I owe my father that much. I owe it to myself. The man can't go free. There's no law to help and I'll never rest easy until he's paid for what he did."

She took and released a shuddering breath, shaken by this sudden turn. "Back off, Kincaid." Her hand reached for her gun but came up empty. She didn't waste a breath but wrenched open the buckle and whipped the holster off.

"Now, Dixie—"

"You dirty, lying, no good polecat. You snake in the grass." She snapped the leather as he backed away from her. "You give me back my gun." It suddenly dawned on her that he could only have taken it while she was sleeping. "You sneakin', thievin', no-account lowlife. Just who the devil do you think you are, trying to tell me what to do?''

''I'm the man who's gonna stay clear of that wicked strap you're swinging, that's who.''

''You snuck up on me while I slept! You stole my gun! You're just no good.''

''Don't get me riled, Dixie.''

''Don't 'Dixie' me!'' She went after him, but he managed to dodge every swing of the leather. ''You're a conniver. You planned this to keep me here. Only heaven knows why. I don't care. Stay still, damn you!'' she screamed when he once more twisted his lean body out of her reach. She had to shove her hair back, for it blinded her. She stood in the middle of the stall, breathing hard and glared at him.

And Ty Kincaid laughed.

She held out as long as she could. He looked utterly ridiculous with his arms splayed against the back wall, as if he were cowering from her. If only it were true. His laughter was contagious and she felt her own bubble up, then free. The more he clowned with terror-struck expressions, the harder she laughed. The hiccup came as a surprise. Ty was moving by the time the second one erupted.

''Now—hic—look what you—hic—did,'' she accused.

''I've got the cure. You need to hold your breath. I'll even help.'' And with that little warning, he lowered his head and kissed her.

Dixie could have pushed him away. She spared a thought toward doing it. But the kiss was too short to stop her hiccups, and too long for her peace of mind. Like a flash flood, it brought back the long, sensuous kisses they had exchanged, but he had already moved aside and picked up the cup.

"Livia's doing the wash. She's got the tub set out for you if you want a bath."

"Ty?" He kept on walking. One more burning-all-the-way hiccup escaped and Dixie thought she was done with them.

She followed him, then ran to catch up with him before they reached the house. Grabbing hold of his arm, she made him stop.

"I meant what I said back there. I have to go after him. You have to understand that. I made a vow on my father's grave, and one to myself, as well. I can't go back on that."

There was a plea in her eyes that he wanted to ignore but couldn't. She wasn't asking for his help. He should be glad of that. For there was the other trap he had avoided thinking about. The one he swore he would never fall into. His skill with a gun came from the necessity to survive. He had never hired out to do someone else's killing for them. He was forced to listen to his warning this time. And while he thought about it, Dixie walked away from him.

And this time he had to let her go.

Livia looked up from her washing as Dixie rounded the corner of the house. "Finished that ruckus with Ty?"

"That man is—"

"More than most women can handle," she finished for her. Livia dropped the shirt she was washing back into the water and wiped her hands on her apron. "Did he give you a chance to eat?"

"Yes. And I'm sorry. I should thank you. I do."

"There's still some biscuits left if you're hungry. Plenty of coffee, too. Don't know if Ty got around to telling you that I fixed the small tub near my bed so's you can have privacy. Water's all heated and waiting on the stove."

Damn, but her eyes were ready to spill tears. What was wrong with her that the least bit of kindness had her set to cry? Dixie glanced away for a moment, the sun a warm blanket over the late morning's quiet. There was peace to be had in this place, she felt it soaking into her. *Someday,* she promised herself, *I'll have a place of my own, too.*

"Livia—" She broke off as movement near the corral caught her attention. Ty was mounted and riding out without a backward look. Dixie turned away, too, forcing him from her thoughts. But without him here, she could make good her intent to leave.

"I'm sorry, Livia. You've been very kind to me, and I have not been gracious about your hospitality. My only excuse is that I haven't had the company of another woman in a long time." She paused, unsure of how to ask where her gun was. Livia, standing with a waiting air, didn't help her.

"Do you, that is—"

"Why not try just coming out and saying whatever it is that's got your tongue twisted?"

"Ty stole my gun. I've got to ride out now while he's not around, Livia. I can't tell you everything, just that I must leave without him."

"Oh, dear. I wish I could help. Didn't know he took your gun. I haven't seen it. And if you run off, well, I believe he'll just come riding after you."

Dixie briefly closed her eyes and gave a little shake of her head. "I wish I could argue with you about that, but I'm afraid that you're probably right about him. My manners may be rusty, but I can help you with chores. I haven't—"

She broke off and ran back to the stable, ignoring Livia's excited questions. Dropping to her knees the second she entered the stall, Dixie tossed hay aside, searching for her saddlebags.

Gone! She sat back on her heels, her hands clenched into fists. She could buy another gun. Not easily, but it could be done. But with her saddlebags gone, so was her gold.

Fury rose inside her and Dixie fought to tamp it down. It was useless to allow that emotion to interfere with the clear thinking she needed to do. There was no doubt that Ty's motive had in part been to protect her. Not that she had asked him outright for protection. Though she admitted to herself now that she had been sorely tempted to. Just as Livia called her from the doorway, she stood up and brushed off the bits of hay clinging to her clothes.

"Dixie? What's wrong? You ran off like—"

"Ty Kincaid stole my gun and my gold." Walking out of the stall, Dixie kicked a clump of hay out of her path and straightened her shoulders.

Joining Livia, she apologized for running off. "You must think I have the manners of a green bronc on a cold morning."

Issuing a shrewd look at her guest, Livia shook her head. "Stop putting yourself down. Land's sakes, woman," she protested with an airy wave of her hand, "look around. This ain't no grand place, and Ty's friends are ours. No need to excuse yourself."

"Guess there's no need to excuse Ty's thievery, either?"

Livia started to walk away, thought better and turned. "He's a bit high-handed at times, but a body couldn't ask for a better friend."

"That's the whole point, Livia, I never asked to be his friend." Knowing there was no sense in berating the woman for something she had nothing to do with, Dixie walked back toward the house with her.

To cover the awkwardness, Livia said, "Whatever the reason, I can't say with truth that I'm sorry you're here. I've not had the company of another woman since Jessie left us almost two years ago. I've been alone more times than I've had company, but I love our home. There's something about this land that gets into a body's blood so that they never want to leave it." Hesitating, Livia glanced at Dixie's set expression.

"You can tell me to butt out, but I'll tell you that you should forgive Ty. He's never done anything that could bring someone harm. Oh, I know all about his reputation. But the truth is that he's never killed anyone lessen he had good reason.''

Temptation loomed to question Livia about Ty. Dixie bit back, then swallowed every single question. The less she knew about him, the easier it would be for her to part company from him. She had a vow to keep. Ty had already proven that he would stand in her way.

She knew this was the right decision to make, even an easy one. But she didn't understand the little nagging voice that whispered she was passing up a good chance to find out more about him.

Dixie glanced at the graduated sizes of the union suits hanging on the line. The playful breeze sent the varying lengths of legs fluttering. Overhead the sky was an intense blue, filled with thick, white clouds that reminded her of lamb's wool. Shading her eyes, she tilted her head back, her gaze picking out what appeared to be an owl's head shape in one of the clouds that seemed to vanish in seconds. It was a child's game she had never tired of playing.

Lowering her hand, she looked again at the clothing on the line and realized it was one more thing that had been stolen from her. From little Julia's flowered print gown hanging next to Livia's longer one, to the boys' and Greg's many shirts, she saw a family's life before her. The hollow feeling in her stomach forced her to look away.

''It's a chore to keep my family clean. But it sure grants me pleasure to do for them.''

''I envy you.''

There was a wealth of pain in those three words, and Livia was not insensitive to them, or to the young woman standing beside her. Impulsively she caught hold of Dixie's hand and squeezed it.

"I know you've got your reasons for being alone. I ain't prying, but I want you to know that you've got more than Ty for a friend. If there's any way I can help, you just ask me."

"You're a good woman, Livia." Dixie returned the woman's handhold, then looked away. Emotions churned inside her, softer, gentler ones that had no place in the life she led now.

"You go on inside. No one'll be back to disturb your bath. Greg took the little ones with him while the boys move the horses in the upper valley. My man's one who understands that a woman needs a day to herself now and again."

Heaping kindness upon her offer of friendship only sharpened the loss Dixie felt. She didn't deny the appeal of a hot bath. Any bath where she didn't have the worry that someone might come upon her and catch her unaware was a gift she couldn't refuse. There was nothing to be done now about Ty. She started for the kitchen door, then stopped.

Without looking at Livia, Dixie said, "If there was a spare rifle or handgun that I could have, Ty would pay you for it."

Bent over her washtub, Livia shook her head. "That's putting me in the middle atwixt you two. What Ty did ain't right. You have your bath an' I'll promise to talk to him. Truth to tell, Dixie, I don't have one. Never could learn to shoot."

Truth or lie, Dixie had no choice but to accept what Livia told her. Perhaps she could soak away her frustration with the high-handed Ty Kincaid.

"You been watchin' that place for nigh onto an hour now, Thorne," Peel Hickman whined. "You can see for yourself them women are alone. So what all are you waitin' on? You know I ain't had me a woman for near three weeks."

"Shut up, Peel. We'll move when I say so."

Appealing to Cobie, Peel tried the same tack about his not having had a women in weeks. When that brought a shrug from the younger man, who went back to cleaning his gun, Peel started in about the food.

"Bet she's got grub to fill and coat a man's belly down there. I's sick of hardtack. You coulda waited till we had supplies 'fore you lit out after Kincaid."

"Never said you had to come, Peel," Cobie lifted his gun and sighted it on Peel's face. "Bang. You're dead."

"Boy, one day you're gonna try trickin' me an' I'm gonna shoot back." Pacing back and forth, Peel doggedly started with Thorne again. "You said our horses are in the corral. Don't make no sense to me nohow to keep waitin' up here when what we all want is down there."

After a few minutes of letting Peel stew, Thorne lowered the small brass telescope he used to spy on the homestead. Tucking the telescope into his saddlebag, he took time to tuck the flap over the initials burned into the leather. The outfit was an extra he had taken from his last job and luckily had taken with him in the saloon. He hadn't gotten paid for that job since he had left a witness alive. But Dixie Rawlins would be found and silenced. Thorne had to make sure of that. His reputation depended upon doing a thorough job. No one left alive to point the finger at him, or the man who paid him.

Peel's whining continued, interrupting his thoughts, and Thorne eyed him with distaste. "You keep on, Peel, an' I'll be thinking to decorate a cottonwood with you."

"Hang me? What for? I was only askin'—"

"That's your problem. Only asking stupid questions. I had to make sure that no one else was around. I had to," he explained with exaggerated care, "make sure that Kincaid did ride off and intended to stay gone. Now—"

"You ain't afraid of Kincaid, Thorne. What the hell did it matter if he was there?"

"You could learn from Cobie, Peel. He don't ask six questions to Sunday. That boy figures things out for himself. I waited until he was gone 'cause I don't want gunfire. I don't want anyone to know where we are. Understand?" He nudged his horse back from the edge of the hill. "You coming? I'm ready to pay a social call."

Whooping, Peel made a beeline for his horse. Cobie, however, still sat on the flat slab of rock and made his refusal heard.

"Thorne, I ain't got no likin for rapin' no women. I came along 'cause I want another chance at Kincaid an' you just said he ain't there."

"But he'll be back. And we'll be there waiting for him. Be a pity if Peel an' me were occupied and you missed your chance at him. Your call, Cobie. Ride with us or stay on your own."

"Com'on boy," Peel urged, barely able to keep his prancing horse still as it caught its rider's growing excitement. "You could get lucky. Kincaid might show up real soon. Catch him unawares an' the man's yours. Bet you'd like that little spitfire that was with him, too."

Cobie flexed his wounded hand. He couldn't outdraw a kid with a peashooter right now, and he knew it. But he didn't want to stay up here alone and wait for Thorne and Peel to get done.

"I'll come, but I won't touch the women. I take down Kincaid an' women'll come after me." He freed the reins and stepped into his saddle. "Still think we should take our horses and ride on. Plenty of places to find Kincaid alone."

"Now you sound like Peel, boy," Thorne noted, riding ahead of the other two men. "Whining about Kincaid? Man might think you're afraid of him."

"I know him, Thorne. Well," Cobie amended, "I been studying his ways. He'll come hunting us for sure."

"Let him. Pity I didn't know you were gunning for him when I hired you on to help me finish a piece of business. Didn't need to lose this time. But I ain't letting him get away with stealing what's mine." Thorne kicked his horse's sides. "We ride."

Chapter Eight

Dixie had lingered overlong at her bath. In her borrowed chemise and drawers, she stood drying her hair with a length of linen toweling. The bath had been a gift of heaven, and even softened her resentment against Ty for keeping her here.

Livia had not only left underwear and a petticoat for her, but a gown, as well. Quickly braiding her hair into a single thick braid, Dixie slipped on the gown and fumbled with the unfamiliar cloth-covered wooden buttons that she had not had to deal with for some time.

The feel of soft, well-worn cotton against her calves and ankles brought back memories of long summer days when she reveled in being barefoot. Leaving her boots, she scooped up her soiled clothing. The sound of drumming hoofbeats didn't alarm her. Not at first. Then Livia's shout alerted her that something was wrong.

She heard someone yelling, and all she could make

out was a man's voice. The sounds grew louder. Livia's scream suddenly shattered the peaceful day.

Dixie dropped her bundle. She started to run through the house, stopped and once more looked about the walls, hoping she would find a rifle mounted. There wasn't a weapon in sight.

The excited whooping sounds frightened her. She had heard enough of them in the mining camps from men drunk on rotgut and looking to kick up a little hell.

Livia's cry was abruptly cut off. Dixie caught up the gown and petticoat, cussed to herself about her bare feet and grabbed a knife in the kitchen. She paused just long enough to look out the window. She couldn't see anyone, but the washtub had been turned over, the sudsy water making a muddy puddle that the ground quickly soaked up.

A glance showed no one near the kitchen door, but a shiver of dread worked its way down her spine as she cautiously made her way to the back door.

There was a stream of vile cursing coming from a harsh male voice as Dixie peered outside. If she hadn't been so frightened for Livia, she would have laughed at the sight that met her gaze.

A man was trying to drag Livia across his saddle, but she had her teeth clamped on his leg. One of her hands reached upward to tear and grab at whatever she could. His howl of pain was heard over the snorting of his animal. He suddenly released Livia and she fell in a heap on the ground. Dixie ran toward her.

Too late, Dixie understood that the man wasn't alone. Another rider charged her. She reached Livia, offering one hand to help the woman to her feet. Holding out the knife, Dixie braced herself. She swore under her breath at Ty for leaving her defenseless without her gun.

There were a few moments when her vision blurred. She shook her head to clear it, uncertain if she was imagining that the man bearing down on her was riding her mare.

In a rush, things came together. These were the men from the saloon. She managed to dodge the first attempt to grab hold of her. The rider drew rein and with sharp kicks turned her mare to come at her again. Livia threw the washboard at him, but he ducked to the side. But it was the mounted man beyond Livia that arrested her attention.

Dixie froze. The man was rubbing his leg where Livia had bitten him. Rubbing the wound with a hand that bore a jagged, lightning-shaped scar. Once more she faced her father's killer. And once more, she might forgo a chance for revenge.

"Livia! Where's a spare gun?" she yelled over a man's order to catch hold of her.

For a moment Dixie didn't think that the woman had heard her. She looked around, a lost, almost distracted expression on her face. She repeated the demand to know where Greg kept a spare gun, but her shout was drowned out by the hollering of the man now circling around her.

The dust choked her. Dixie saw that her mare's mouth was flecked with blood. The horse had a gentle mouth, and the animal who rode her used her cruelly. Pity for the mare rose inside her. The horse's eyes rolled wildly, but the spirited mare fought her rider for control of the bit.

Swiping at the rider with the knife, Dixie kept him from getting too close to her. Between the two horses weaving around them, Dixie couldn't see the third man, the young gunslinger who had challenged Ty. She worried about where he was, but there was little time to look when she once more defended herself from being caught.

"Get inside the house," Livia shouted to her. She ran and tried to grab hold of Dixie's arm to pull her along, but once more the rider came between them. "If you get in, bolt the door."

"We'll both make it." Dixie coughed, and wished she felt as certain as she sounded. She saw that the wash line had been torn down, the clothes dragged into the muddy puddle. It was foolish to become enraged over the soiled clothing, but a fury rose in Dixie that men like this only knew how to destroy.

She shoved Livia ahead of her while the men were once again getting ready to charge.

Too late she saw that their escape into the house was cut off. The young gunslinger stood in the doorway. His eyes were as cold and hard as the biscuit he was eating.

Then the man with the scar was dismounting and Dixie felt fear take hold. She knew what he was capable of. Even as she swore she would kill him before he ever touched her again, the cold, dreaded fear wrapped tight around her and squeezed until her knees felt like jelly. He, too, now stood between them and the door.

Dixie grabbed Livia's arm. "Run for the stable!" All she could think of was getting to the horses, if not them, then the tack room. She beat back the fear of fire. Fire that could easily smoke them out into the open once again.

Her unsecured braid had come apart, and her loose streaming hair made a perfect handhold as Peel leaned from his saddle and yanked hard.

"You little wildcat bitch! I'll teach you to knife me!"

"Run, Livia!" Dixie shouted her order, then turned in a blind rage. She had sworn no man would ever make her feel helpless again. She knew her rage made her wield the knife in a clumsy manner, but the man's swearing hit a new high, so she knew she found a mark.

Praying that Livia was free and that she would ride for help, Dixie blocked out the pain of her hair being torn from her scalp. Tears filled her eyes. Tears that blinded her as he wrenched her head back and dragged her tight against his leg.

Her heart pounded, and sounds receded until all she heard was her own blood in a drumming beat. Her breath was dragged into her lungs and released in heaving pants as she tried not to cry out with the agonizing pain. She made an attempt to stab at him, but his laugh told her she had missed. The tangled fall of her hair truly blinded her. She didn't know if Livia had made it to the stable or not.

Dixie barely avoided having her bare foot stepped on by the horse. She was hauled alongside the animal. Trying to still the panic taking hold, she warned herself to bide her time and wait for a chance to get free.

"What the hell are you standin' there for, Thorne? You let that other one go."

"But you caught what I've been hunting, Peel. That's all that matters. We got unfinished business, her and me. I didn't recognize her that night in the saloon. But in a gown, with that hair all wild recalled my memory."

Thick, guttural, the sound of his voice brought back Dixie's memory, too. The terror-filled nightmare came rushing back from where she tried to keep it buried.

Black spots danced in front of her eyes. She no longer heard the men's taunts. Within her was a strong yearning to give in to the darkness welling up to embrace her. Seductively it whispered that it was the only way she could block out the sound of *that* voice.

But right now, she needed the hate fueled by once more hearing a voice from hell itself. A voice that now had a name to go with it—Thorne. Hate gave her strength. Memory proved stronger.

She saw herself standing in the kitchen that long-ago night, folding the napkins, then putting away the supper dishes. Her mending basket waited, but first she would join her father for their nightly walk down to the barn. They had two mares ready to foal, blooded stock bought with a gambler's winnings whose offspring would bring them good prices to increase the cattle herd they had started.

Faster and faster the images rose, and with them came her silent scream to cease.

The first shot had torn through the night just as she had blown out the lamp. Screaming for her father, she had run to the door when a torch came sailing in the parlor window. Shattered glass snapped beneath her shoes as she stamped it out before the curtains caught on fire. Her cries to her father for help went unanswered. The smell of pitch from the torch stayed with her.

Laughter. How could she ever forget the laughter? Wild and wicked sounding, filling the night.

And the shots. There had been too many of them to count. The air burned as if all she could inhale was the gunpowder.

Even then she had known this had been caused by her father's refusal to sell off his water rights. He had been worried but not fearful. He had never warned her to expect an attack like this.

It shamed her now, as it had then, to remember herself cowering inside, too afraid to go out and see what had happened. Terror had kept her scurrying like a frightened mouse from room to room until she had smelled the smoke from the barn.

Memory brought back images, and with them an intense pain that sought relief. Dixie couldn't stop the keening wail escaping her lips. Regardless of the added pain it caused, she rocked her head from side to side. She wanted to block out what she saw. She had to.

Once again, memory proved stronger than her will. And the nightmare she had lived with all these months continued to play itself out.

She had grabbed the pan of dishwater by the back door. At a run, water sloshing over her gown, she headed for the barn. Smoke was thick. Her eyes watered and stung, but she saw the flames licking up the back wall. Fear didn't stop her from running inside with her empty dishpan.

Her only thought was to save the mares. A scream came. Faintly she heard it, but then she had screamed over and over that night, too. Blood was smeared on the barn doors. Smeared on the posts, on the stalls. It had been too late. She had been too late to save her precious horses. Her hands were covered with blood when she ran, choking and crying down the length of the barn and into the night.

Both horses were dead. Butchered in their stalls. There would be no foals. No money. No future breeding stock. No more dreams.

And no matter how she screamed, her father never once answered her.

But *he* did.

She was branded by the sound of his laughter when she tumbled out of the barn and ran for the house. She would forever carry his taunting voice telling her what he was going to do to her.

Panic lent strength to her legs. Terror sent her fleeing. She couldn't breathe. Couldn't contain the beat of her pounding heart. Or the icy fear that encompassed her body.

Run! was her only thought. The only action she was capable of, the one thing she could do.

Alone. Hunted. Then, as now, *he* had come after her on his horse trying to ride her down, attempting to rope her like a calf for branding.

She had stumbled and fallen to her knees time and again. Like a wild creature she struggled to her feet, dodging, running, driven by terror of being caught. And always the laughter returned, sending a new frenzy of panic streaming through her.

Clawing her way up the porch steps, she had touched hard leather. Even through the fear that filled her, she knew it was a boot. She listened again to the childlike whimpers that had escaped her throat. Knowing, before she could reach up and touch the now-still face, that it was her father's body sprawled in death.

Whimpers became screams. She had never heard the whistling of the rope that settled taut around her body. With a jerk she was down, scrabbling for purchase, holding on to her father's body as she was dragged like a broken rag doll off the porch.

Even now, she spat dust, like that night, feeling how it had filled her nostrils and sucked every bit of moisture from her mouth. Her body hurt. Grit filled her eyes.

She remembered the searing burn of the rope around her body. The utter despair of being so helpless to stop him. Around and around the yard he had ridden, dragging her behind the horse. Bruised and bleeding, she was barely conscious when the rope suddenly went slack.

He had come for her then. She had begged for mercy. And his harsh laughter grew, grew until it was all she heard. Where the strength to continue to struggle had come from, she never knew. It was all in vain. He dragged her inside.

She had wanted death. *He* wanted her to see hell first.

Glass had crunched beneath his boots when he flung her to the parlor floor. From her lips came animal-like snarls. His laughter abruptly stopped when she threw glass at him.

And still he reached for her.

She had to stop the laughter. Life was suddenly very precious. He had destroyed what she loved most. She could not let him destroy her.

She couldn't!

Tearing cloth. Fetid breath. A feeling of being smothered. The glass. She remembered the glass he held. His howl of pain. The surging demand for survival rushing through her. The sudden freedom that renewed her fight.

The smash of broken wood. Her mother's candle stand shattered. Her flight to her father's body. In the glow of the burning barn she knew it had been too late to save him. The image of herself backing away, sickened until she was racked with tremors and a cold sweat, had never left her. The sight of that hand, torn and bleeding as it came through the doorway of her home, was all she had remembered of the animal who destroyed her life.

And she had never forgiven herself for running.

Now it was happening again. She was caught, helpless to stop him.

Only he wasn't alone. She fought back the smothering blackness that threatened to enfold her. A ringing filled her ears.

The present rushed back with the pain of her hair being twisted and yanked. It was moments before Dixie understood that the ringing was real. A bell pealed with a frantic clanging. Livia had made it to the barn. She had to be signaling for help.

Time had lost meaning for Dixie. A body neared and she kicked out, impeded by the gown and petticoat. She dropped the knife and, with both hands, reached up and behind her to grab hold of the man's arm that held her. The yells and shouts returned as her hearing cleared. Holding the bony arm in a death grip, she threw her body forward.

The move was unexpected. Suddenly she was free, stumbling to her knees, barely breaking her fall with her extended hands. There was no time to catch her breath. She heard the thump of his falling body behind her. Not waiting to see what he'd do, she was up and staggering toward the barn.

The bell had stopped ringing. She heard shouted orders but made no sense of them. Halfway across the yard, Dixie looked up to see Livia, mounted bareback, come charging out of the wide double doors. With expert skill she cracked a bullwhip, driving the calves and horses into the yard. Confusion reigned. Calves bawled. Horses shied and pawed air, trying to avoid the milling smaller creatures.

And over the animals' heads, Livia swung that fifteen-foot lash with a strength and repeated skill that almost stopped Dixie in her tracks. But she had not forgotten the nightmare she had just relived, and veered around the swarm of animals until Livia and her deadly whip stood between her and the men.

There wasn't a moment to lose. Livia could only hold them off as long as no one shot her. Even as Dixie darted into the barn, searching for a pitchfork to use as a weapon, she was struck by the fact that not one of those men had used their guns. It gave her pause. The answer came to her in the same moment that she spotted the pitchfork.

Shots would alert Greg and Ty that there was trouble. For some reason those men didn't want them down here. She grabbed hold of the pitchfork, intending to return outside to help Livia. Then she remembered the bell. Had Greg heard his wife's warning? Were he and Ty even now riding back?

Gunfire erupted.

Chapter Nine

Dixie ran out from the barn, carrying the pitchfork. She cursed Ty in one breath, then thanked him in the next when she saw that he rode with Greg and the older boys. Like four avenging angels, they came down the sloping hill toward the homestead.

The gunfire had sent the loose horses fleeing. The calves scattered. She couldn't find Livia in the milling mass of animals. Another burst of shots made her realize that Ty and Greg were firing in the air, not yet close enough to sight clear targets.

She found Thorne. Their gazes locked for a long, endless moment. He was readying to mount. Where the other two men were, Dixie didn't know and didn't care. She was not going to allow her father's killer to escape again.

The pitchfork was heavy and awkward, but she found the inner strength to make a rush at Thorne.

Someone shouted her name. Dixie ignored it. A calf ran alongside her. She was halfway across the yard when a single shot sent Thorne reeling from his saddle.

"No!" she screamed. This was to be her revenge. No one was to cheat her of it. Thorne's death would wipe out the stain of being helpless, of losing everything her father had labored to gain.

The calf butted her side, making her stumble. She swore at the animal. The pitchfork saved her from falling, but she wasted precious seconds before she could heave it up in front of her again.

A shot kicked up dirt at her side. Thorne was mounted! He aimed at her again, but the bawling calf knocked her off her feet and the shot went wide. From behind her, Dixie heard shouts, but nothing mattered now. Thorne, with the young gunslinger at his back, was riding out and she was once more left in the dust.

She didn't know how long she lay there, her sobs of sheer rage soaking into the earth, before she felt Ty's hands on her shoulders.

"Dixie? Are you hurt?" Guilt pierced Ty. He had ridden off and left the women alone. He could feel the sobs that shook her body and his concern for her grew. Muttering curses, then whispering to her, he felt his fury build higher when he spied the pitchfork.

"You used that? Worthless as a barrel of shucks! What's the matter with you, Dixie, going after them with a damned hay-tosser? Dixie? Dixie, let me help you turn over so I can see where you're hurt."

She tensed the moment he tightened his hold on her shoulders in an attempt to see her face. Ty wished she was a soft, dependent sort of woman right now, one

who showed some appreciation of the fact that he had
helped to run those varmints off.

Not that he didn't admire her spirit. But there was a
time and place for it, and as far as he was concerned,
now was not the right time. He had known she was
trouble from the first. He had no one but himself to
blame for getting his boots tangled with an ornery
critter like Dixie Rawlins.

"Dixie, honey," he whispered, leaning over her so
that his words were for her ears alone. "Don't get all
mule stubborn on me now. It's the wrong time to show
off your thickheaded independence. Let me hold you.
Let me just see for myself that you're all right."

"Then see for yourself!" She spit the words at him
and, like a Texas twister, rolled away from him. "You
bastard! I could have killed him, Ty. If I had had my
gun. That's twice now, Kincaid. Twice that I missed
him. I wouldn't have needed you or any man to protect me and Livia. Damn you!"

Ty made a move toward her, and she scampered
backward. "Don't you touch me. I'll never forgive you
for this. Never, Kincaid. You just leave me alone. Give
me back my gold and my gun." Swiping at the tears
that blurred her eyes, Dixie rose on unsteady legs.

She stared down at him. Ty was hunkered back on
his boot heels, his dark hair tumbled over his forehead, and his steady, dark blue eyes regarded her with
an unreadable expression.

"Don't cut my trail again. Soon as I get my gear, I'm
going after them."

He remained where he was, watching her limp away from him. He didn't even acknowledged Greg's strong hand on his shoulder until the man shook him.

"Ty? What the hell was that all about?"

"The men from the saloon. One of them killed Dixie's father." Ty looked up at Greg, then at Livia beside him. "I can't tell either one of you how sorry I am that I brought trouble here. Words just won't cut it this time." He came to his feet, seeing the last of Dixie's back disappear into the house.

"You can't let her go after them alone, Ty. She's a mighty strong woman, but I'd think less of you—"

"You couldn't think less of me than I do about myself, Livia," Ty returned in a hard-edge voice. "Greg? Help her pick out a good horse. And give her whatever else she needs. She'll likely argue you near to a grave, but make sure she's fully outfitted." Rubbing the back of his neck, Ty started to walk away, then turned.

"I owe you, Greg."

The bleak look in his friend's eyes had Greg shaking his head. "You promised to look in on Jessie for me. I figure that makes us even. Livia and me don't want to hear no more talk about owing."

A curt nod was all that Ty could manage. Like he said before, sometimes words just didn't cut it.

Anger had carried Dixie as far as the Rutlands' sleeping area, where she pulled the blanket across to give herself a little privacy.

Waves of anguish washed over her. Her shoulders slumped, her head bowed, and she gave in to the aftermath's shivers that she had held at bay. Snapping and snarling at Ty had come from her own guilt, her own feeling of being overwhelmed by the vindictive task she had set for herself.

It was only now, with none but Julia's cat Witchy and her tiny kittens as witnesses, that Dixie gave in to the terror of facing a killer again. No, she silently amended. She had a name—Thorne.

With a feeling of doom that she would never be able to keep her vow, Dixie began to pick up her scattered clothes. A deep weariness overcame her, as if more hours than in one day had passed since she had emerged from her bath. The water still stood in the tub. It was irrational that she should be upset that she forgot to empty the water. What was happening to her?

She didn't want to answer her own question. There was fear attached to finding out the answer. She set aside her clothes and dipped the buckets into the tub. Gripping the rope handles, she started to leave. The moments of being seized returned and she swayed where she stood. Her skin crawled with the memory of hands on her. There wasn't, she was sure, enough scalding water to rid her of the feeling.

Stepping around the blanket, Dixie stopped short. Greg stood near the fireplace with his arms around his wife. His eyes were closed and he rocked her to and fro.

Unwilling to intrude on their private moment, Dixie let the edge of the blanket fall. Quietly setting the buckets down, she backed away until the edge of the bed made her stop. Curling her fingers into a fist, she pressed it against her mouth. She had thought she felt alone before, but the depth of the loneliness that took hold of her now was unbearable.

She, who had been so certain of her mission, was forced to take another look at herself. Admitting the truth, she fought against it. If she gave in to the doubts rising and plaguing her, she would face the emptiness of her life.

And there was her vow. She couldn't let her weakness make her forget that promise made on her father's grave.

She rid herself of the black mood the same way she had rid herself of the distaste and fear when she began following a killer's trail. The mind had a great capacity to store unwanted thoughts.

Ty Kincaid belonged in that graveyard, too.

As if summoned by her despondent state, the cat purred and rubbed against Dixie's skirt. Witchy's eyes were bright yellow, her fur soft and thick, mostly white but for the black curved half-moon mark that encompassed one ear and eye. It gave the cat a rather wise look, and Dixie couldn't resist sitting on the floor to pet her.

"I envy you, cat," she whispered.

"There's no need to, you know," Livia said, slipping behind the blanket. "Ty told us what you plan. It's not a woman's place—"

"Don't, Livia." Dixie came to her feet. "I was going to empty the buckets. I'll change my clothes." She looked down at the tears and dirt on her borrowed gown. "I've ruined this for you. I'm sorry, more sorry than I can say for the trouble we brought with us."

"You're hard on yourself, Dixie. No one's pushing you away. You can stay here with us. Ty will—"

"No. It's not his place, not his fight."

They both heard the younger children call out for their mother, and with a last look at Dixie, Livia left to see to Julia and James.

Dixie blocked the sound of their excited voices asking what had happened, and Livia's calm one answering. She made quick work of changing her clothes, warring with a body that wanted to leave and a mind that didn't want yet another confrontation with Ty.

Julia settled the matter. "Miss Dixie," the child called, "Pa says to com'on out."

Carrying her empty gun holster, Dixie parted the blanket.

The little girl scooted past her to get to her cat. "I was so worried 'bout her an' the babies."

"They're fine, Julia. Those men never got a chance to hurt them. Your mama's whip kept them away."

"Me an' James had to hide in the rocks. Elwin says we was too little to...to do a lick o' good," she finished in a rush. Bending down to pet Witchy, she reminded Dixie that her father was waiting outside.

There was no one inside the house, but Dixie found Greg with Livia and their sons waiting together outside. The two older boys were mounted, and James clung to his mother's gown.

Greg held the reins of a dark red bay. He offered the reins to Dixie. "She's a fine mare and yours."

"I can't take your horse. The one I rode—"

"Now, Dixie," Livia cut in, "we don't want to hear that. Take the horse. She's a gift from us so I don't want a word about paying for her. The boys packed bacon and coffee, flour and jerky for you. I still wish you'd change your mind, but I won't whistle to the wind hoping. You just remember that you're welcome here."

"I don't understand why I can't ride the horse I came here with."

"Ty's already taken those horses with him." Greg stared at her, as if daring her to say another word.

"I see," Dixie said, but she didn't. Ty had ridden off without a word. She'd gotten what she wanted. She gave Livia a quick, tight hug. "I can't thank you both enough for all you've done. But I do have the gold to pay you for—"

"Won't take it." Greg patted her saddlebags slung behind the cantle. "Your gold's right there. Your gun, too. Our boys will ride a ways with you. They've got to round up our stock."

"You're good people. But before I leave, Livia, I need to ask where you learned to handle a bullwhip like that."

"Her daddy was a bullwhacker," Elwin supplied.

"Yeah, Grandpa was gonna teach us like he taught Ma, but he got lung fever."

Dixie murmured her sorrow, but her thoughts returned to where Ty had gone. She wouldn't ask Greg if he had said anything, not after the way she had lit into Ty in front of them. To cover the awkward moment, she held one hand beneath the mare's nose to allow the horse to learn her scent. The mare's points were all black, ears, stockings, mane and tail. Her eyes were clear, and while gentle, showed intelligence. Dixie knew horse stock and she couldn't have picked out a better one for herself.

"She's a beauty, Greg." Patting the mare's outstretched neck, Dixie continued her inspection. She felt the fetlocks, shoulders and stroked the downy soft muzzle. The mare lifted her head and gently butted Dixie's shoulder. The first smile of the day crossed her lips as she leaned close and once more rubbed the horse's muzzle.

"Gilby's been working with her for almost a year now," Greg said with pride. "She'll turn on a spot and has one of the softest mouths I've ever seen. She'll go a distance for you, Dixie. Sure you won't reconsider and spend the night?"

"Can't," she answered, holding the reins in one hand while she stepped up into the saddle. "I don't want their trail getting cold on me again." She murmured her goodbyes and with the boys following, rode out.

High on the hilltop overlooking the homestead, Ty watched Dixie's leave-taking. He had discovered very little about the three men and the place where they had watched and waited, too. One of them smoked with a habit of ripping open the end of his butt and making a small pile of the remaining tobacco. One horse had a notch cut in the left back shoe. There were only two sets of footprints. One he was sure was made by the young gunslinger—the boot had a higher heel and showed a big man wasn't wearing it by the depression left behind. The other boot heel revealed a man who favored his left leg, not a great deal, just enough to show a slight drag in the walk.

It wasn't a hell of a lot to go on, but it was all he had. Bits and pieces and two horses. They had made this personal when they knifed him. Attacking his friends' home made this his fight.

And as much as he wanted to avoid thinking about her, there was Dixie. Noose waiting for them or not, he couldn't let her go after them alone.

The sun was already beginning its descent, leaving a pale blood hue across the sky. He knew he had to give her plenty of time before he went after her.

Her pride and vow aside, the woman with a smile of an angel had left her mark on him. Until he sorted out what it was she made him feel, he wasn't letting her go.

Dixie was sorry to lose the boys' company. She waved goodbye to them and rode on, refusing to allow her thoughts to stray from finding a high spot where she could search for sign of the three men's trail. She knew it would not be easy to find them again, but a prayer to lady luck might grant her this one favor.

The sun was slipping beyond the horizon, leaving behind a hue that reminded her of crushed gooseberries floating in water. The sky had incredible hues of pink and orange and lilac, promising a scorcher of a day to come. It was a warning to her, too, to find a camp spot soon. Since this was the first time she had ridden this mare, she did not want to push the animal or risk the chance of injury.

Drawing rein, she scouted with an intense gaze for a hint of water. Up ahead was a rocky slope that at least promised the high spot she had wanted. Dixie headed for it, letting the mare pick her way. She was thankful that the horse appeared surefooted on the loose scree.

Shadows had already deepened by the time she reached the top. Closing her eyes as she inhaled, opening them as she released a deep breath, Dixie fixed her gaze on the land below. There was a water hole a short distance away, and she caught a glimpse of shining eyes, but dusk made it hard to see what animal was there. Nothing moved. With a mental shrug, she urged the mare around and headed back. She'd get an early start tomorrow, she promised herself.

Halfway down the slope she found what she was looking for. There was a rock shelf overhang that would offer some protection from the weather while allowing her to build a fire that couldn't be easily seen from a distance. The mare tossed her head as she dismounted. Dixie stood holding the reins loosely in one hand, the other on the butt of her gun. The horse had her ears up in an alert manner. Dixie had a healthy respect for any animal's senses.

A few minutes passed and still the mare stood, adding a pawing motion with her front hoof.

"I wish I knew you a little better, pretty lady," Dixie whispered. "I can't tell if something's got you worried or if you're just as hungry as me."

She led the mare toward the overhang, stumbling when the horse nudged her shoulder with her muzzle. Dixie saw it then, the sparkle of a tiny trickle of water that was filling a scooped-out depression in a boulder. Her own canteen was full, so she allowed the mare to drink her fill. Ground-tying the horse, Dixie set off to search for dry grasses and some deadfall for her fire.

An hour later she was back with plenty of grass but not a twig for a fire. "Cold camp tonight, lady."

As she sat chewing jerky and washing it down with water, Dixie couldn't avoid thinking about Ty any longer.

She knew it was contrary to have expected him to show up when she had made it perfectly clear that she didn't want him around. Didn't want him, or need him interfering with his high-handed ways.

But contrary or not, the fact remained that she had expected him to show up by now.

Her appetite gone, she repacked the jerky and found herself worrying about his shoulder. Would he remember to keep it clean? Livia had given him a salve she made from lard and crushed herbs, which her family had used for years. She tried to dismiss her worry. After all, Ty Kincaid was a man, not a boy. He didn't need a nag to keep after him to take care of himself. The man had survived without her help for all this time. She just needed to remember that.

Thoughts about him kept coming to mind, images of his smile, the steady regard of his dark blue eyes, the way his hair tumbled forward on his forehead so that she wanted to brush it back. She remembered the feel of his lips on hers.

With a rough little shake of her head, she tried to banish that memory. Taking a last sip from her canteen, she wondered if she was so exhausted that the mental barrier no longer held.

She didn't want to think about Ty's kisses or remember the feel of his arm around her, holding her against his hard body. She could not deal with the strength of the desire she felt for him and that memory made it so easy to recall.

Smoothing the ground of loose rocks, she spread her blanket beneath the overhang and wrapped herself in it. Sleep was all that she needed now, and her body wanted it. She had slept little these past few nights, but her mind churned with thoughts and refused to allow her escape into sleep.

Where was Ty now? Greg had said that he had taken the two stolen horses with him. What did Ty intend to do with them? If he was caught...she didn't want to think about him being hung as a horse thief. But that was exactly what would happen to him. No one would ask questions, no one would care that the men those horses were stolen from were guilty of worse crimes.

She knew too well that there weren't any laws to punish someone like Thorne. But she suspected he'd been hired by a wealthy man to murder her father for their land and water rights. Trouble was, she couldn't discover who it was. Only Thorne could tell her.

Dixie pulled the blanket up to her chin, to ward off both the night chill and the inner one that beset her.

The saddle made a hard pillow. Cupping one hand beneath her head, she stared out into the darkness.

Mercifully her mind ceased thinking about the man who had ordered her father's death. Images of Ty came to mind, until he was all she could envision.

It was hard to believe that she missed him. Only a few hours ago, she couldn't wait to be rid of his company.

If lady luck rode with her, perhaps someday she could find Ty again. There were all those questions about him she wanted answered....

All she had to do was survive.

Her eyes closed. She drifted into sleep holding the image of Ty's reflection in the mirror as she brushed her hair, and the warmth that curled inside her.

In the middle of the night she cried out, "Ty, where are you?" No one heard. No one answered.

Chapter Ten

"You real sure, Cobie?"

"Thorne, I tol' you and tol' you. Kincaid's bedded down not more'n two miles back. An' no, I ain't seen a sign of the woman." Hunkered near the fire, Cobie poured himself a cup of coffee. It was a good thing he had had the sense to see to their supplies while Thorne and Peel had made fools of themselves attacking two women. Now, at least they had coffee and smoked ham, as well as flour, to see them on the trail.

Cobie hid his disgust that while neither Thorne nor Peel had thought about getting the supplies, his traveling companions had no problem eating what he cooked. He flexed his hand, figuring to himself how long before he'd have full use of it again. Maybe he should start thinking about cutting loose from these two.

Cobie rolled a smoke, took a brand from the fire to light it, then moved to sit a little away from the fire with his back against his saddle. Thorne appeared deep in thought and Peel was busy honing his knife.

The way they ignored him was fine with Cobie. He hadn't questioned Thorne as yet—he wanted to scout out a few more things before he said anything—but he was sure that Thorne knew one of those women. The one that Peel had tried to grab.

From his place in the doorway, it wasn't hard to see that the woman had recognized Thorne. If he had ever seen a pair of eyes ready to kill, the woman had them.

He knew one law. Survive. Only the strongest did that. Cobie aimed to make himself survivor. He was going to build a reputation as a fast man with a gun so that folks would do anything to keep him calm and happy.

Sipping his coffee, he frowned. That wasn't quite the way it was for Kincaid. The man might be fast with his iron, but he didn't know how to make that work for him. A fool for sure. Cobie was no fool. He took another drag of his smoke, pinched off the lit end, then set his cup down. One of the few habits he had carried away from the mission where he'd been raised, was never leaving a sign that he'd been someplace.

With this in mind, he shredded the thin paper, letting the tobacco fall into a tiny pile. A good rain would wash the sign away. Cobie looked up then and saw that Thorne watched him from across the fire.

"I've been doing some thinking, Thorne," Cobie began.

"It ain't what you're best at, boy."

Cobie stifled the swift rise of anger at being called "boy." His instincts were right. It was time he cut loose from these two. And since he wanted to do that without a fight, he chose to ignore the remark.

"When we hooked up in Prescott you promised me money. I ain't seen dollar one."

"But you got a chance at Kincaid. A chance you fouled up but good."

Cobie shot a look at Peel. If he was paying attention to their conversation, he wasn't revealing it. The steady motion of blade against whetstone never varied, nor did he look up at either him or Thorne.

"Ain't gonna make excuses for that. But you got me mixed up in something that don't smell right. That woman back there, she's got past history with you. Killing kind of history."

"You asking, boy?"

There was a deadly softness to Thorne's voice that Cobie had a healthy respect for. He shook his head. But his mind was made up now. He was cutting loose of the bad smell of trouble coming his way.

"'Pears to me that you're getting a yella streak, boy."

"Shut the hell up, Peel. No one asked you." Thorne kept his steady and warning gaze pinned on Cobie. "You ain't got a yella streak. You ain't got questions. You're gonna ride along an' do what I tell you 'cause you want a chance at Kincaid again. An' this time you ain't gonna foul up. Are you, boy?"

"Whatever you say, Thorne. You're the boss." Cobie scooted down until he was prone and pulled his hat low. Every muscle in his body was tense with the need to climb all over Thorne and show him who he was dealing with.

"You remember that, Cobie. Remember it good. Turn in, Peel. I want us to get an early start come daybreak."

Thorne rolled over with his gun nestled within his hand. He didn't like Cobie questioning him. The kid was smarter than he let on. He'd have to do something about the boy, but not until he had taken care of the Rawlins woman. He hadn't questioned the luck that had placed her in his path, but cursed hers for escaping him again. Damn! but that little bitch was a fighter!

Under the cover of darkness, he traced the scar he bore. The scar she left him with. He had almost had her that night. He'd never figured she had any spit and fire left in her. It was a mistake he'd never again make.

He didn't much like the idea that she had split off from Kincaid. It would make things neat and tidy for him to catch the two of them together. Kincaid had gotten in his way, and he owed him for the bullet crease that left his arm aching. Unless... Thorne shook his head. She couldn't have hired Kincaid to help her. He knew she was gambling, he'd heard the rumors that she was buying what word she could about him. Kincaid would command a high price. After all, he knew how much he got paid for a job, and he didn't have Kincaid's reputation.

He chewed over this new, possible complication, half-listening to the restless stirrings as Peel tossed and turned in his bedroll.

The only solution he could come up with was to let Cobie have Kincaid. But he had to be the one to set it up so that the kid would owe him one.

That was something he'd learned from his boss. It was not enough to pay a man to do your dirty work. You had to have something to hold over his head so that he never got free of owing you.

A setup... he'd need to ponder that come morning. A hiss and flare came from the fire where a bit of sap burned. Thorne carefully turned over and watched for a few minutes to make sure that Peel and the kid were asleep. He slipped out of his blanket, waited again, then slowly crawled toward Cobie's bedroll.

Thorne ignored the lancing pain in his arm each time he braced his weight on it. He wanted the kid's saddlebags. Foolish men kept personal mementos, and Cobie struck him as a foolish kid still wet behind the ears.

He gauged the boy's steady breathing with his own. Satisfied that Cobie was asleep, Thorne leaned forward to lift the saddlebags.

The chill press of cool metal against his throat warned him he had made a mistake.

"You want something, Thorne?"

"Just came to talk." He set the bag down and coughed, hoping it distracted the boy so that he wouldn't know what he'd been up to. "Had a thought on how we can corner Kincaid."

Still keeping his gun in the open, Cobie sat up. "I'm awake and listening."

"You ever walk-down mustangs?"

"Never did, but I heard tell about it."

"There's three of us and only one of him," Thorne said, shifting slightly away from Cobie. "We keep him on the move, never giving him a chance to rest or water. We do it in relays. Just need to keep back out of firing range. Won't last long that way."

Cobie fought the tug of a smile. It wouldn't do to let Thorne see what he thought of his lie. "You figure that's how I want to take the man? Bone dogged, too weary to draw on me?"

"What the hell difference does it make how the hell you take him? Fact is, you'll have the notch you're aiming for."

Still holding his gun, Cobie lay back down. "I'll sleep on it, Thorne. You want that early start in the morning, I'd suggest you do the same."

Thorne crawled back to his bedroll. He didn't much like the feeling that the kid had the best of him. Funny thing was, he couldn't figure out why he had that suspicion. Once he had presented a walk-down as a way to get rid of Kincaid, he found himself liking the idea. Then he would go after the Rawlins woman to tidy up that last loose end.

Come morning...

When the barest hint of daybreak was lighting the far horizon, a shout from Peel sent both Thorne and Cobie scrambling from their bedrolls.

At first Thorne couldn't see anything wrong. There was no gunfire, no sign of anyone, and he cussed Peel as he made his way to where the man stood.

"What the hellfire was that about?" Thorne demanded.

"Count them," Peel answered, pointing to the rope picket where they had tied the horses.

"Count them?" Thorne repeated, rubbing the sleep from his eyes.

"There's four," Cobie announced. "That little wildcat's mare is missing but we got our two back. Now we won't have to listen to Peel's bellyaching about his mount." He glanced at Thorne. "Still figure to do a walk-down on Kincaid?" He walked away before Thorne could answer him.

"How'd this happen, Peel?"

"I was sleeping. You never said to stand guard. He come an' fooled us good, Thorne. Yep, that Kincaid's gonna be a tough son to take down."

"Go make coffee, Peel, before I figure to take you down in his place."

Peel spat off to the side and left Thorne. He didn't blame Thorne for his surly voice. He was a mite put out that Kincaid had snuck up on them without making a sound. A shiver of dread walked up his spine and Peel looked around, not once, not twice but continuously as he filled the coffeepot with water from the canteen and built up the fire.

"What d'ya make of this, boy?"

"Me? I tell you, Peel, I figure Kincaid's served notice that he's riding us."

"Maybe so. But there's three of us an' only one of him."

"And still he managed to sneak in here last night. Don't think more of us is gonna stop him, Peel. Kincaid's smart."

"Yeah? Thorne's the smartest man I know. He'll figure a way. You just wait and see if he don't."

Ty found himself a shaded place to grab a few hours of shut-eye. He would have liked to have been there when the horses were discovered this morning, but he had a lot of ground to cover.

With any luck he'd have a good four hours to sleep before Dixie caught up with him. And he knew he would need every bit of it when he presented himself to her.

The setting sun's promise had been kept and by midday, Dixie was sweating. She wished she still had her hat, but she wasn't about to veer off the trail she had found to head for a mining camp to buy one. Three sets of horse tracks were headed south and, as near as she could determine, the riders had about a four-hour lead on her.

Instinct was all she had guiding her that she was on the right trail. Time and again she wondered where Ty could be but ruthlessly pushed the question aside. She couldn't afford the distraction. The mare proved herself surefooted over the vast steppes she rode between two ranges of mountains.

The grass was plentiful, and she knew that a source of water had to be close. Anyone with sense would think about resting in the scorching heat of the day then moving on in midafternoon when the sun began its descent. She longed to stop and bathe in cool water. And she knew she was breaking a good rule of the trail. Thinking about it increased her thirst, as well as made her feel the heat more intensely.

Dixie didn't know who was more startled—her or the mare—when the sheep suddenly cut their path. The mare quickly settled down as four thickly coated churro sheep ambled up into the rocks. She watched them for a few minutes, their coats earthy in tone from brown to pale cream, gray to black. She knew the Indians raised the sheep, for she had seen the weavings made from the colors of the sheep's wool.

What struck her as strange seeing the sheep loose like this was that less than ten years ago in the crushing finale of the Navajo wars, the army had swept through the Navajo homelands killing the sheep and burning the crops. She had heard that sheep had been brought back to the reservations.

Just as she urged the mare into a walk, one of the four horned rams crossed her path. There were twigs caught in its thick shaggy coat. Dixie glanced at where the sheep had come from, knowing that water had to be close.

But she was leary, too, and proceeded with caution to walk the mare up a granite gravel slope where she could study the land before she went farther.

Twisting around in the saddle, Dixie found Black Butte to the far north, which helped her get her bearings. To the east and south of where she was would be the Big Horn Mountains. Below her, a winding ribbon of water flashed beneath the sun. In places she could see how clear and shallow the wash was, for its rock-strewn sandy bottom was visible. If she followed its path, Dixie knew she would find deeper pools along its banks.

The temptation to find a safe place where she could bathe the stench from the trail grew too strong to resist. She thought of the few hours' lead time Thorne had on her. If she rested herself and the mare, she could push hard and close the distance between them.

Glancing up, she saw a lone hawk floating high above. Like the tattered remains of a shawl, a drifting cloud revealed the sun once more in all its blazing glory. The heat intensified. Dixie made up her mind.

She slipped the rawhide loop holding her gun in the holster, for there were too many hiding places in the rocks below. Regret for the loss of her gear, including a Spencer repeating rifle, filled her. She had no more than her own instincts and that of her horse to warn her of any trouble.

It had to be enough.

She found the spot she wanted within an hour, then sat and watched it for an hour more. Satisfied that this small dip in the curve of the wash was deserted, Dixie rode down. She stripped the mare of the saddle, let her drink her fill, then ground-tied her close by the sheltering branches of an aged cottonwood, where there was sacate grass growing in a small patch. By its thick growth, Dixie knew no animal had foraged here in some time.

Dead branches lay in abundance, and she gathered enough for a fire to dry her clothes. Keeping a close watch on the mare, for she would alert Dixie if anyone was coming, she stripped and headed for the thigh-high pool. The sand was both soap and washcloth for herself and her clothing. There was one vulnerable moment when she had to duck her head beneath the water and Dixie steeled herself to do it.

She rose with water streaming down her face, momentarily blinding her as she struggled to keep her footing in the sandy bottom and push her wet hair aside.

Smoke curled from the wood within the stone circle she had left ready.

A glossy-coated roan hid most of another horse that had joined her mare on the grass patch. Still clutching her wet clothes, Dixie fought the fear that speared through her, leaving her shaking.

She eyed her gun lying on top of her saddle. She wondered what her chances were of reaching it. Once more she scanned the small clearing. There was no sign other than the two horses that anyone was here. But the chill penetrated deeper inside her. Forcing her legs to move, she started for the bank.

"I was just betting with myself if you'd come out or take root where you stood."

"Ty?"

"None other."

Dixie followed the sound of his soft, amused voice and found him wedged in a shadowed rock crease above her. She was glad to see that he was all right and knew she couldn't hide that from him. It wasn't until he moved with that lazy, lithe grace to come down that she once more became aware of her state.

"Go away."

"Nohow, Dixie. Just think what could've happened if it hadn't been me that found you."

Feeling utterly ridiculous standing there, Dixie had no choice but to climb up the bank. She ignored him as best she could while she wrapped her blanket around her. No heroine in a penny dreadful had ever confronted a man she thought of as both hero and villain. But Dixie did.

Forcing a calm that was as phony as her smile, she eyed him from his head to his boots, then slowly drew her gaze back up to his face. "You don't look any the worse for wear." But she could see the faint lines around his eyes, as if he hadn't slept well.

"And you," he noted softly, "look a hell of a lot better than the last time I saw you."

"Which wasn't all that long ago, Ty. Why did you follow me?"

"Angel, if you were standing in my boots, seeing yourself with my eyes, you wouldn't be asking me a schoolgirl's question."

"But I'm not." Her hand closed nervously over the tucked end of the blanket. "And I was never a schoolgirl. There wasn't time, or a place my father and I stayed long enough for me to go to school."

Ty could see the rapid pulse in the hollow of her throat that betrayed her nervousness, and he felt a sudden surge of tenderness. She faced him with more courage than men he had known. He still wasn't accustomed to the swift rise of wanting he felt for her, but he knew she aroused him more when she faced him proudly than any other woman.

"I'm not a child, Ty. I won't be treated as one who needs—"

"I," he said in a near whisper, his gaze traveling to the hint of cleavage edged by the blanket, "can see that for myself."

Warmth curled in her belly. Dixie had to look away from him. Within seconds, memory supplied the feel of his hands holding her, the press of his hard body against her own, his lips tantalizing hers with the promise of a kiss. She closed her eyes, willing the images away.

"Dixie? What's wrong?"

She knew he was too close. Even before she opened her eyes to find him standing before her, she knew she had to refuse the invitation in his gaze.

"My clothes need drying." She wet her lips and swallowed hard. "The fire's hot enough—"

"I know that, too." He lifted his hand to brush the wet hair from her shoulder. Beneath his palm she was tense, but her skin felt smooth, and he could feel the heat below her skin. "There's unfinished business between us, Dixie. You'll run and I'll likely chase you until one of us gets tired of running, but in the end—"

She jerked away from him. "It won't be me. Nothing you do or say will stop me from doing what I must."

"I just wanted you to understand how it'll be with us. As for going after them, you won't be doing that alone anymore."

Chapter Eleven

Dixie refused to be drawn into an argument with him. "Suit yourself, Kincaid," she said with a shrug.

"I intend to."

When he lifted her clothes, Dixie started for him but thought better of it. The best thing she could do was to keep her distance from him. Seeing the way he held up first her shirt, then her pants, a frown deepening on his brow, she tartly asked, "What's wrong? Didn't I get them clean enough?"

With a devil's light glinting in his eyes, Ty turned toward her. "Ain't the problem. I was just wondering where the rest of them are."

"The rest? Of what? That's all I was wear—" Dixie felt the heat climb into her cheeks. Her chin rose. With a narrow-eyed stare showing the battle glint in her eyes, she marched over to him and snatched her clothes from his hand. "I'll tend to these, Kincaid."

Ty let them go. "You know," he remarked, ducking beneath the dripping branches to settle himself against the tree, "you can't keep me at a distance by calling me Kincaid. You only do it when I'm getting too close."

"It doesn't work, does it?" she snapped, trying to figure out how to stretch up and hang her shirt and pants without losing the blanket. "Telling you plain out to leave me alone doesn't make a dent in that tough hide of yours, either."

"Well, at least you're thinking about my body."

"Kincaid! You'd give a saint callused knees and the good Lord knows I'm no saint." She wished she could see his face, but he was nearly hidden behind the thick leafy growth. His soft chuckle set her temper on low boil.

"I thank the Lord that you're not a saint. Don't know a man alive who'd want one."

He swung aside the smaller tree limbs and stepped out into the open. "Will you give me those before I lose what little control I have left wondering if you're gonna lose that blanket any second?"

Dixie slapped the wet clothes against his chest and walked back to the fire. She was a fool to argue with a man whose skull had the density of rock.

"Why don't you tell me the real reason you're here, Kincaid?"

"I brought you a present."

"A present?"

"Did you get water in your ears, Dixie, that you need to repeat—"

"No. And stop trying what little patience I have left."

He smiled to see her sneak a look around without letting on that she was curious. "Angel, you're looking for something small. The present I brought you is quite large, although I guess I did a good job of hiding it. Try looking behind you, a little to the left."

Dixie turned and saw her mare, and with her was a glossy-coated roan that she assumed Ty had ridden. The swish of a longer, black tail called attention to the rump of the third horse. Kicking the trailing edge of the blanket out of her way, Dixie moved closer to the animals.

"Kah?" She couldn't believe it was her own mare, the one that had been left behind at the saloon then ridden so cruelly by Thorne. The welcome nicker as Dixie rubbed the white blaze marking on her head made her realize what Ty had done.

She knew he stood behind her and, without turning, she said, "I never thought I'd see her again." Dixie leaned her cheek against the horse's sleek arched neck. "Her name is Apache for arrow. My father—" Her voice broke. She pressed harder against the mare's neck. Ty's hands were warm and comforting on her shoulders. His voice and words more so.

"If you wanted to cry, I wouldn't think you weak, Dixie. I've already told you that I admire your courage. I wish I could—"

With a sob she turned and pressed herself against him. "I don't want to cry. I don't want every memory of him to bring me pain. Can you understand why it's important to me that his killer doesn't go free? He was a good man, Ty. He shouldn't have been killed because someone wanted his land. He shouldn't have died when I needed him."

Her grief-laden voice tore into him. He rocked her within his arms, wishing he could make her world right again, vowing in the next breath that he would.

"Honey, listen to me," he whispered, smoothing the damp, tangled hair back from her face. "I've seen men bigger and stronger than you push themselves past the last of their endurance. You've reached that point and more."

She lifted her head, her eyes filled with the shine of tears that she refused to shed. Ty wanted her so badly that he shook with need. But he found that he could put aside his own need to care for her.

"I want you to promise me that you'll rest here tonight. No, Dixie, let me finish," he demanded when she tried to speak.

"They're camped about four miles down the wash, still trying to figure out how I switched horses without them waking up. I overheard enough to tell you that the kid's having second thoughts about staying with them. It doesn't matter if he does. I still want all three of their hides.

"If that's not enough, I can tell you that thunder-heads are piling up and if we get a storm, they won't be riding out anytime soon. Now, will you promise me?"

Whatever Ty thought he expected, it wasn't to have her nod, then slip from his arms. "Dixie?" He waited until she turned. "It will be all right." Then, in a cold, hard voice he promised, "I'll make sure of it."

She gazed at his face for long moments. "You were right about my going past the point, Ty. I can't keep on fighting you."

Dixie moved to sit in the sun, and Ty scooped up her clothes and spread them over the low-hanging branches. He winced with every stretch of his arm, for his wound was yet open. The defeat in Dixie's voice bothered him. He'd rather have that hot pepper tongue firing spirited comments at him.

She had her eyes closed, head tilted back toward the sun. Ty knew he couldn't push her now, but he couldn't seem to keep away from her, either.

Dixie heard him moving around but thought it safer to remain as she was, quiet, with her eyes closed so she wouldn't be tempted to watch him. She couldn't tell Ty about the fear he raised in her each time she was near him. She wasn't at all certain that he would understand how vulnerable he made her feel with the tantalizing thought of being a woman with dreams again. The one thing she was sure of was that she wasn't about to risk telling him. That would require an act of trust on the deepest level for her.

Trust, like control, was not easy for her to give to anyone now.

"Dixie?" Ty whispered, coming to kneel behind her.

She merely murmured in answer, for the warmth of the sun and perhaps his presence made tension leave her and she was growing drowsy. But she opened her eyes quickly enough when she felt his hand on her head, drawing her hairbrush through her damp hair.

"No, don't move. I've wanted to do this, Dixie. Let me. Just for a little while, let me take care of you."

She thought of his telling her about that night he had watched her by her camp fire brushing her hair, and the tempting pictures she had made. Ty had a light hand with the brush and it made her feel good.

She couldn't remember the last time anyone...no, she refused to allow thoughts of the past to intrude now. There was peace to be had from this place, with Ty, and she wanted it, needed it so badly that she offered no protest.

"Your hair's the dark of a mink's winter pelt shot with all the tawny shades of a cougar's coat. And just as silky soft to touch," he whispered, then smiled as she leaned her head to one side. Ty couldn't resist pressing a light kiss to the arch of her bare neck, quickly retreating before she could deny him.

Her smooth skin gleamed with warmth in the sunlight. Above the edge of the blanket her breasts swelled temptingly, tiny drops of water beaded like diamonds in the shadowed cleavage. His hand stilled. Her cold-hardened nipples were clearly defined by the soft drape of the blanket. He wished it had been the heat and moisture of his mouth that had made her nipples hard. A slight tremor that he couldn't control shook him.

"Ty? What's wrong? I know my hair's a terrible tangle after I wash it."

"Nothing." He resumed brushing her hair, trying to be satisfied with her sleepy, contented murmur.

Dixie was thankful that her voice had not betrayed her. It was becoming difficult to stifle the sounds of pleasure that she longed to free. His hands were gentle, and she felt as if he touched her as if she were something fragile and precious, to be cherished—not hurt or broken.

Since Ty made no move to increase the intimacy between them beyond that light, fleeting kiss on her neck, Dixie let the last of the tension she felt go. She knew that he wanted her. There was no way he could disguise the blunt ridge of his flesh rising within his denims. But she was also aware that Ty wouldn't push her, demanding something she wasn't quite sure she wanted to give.

Ty rubbed her scalp, absorbing the warmth with his fingertips. He thought about feeling the long, silky strands of her hair covering his body and felt the new heaviness of his blood. His hands stilled.

She opened her eyes, blinking against the brightness of the sunlight, and closed them again. "You don't have to finish, Ty. It's a chore, but this is the one vanity I've allowed myself."

"Don't ever cut it, Dixie. And it's not a chore. I'd guess I'm getting as much pleasure out of this as you are." Seeing the corners of her mouth lift upward, he bent to kiss her head. Her dark lashes formed delicate shadows over her cheeks, and he wanted to place kisses there, too, but he resumed brushing her hair until it lay like a polished mantle over her back and shoulders.

"I take back what I just said. There's no guessing to it at all. Touching you is a pleasure all its own."

He dropped the brush and stroked her hair with his hands. "A crowning glory," he whispered, feeling deep inside him the way the silken strands of her hair clung to his fingers in a soft caress.

In an unexpected move, Dixie reached back and caught hold of one of his hands. She drew it forward with her fingers curled within his and pressed a kiss on his palm.

"Thank you, Ty."

"The pleasure, as I said, is all mine."

Dixie felt the heat of the sun disappear from her face. Her eyes drifted open to find Ty leaning over her. Dark and dangerous, he appeared both a dark angel and a tempting devil with his intense gaze studying her. A powerful yearning swept through her.

He disengaged his hand from hers and raised it to her cheek. Gently rubbing his knuckles from her cheekbone to her chin, he eased her head back until his breath blended with hers.

"You know you're safe with me, Dixie. As safe as you want to be."

His words, like his touch, were another kind of caress to her. And another break in her defenses. She had to close her eyes against the intensity of need that rose within her to feel his lips upon hers.

Hunger. She had not known its like. Thoughts of revenge slipped from her thoughts. That shocked her. The desire she had for Ty ripped aside every layer of control she had used to protect herself these last months.

Her whole body tensed with pleasurable anticipation of feeling the fire burn again. Ty had only to kiss her to make it happen.

She felt the press of his teeth on her earlobe, sending a sharp burst of wild sensations through her. Instantly he soothed it with his tongue, then the warmth of his mouth. She forgot to breathe as he traced the tiny indentations that shaped her ear. And she discovered that kisses came in many forms, but from Ty they all made fire burn.

"Stop running from me, Dixie. There's enough hunter in all of us so that when you run, I chase. One of us is going to get caught. But I'm not taking any bets on who."

The thought of having Dixie made his body flood with heat. The telltale catch in her breathing, the slight tremor of her body told him he could press the matter now. He stole a quick, light kiss from her lips.

The sun's heat warmed her face and Dixie knew that he had moved away before she opened her eyes.

"Ty?"

"Right now that water looks mighty appealing." He stripped off his shirt, blinded for a moment while he pulled it over his head. When he turned, still clutching the bunched-up shirt in one hand, Dixie was gone. And so, he noted with a hard, scanning gaze, were her clothes.

"You running again? I warned—"

"No, Kincaid. I'm not running. I'd just feel...better dressed."

He didn't miss her slight hesitation and mentally supplied safer for better. He was a fine one to warn her about running. He was doing a little of it himself right now. He hadn't thought about moving off, just did it to prove to himself that he could. But his body was not complying with his mind's dictate. He wanted her and the thought of having her spiked the heat of his blood higher.

"Be foolish to get dressed now. Your clothes are still damp," he pointed out, turning toward the water to give her some privacy beneath the tree.

"I've worn them wet before. Stop worrying about me, Ty."

"Can't help it."

Dixie heard the light splash of water and peered between the leafy branches at Ty. Sunlight washed over the lean, hard muscles of his back. Only the white strip of linen from the bandage that Livia had wrapped around his wound marred his deeply tanned skin. His hand was rubbing the back of his neck as though to relieve muscles tightened by fatigue. Or was it desire? The same desire that had made her run and hide time and again.

Her hand stilled, clutching the edges of her shirt together. She told herself that she couldn't trust him entirely, yet she had accepted his word about where Thorne was. She had accepted his prediction about the possibility of a storm that would keep her father's killer from getting away.

And she stood watching him rubbing sand from the streambed's bottom, envying its touch on his body. Even under the sheltering branches, she felt hot. Sweat slicked her skin and she thought longingly of the cold water that glistened on Ty's skin.

He leaned over, struggling to keep his footing and not get his bandage wet while he scooped up water over his hair. He shook his head, spraying water every which way, then turned around.

"I wouldn't mind company, Dixie."

His soft, husky invitation sent a flush stealing through her body. He had known she was watching him, and in an effort to be open with him, Dixie stepped out from the sheltering tree.

Tiny water diamonds were caught in the wedge of dark hair that delineated the center of his chest. As if her thought was his, Ty raised one hand and rubbed the very spot she stared at. She could see the pink flesh of a scar that began on his right hip and disappeared lower where the water lapped him.

Even the breeze was sultry and heavy with the promise of a storm. But Dixie was battling a storm of her own emotions.

She wanted Ty, but giving herself to him meant giving her trust, too. He claimed he wanted no complications, and she longed for more. If she had learned nothing else in the almost two years she had tracked Thorne, Dixie knew that what she wanted and what she could have were never the same.

"Dixie, I'm coming out."

She came to, aware that he warned her, and she found herself taking her damp, discarded blanket to the edge of the water.

"Then you'll need this," she said, holding the blanket out to him.

His eyes darkened until the blue almost disappeared. She followed his gaze to where her shirt gaped open. For long moments she stared at the clean, powerful lines of his body.

Abruptly she dropped the blanket and walked back to the fire.

Ty didn't say a word. He came out of the water, scrubbed the blanket over himself to get barely dry, then slipped into his denims. He blamed himself for making her retreat once more. But even as he regained control he knew that it was for the best.

"I don't want you to think I'm running away again, Ty," Dixie began, struggling to fasten her shirt.

"You want to leave."

It wasn't a question, but she answered anyway. "I think it best that I do. You told me you didn't want any complications. Neither do I. Maybe when it's over there'll be time."

"Just tell me one thing, Dixie. Do you believe me about where Thorne and the others are?"

"I—"

"A yes or no'll do. Tell me if you trust me to tell you the truth. 'Cause if you can't, then ride the hell out of here."

She hated the way he forced her to make choices she wasn't ready to make. But there was no arguing with the low, deadly tone of his voice. She was tempted to turn around and look at him, but she resisted.

"I believe you." The words were a mere thread of sound, but she knew he heard them. Knew it and wondered what she had committed herself to.

"Then stay with me," Ty whispered.

Chapter Twelve

Eyes closed, Dixie threw her head back as if she were seeking guidance. "Don't do this to me," she pleaded. "You frighten me with the need you make me feel for you."

Stripped of all pretense, her voice cut into him. But then, he reminded himself, Dixie had never used any women's wiles on him. Her honesty demanded the same from him. And Ty discovered that there was no shame in admitting his feelings to her.

"You think it doesn't scare the hell out of me? I've never wanted a woman the way I want you. Don't ask me for answers. Seven questions and six ways to Sunday I couldn't give them to you."

A distant peal of thunder drowned out her reply. Ty glanced at the mountaintops. "Storm's coming. Just like I said it would. But there's a bigger one brewing right down here where we're standing, Angel. Your move."

First he forced her to make a choice, now he flung a challenge at her.

"What do you want from me, Ty?"

The touch of his hand on her shoulder didn't surprise her. She knew how soundlessly he could move. She felt the heat, and the strength of his long fingers shaping the curve of her shoulder. Like lightning, the touch became a lover's caress.

"Tell me what it is you want me to say, Ty."

And he leaned close to whisper, "That you're not afraid of me. That you know I wouldn't hurt you. Tell me you believe I don't want to just take from you but share pleasure that two people who want each other can have."

She lowered her head and leaned back against him. "Is that all?"

"It'll do for a start." He slipped both arms around her and held her close. "Dixie, I know you've had a rough time of it. I haven't asked you to tell me everything that happened to you, and I won't. You've a right to share what you will about your past and respect my right for the same.

"I want you. I want you to say the same and mean it. No recriminations later that I took advantage of—"

"There's something you should know, Ty. I've never been with a man." She couldn't resist twisting around in his arms to see his expression. When her gaze locked with his, she saw the surprise he couldn't hide fast enough. She didn't like the way his nearness clouded her senses. He made her feel out of control again.

"Have I shocked you?" she asked, tilting her face up.

"No," he answered with a quick, rough shake of his head.

The tension in his body became hers. "How's a little honesty, Ty? You're lying to me. I can feel it. You never expected that?" No matter how she had willed her voice to be steady, she heard for herself the betraying tremor that gave away how much it hurt. She knew how she had changed. She just never thought it mattered what he thought of her.

His hand tangled in her hair as if he sensed she would bolt and run from him. "You've got me so confused, Angel, I can't tell if I should be baying at the moon or getting down on my knees and begging."

"You're not a man to do either one, Ty."

There was that honesty again. He had no weapon against it but more of his own. "I never have been. But it doesn't matter. You do. Say the word, Dixie, and I'll leave you alone. Tell me no."

"Ty, I wish I could. I wish I even wanted to. But I can't lie to you."

"I'm not making any promises." He wanted to recall the words the moment he spoke them. Her eyes clouded and for long seconds she looked away, before she directed a steady, level gaze at him that still held too many secrets for his peace of mind.

But within her dark eyes was hunger. And it made him ache to see desire touched with curiosity. Emotions he couldn't name seethed through him.

Shaking with need, Dixie lifted her hands to cup his hair-rough cheeks. "I didn't ask you to make any promises, Ty. And," she whispered, slowly drawing his head down to hers, "just to keep things even between us, I won't make any promises to you."

Her heart raced when he moved like lightning to close his mouth over hers. If she had made even the smallest struggle, given a token protest, Ty swore he would have let her go.

But she rose on tiptoe to fit her body against his. He buried his surprise. She claimed innocence. He did not want to doubt her. No man . . . Ty didn't want to think about it.

His lady with a smile like an angel and the touch to make his blood heat came to him like a storm to a thirsty land. No coyness. No retreat. Just a generous passion that made him ache.

He wanted to be gentle with her.

She wouldn't let him.

There was raw heat. Exactly what he had remembered and needed. The taste of her filled him but never eased the craving, it only intensified it. She was as slim and as supple as any man could want. But there was strength here, too. Her arms locked around him, her fingers clutching his head, just the way his held hers.

She opened for him. He took what she offered and demanded more.

The low, deep sound of approval vibrated in his throat. Dixie heard it and answered with one of her own. She could have stopped the madness. Should have. But there was such power in his kiss, such strength in his arms holding her that she wanted more. Later she would think. Much later.

Like a raging river, her blood raced to the beat of her heart. She pressed closer to the lean, hard length of him. His hair was thick and damp, her fingers tangled deeper to hold him. With the mad beating of her heart came a strange weakness flooding her. The tremors started in her legs and burned their way upward until she felt as if she were shaking from the inside out.

An emptiness ached inside her. Hunger to be loved spread. Her body yearned for his. Even as he gentled the fierce kisses, she knew the risk she took. Ty was a man to share with, more than passion. She fought hard to bury the hope that rose. The pain would be too much. It was easier, far easier to let the passion storming her senses sweep her on its tide.

Murmuring her name, Ty ran his hands over her with greedy speed to touch, to take and possess. He tore his mouth from hers to press it against her throat. He felt the bite of her fingers into his shoulders, and she arched back, moaning when he placed his hungry mouth on her heated skin.

He wanted her now. No. He realized he needed her now. The same way he needed food and rest after a hard day's labor. The same way he needed water after a vicious day in the desert. He stroked her spine and found the tiny pulse in the hollow of her throat, pressing kisses there in an effort to slow himself down.

The leash he held on his control was slipping. Ty fought to keep it. He pulled back. She was beautiful, her hair loose and tumbling into his hands, gold strands glinting in the sun. Her eyes were dark with passion. And her mouth—lips slightly parted, full and red from his kisses. Waiting.

She remained pliant in his arms and he leaned close to kiss her lips, slanting his head and nipping lightly. He felt her tremble. His arms shifted slightly, subtly moving her closer without making her feel trapped. Each breath was labored, but he noticed that hers were the same. And against her lips, Ty smiled, knowing he wasn't alone in what was happening between them.

Dixie opened her eyes and watched him with an intensity that she didn't quite understand. Every harsh breath that he took, every movement of his body against her own, each touch of his fingers against her sensitive skin, sent new shivers of awareness through her.

She needed more from him. She needed, yet couldn't ask. The need itself was frightening, for it seemed to seethe through her. His eyes were almost black with the passion that stained his high cheekbones. She followed his gaze as he eased back from her. Damp from his skin, her cotton shirt clung to the erect tips of her breasts.

"Ty?"

He looked up and saw the small spark of fear in her eyes. "It's all right, Angel. You just set a fire that burns all the way to the soles of my feet."

His wholly male, hot smile confused her. "That's something good? I burn like that, too. Inside I—"

His kiss stole her words. Long fingers tangled in her hair, bending her head back and arching her body so that her breasts pressed against his hard chest. His other hand slid down to her hips, lifting her into the cradle of his thighs, rocking her slowly over the hot, erect male flesh that strained against the buttons of his pants. In the same sensuous stroking of his tongue, his powerful body moved against her. Ty found his quick reward as Dixie returned those sensuous rhythms to him with her tongue, her body.

When he felt the wild tremblings that shook her, he released her, rocking her against him. He tried to tell himself to go slower, that she was innocent, even if she came apart with the feelings riding both of them. Ty couldn't stop stroking her body, easing his way over her breasts to find the sensitive peaks.

Her back arched in a reflex as old as passion itself and he didn't have to ask if his touch pleased her. Her breath was a near moan, her eyes had drifted closed and her lips were parted.

He caressed the hard tips that rose to his touch, wanting the thin cloth gone, wanting to feel her flesh against his.

"Ty, please . . ."

Her voice was husky, another caress to burn through his control. He opened the buttons on her shirt, drawing her against him.

She felt vulnerable and exposed as she had never been with any man. She shook her head, sending tendrils of long hair whispering across her shoulders. Ty gently brushed it back.

"No," he said quietly. "I want to see you against my skin." His hands tightened on her back and he gently abraded his chest against her breasts. He heard her broken sounds as she tilted her head back and caught her when she couldn't stand on her own.

Ty steadied her even as he lowered her to the ground. "It's all right, Angel," he murmured, kissing her throat, nipping her ear delicately and making her shiver. He lay on his side, one hand cupping her head, the other spanning her rib cage.

Dixie saw that he looked at her with heated approval in his eyes. She felt weak at the fire and pleasure that was spreading through her. There were no lies between them and that made her brave enough to reach out to touch the soft, curling hair on his chest. She heard the hiss of Ty's breath come swiftly, suddenly, and her hand stilled.

"No. Don't stop," he said huskily, leaning over to steal a quick, hard kiss. "Touch me, Angel. As much as you want. That's how I'm going to touch you."

Dixie's fingers tightened. His hand cupped her breast. Before she could ask him what he meant, his lips trailed a string of molten kisses across her sensitive flesh. The heat of his mouth was added to the warmth of the sunlight and a sheen of sweat dampened her skin. She cried out as her nipple became more erect beneath the moist caress of his tongue. Filled with the wild pleasure he was giving her, she held his head hard against her breast. Her breath came out a ragged moan when he responded with a taut, hungry suckling.

Ty was drowning in the sun-sweet scent of her. She was warm and slender and her taste was enough to drive a man over any lines of reason. Beneath his lips he could feel the race of her heart, a beat wild enough to match his. Her hair smelled of the water, and he heard his name cried in a desperate whisper as she pressed her lips to his head.

There was no plea. No soft cry. Dixie understood that softness had no place here. Innocent, yes, but she knew this was raw, primitive passion that they brought to each other. His mouth tightened over her breast, hot and greedy, and need erupted and shattered her.

She lay dazed as Ty shifted and used lips, teeth and tongue to draw another cry, a deeper tremble from her. She was filled with hungers that had no names. Her hips moved in the same wild rhythms of his mouth tugging at her. Wave after wave of pleasure spilled through her. His right hand caressed her other breast, his thumb brushing the taut peak so that she arched her back with a sensual abandon she had never known.

Naked skin slicked over naked skin when he found her mouth with his. She felt his groan of pleasure, as well as heard it. There was no time for thought. Fire burned, hot and fast as they raced over each other in a mutual burning discovery.

He tugged her arms free of her shirt, she fumbled to open the few buttons on his denims. Her fingers traced the long scar from his hip to his thigh. A murmur of pain escaped her as if the scar and its pain were her own.

Ty found how strong she was when she bore him back to the ground, her lips racing over him, pressing kisses to his scar, only to retrace a path of fire until she joined her mouth with his. He cupped her buttocks, pressing her against him, and she melted and ran like hot honey.

He rolled her over, pulling back to work her pants off. Ty tossed them aside and stroked from her trembling thighs to her ankles. Her skin was almost milk white against his darker, tanned hands. He looked up to see that she reached for him, her gaze both demanding and vulnerable.

"Please, Ty, I feel so..."

"Naked?" he finished for her. "Me, too." And he rose to strip off his pants, making it a fact. "Now there's nothing between us," he whispered, once more coming to lay beside her.

"I want to touch you," she murmured, restlessly turning. The desire she saw in his eyes took her breath.

"And I dreamed of feeling those hands on me. But not now, Angel. Later you can touch all you want."

"Ty—" What she longed to demand ended in a helpless moan. He touched her bare stomach, her thighs and pressed gently at the apex of her legs. Dixie was too aroused to be shy, she shifted her legs for him, but she refused to close her eyes. She wanted to see him, needed to know why this one man made her feel surrender wasn't losing but winning. A gamble. One she had never taken. Never been tempted to take. But she would for Ty. And with him. If she was yielding to the emotions that churned inside her, he was no less involved.

She clung to him, the gentle, clever ply of his fingertips arousing her to a new level of need, one of more intense pleasure, but one that showed her new hunger.

Time and again she cried out to him while he held off that last, ultimate joining. She heard his whispered praise and watched him with eyes dazed with passion. His face was taut, faint high color stained his cheeks and his eyes blazed with desire as he touched her.

A whimper caught in her throat. She dug her fingers into his arms, wanting to drive him to that last intimate joining, terrified of where he would take her, even as she stirred restlessly beneath him in invitation. His mouth feasted on hers, then sought aching flesh.

He knew he wasn't gentle enough. His mouth was too greedy for the taste of her. His blood pounded with her sweetly given response, the arched invitation of her body up to his, the fierce kneading motion of her hands that held him against her. Her long, throaty moans followed one after the other, sending a pleasure he had never known streaming through him.

He knew he wasn't giving her enough time. Hunger refused to allow him to give her respite. Every muscle trembled in his body when he took her mouth again, delving deeply with his tongue. Ty settled himself deeper in the cradle of her hips, swallowing her gasp, then her cry as he plunged into her.

Dixie jerked her head to one side. There was an incredible stretching fullness that burned through passion's fire. He subtly shifted and she turned her head, sinking her teeth into his shoulder to bury the scream that rose.

Ty went tense and still above her.

"No," she whispered as he lifted his head to look at her.

He braced himself above her and stared down into her face. His groin tightened. He had to lick his lips against their sudden dryness. "I never meant to hurt you."

"I know that, Ty." Dixie reached up with one hand to touch the bite mark she had left on his shoulder. "Now you have two wounds. I never meant to hurt you, either."

"I'll make this good for you, Angel. I promise I will." *Don't tell me to stop.* The words went no further than his mind. Nothing could feel this good. Nothing had ever given him so much pleasure. He wanted to settle his weight on her, wanted to burrow his face in the soft, fragrant hollow between her neck and her shoulder.

Her fingertips rose to touch his lips. Holding his gaze steady with her own, she said, "No promises, remember, Ty."

"I remember." But the words were low, gritty and hinted of his longing to recall them. Because he suddenly wanted promises. He wanted to hear her whisper that she was his. That no man...

He lost his thought with the feel of her supple hands riding his back. He held his breath as she touched his hip, her eyes closing, a soft smile playing on her lips.

"Dixie?"

"It's all right now," she whispered. To make him understand what she couldn't explain, she used both hands to trace the lean, hard muscles of his thighs. His belly convulsed in reflex. She held his hips and murmured, "Kiss me, Ty. I want to feel the pleasure that came before the pain." To reinforce her demand, she ran her hands along his thighs, then cupped the hard curves of his buttocks to draw him deeper inside her.

"Yes . . . that," she moaned. "I want—"

"No. That's not what you want, Dixie. Say my name. Say you want *me* deeper inside you. Say it's me you need now."

She struggled with the words, dragging in shallow breaths as he slowly penetrated deeper, then as slowly began to withdraw.

"No!" she cried out.

"Then say it," he demanded once again. And Ty discovered what hell felt like. The tight resistance that gloved his flesh seemed to stroke him with every ragged breath she drew.

"Ty, please." She barely managed a subtle shift of her legs. The sudden, grinding, circular motion of his hips robbed her of breath. She couldn't close her eyes. She stared up at his face looming over her and saw the sweat bead as he held himself still and waited. He was dark, almost savage looking, his eyes near black and making the same silent demand.

"I want you," she cried in a broken whisper. "I want you inside me. You, Ty. Only you."

He began to move, rubbing his open mouth over hers to drink her pleasure cry.

Dixie closed her eyes. She drew in the scent of the crushed grass beneath her. Heat seared her body inside and out as she stroked his skin warmed by the sun. He quickened his pace, pressing into her, and she knew his control had snapped. There was a wildness to his thrusts, as if he had no thought but to take possession of her. She listened to his harsh breathing and the faint peal of distant thunder. But its rumbling was no match for the racing beat of her heart.

And his.

Her head thrashed back and forth. Tension built and spiraled into unbearable need. She cried out his name in both plea and demand.

She listened to the harshness of Ty's breathing.

And her own.

She thought of the powerful, hard strength of his body and her own helplessness against it. Pleasure caught her in rhythm that was wild, deep . . . hot.

She was burning.

She couldn't breathe.

Complete surrender. Nothing held back. Ty offered what he was asking from her.

"Now . . . it has to be—" Ty bit off the words. The tension exploded, shattered.

"Hold me!" she cried out.

He gathered her into his arms as pleasure so intense showered her with feelings that left her stunned.

"Mine," he whispered as tremors claimed him.

No! she denied in silence as she trembled with her own fulfillment.

Chapter Thirteen

As if he had heard that silent denial, Ty reared his head back and stared down at her face. Her eyes were closed, shutting him out. He had claimed the secrets of her body, but not her heart or her mind.

No promises, remember? He blocked out the reminder he had to forget. The rules had changed.

Slowly he lowered his head to nuzzle his lips against hers. He stroked the tangled strands of her hair back from her face, then framed her cheeks with his palms.

"Look at me, Angel. I want to see for myself if you're all right."

In blissful lassitude Dixie murmured soft sounds, unwilling to be torn from the exquisite pleasure that still radiated through her.

"Did I hurt you?" Ty asked, hearing a tremor he could not control ride his voice. She had not moved, yet he felt her withdrawing from him. The sudden anger caught him by surprise. He let his arms take his weight as he braced himself above her. It was agony to separate himself from her, for he could still feel the tiny shivers that rocked her body.

He lay beside her, flinging one arm up to shield his eyes and wondered how something that felt so good, so right, had gone so wrong. The fault was his. A woman deserved soft words, gentle touches and he had fallen on her like a man starved for sustenance. He'd always had a way with women. It was one thing that he shared with his oldest brother, Conner. Not so with Logan. He was a hard man to please and swore he'd never marry. Ty agreed with his middle brother.

He'd sworn never to marry, too. Marry? Where the devil had that thought come from? Irrational as it was, he moved his arm to his side and turned to look at Dixie, knowing it was somehow her fault for the direction of his thoughts.

Cause and blame fled the moment he saw the tears sliding down her cheeks. She didn't make a sound, but he had a feeling these weren't tears of joy she shed.

"Dixie?" He curved his hand over her cheek, turning her face toward him. "I should be shot for what I've done to you. I swear I'll make it up to you, only don't shut me out. I couldn't deal with that now."

His thumb brushed the tears from her cheek while he waged a battle with himself. He knew the perils of the territory, had survived brushes with death, but he stood in peril of losing his heart to this one spirited, lovely woman he needed to claim as his.

The land was unforgiving and Ty was just as hard on himself. He knew the mistake he had made. The fever she raised in him hadn't been cooled. Once wouldn't do it. Forever might. She had to know how he felt, but the words stuck in his throat. All he could do was whisper for her to open her eyes, to look at him, to tell him that he hadn't hurt her.

Shutting him out. Dixie repeated it over and over, knowing it was the only protection she had left. Ty made her wage a battle with herself, had from the first moment she understood how dangerous he was to her.

In his arms she had become a woman for the first time. Yes, she had felt pain, but the fire of passion had swept it away. She tried to block out the soft murmur of his voice, tried repeatedly and knew she was failing. His gentle kisses, his touch, all awakened the desire that yet simmered within her.

She could admit to herself that she wanted him still.

But she couldn't forgive him.

She rolled to her side, breaking his hold on her.

"Damn you, Dixie! Talk to me."

Words wouldn't come. And even if they did, Dixie knew she couldn't say them to him. He made her dream again. The one thing she had had to deny herself to have her revenge. That Ty could make her forget, make her want to forget it, was unforgivable. For herself, more than him. And it pained her to know that the beauty of what they had shared was tainted. To tell him would strip her to her soul. She would no longer have the power to be in control.

But even as she struggled to push off his hand and rise, she wanted nothing more than for him to hold her.

"You bitch."

She flinched at the very softness of his voice, absent of hot fury, filled with cold fire. She had to be strong. Strong as she had never been, to walk away from him. Ty must never know how much she cared.

It was an effort to gather up her clothes and avoid looking at him. He hadn't moved. He watched her though, watched her with eyes that burned with the same cold fire that had coated his words.

"Where the hell do you think you're going?"

"To finish what I started," she answered in a voice devoid of emotion. Her hands trembled and she swore when she couldn't fasten her shirt. Dixie sent a quick, yearning look at the water. Her body wanted soothing. If a cold embrace was all she could have to ease the burning, she would take it.

But a darting glance at Ty's prone form killed the thought. She couldn't stay here a moment more than she had to.

Ty followed the direction of her gaze toward the water. The wind had freshened and ripples danced over the wash's deep pool surface. He should be moving, doing something to stop her, but anger held him back.

After what they shared—and he knew how good it had been, even if she didn't—she still couldn't trust him. No. It wasn't that Dixie couldn't—she wouldn't. Damn her stubborn hide!

The woman was a complication he wasn't sure he knew how to deal with. But even as he tamped down the anger and swore he'd let her go, he rose and grabbed his pants.

"Hold on, Rawlins," he snapped. "You're not going anywhere alone."

Dixie refused to dignify that statement with protest. She fought hard to ignore him, and just as hard to ignore whatever he said.

"Your stubbornness has no place here. Take a look at what's coming in over the mountains, Dixie. Shelter's all we should be looking for. Thorne won't be going anywhere."

She rounded on him, which he hadn't expected, and Ty dropped his boot.

"Why do you have to include yourself in my plans? I never asked you to. I want you gone, Ty Kincaid. You've taken enough from me."

"Maybe by your way of reckonin' I have," he drawled.

She hadn't wanted to look at him, but that compelling gaze of his forced her to meet it. She wished she could read what was there in his eyes, but the emotions were complex. Anger, yes. She saw that clearly. But there was hurt and betrayal staring out from his dark blue eyes, too. How could he feel the same emotions that she did? How could she get him to cut her loose so that she could lick her wounds without him around?

Dixie took a deep, steadying breath and slowly released it. His spread-legged stance bore aggression, his features the stamp of arrogance. The rising wind ruffled his hair and snapped the loose tails of his shirt out from his lean, hard body. Her eyes closed for a brief moment, fighting the memory of having touched the body that even now, even through the anger she fought to cling to, had desire curling through her.

"You're right, Ty. By my way of reckoning I have lost. I—" She broke off when he stepped closer, fury coming off him in waves. And Dixie suddenly had her answer.

Her chin rose and she leveled a biting stare at him.

"I feel as if I've lost part of myself—"

"Well, hell! You did!" Ty closed the short distance between them. He wanted her pliant and warm in his arms. He wanted her to let him whisper soft words and offer the tender wooing that should have been hers from the start. He wanted anything but the anger, betrayal and hurt that sheened her eyes.

"Listen to me, Dixie." He blocked her move to go around him, then grabbed hold of her upper arm and yanked her against him. "Stay right here. I'll admit it pleased me something fierce to be the first—"

"Bastard!" She tried jerking her arm free, but his grip tightened.

He dragged the sultry air into his lungs, striving for calm. He might as well have asked to be in another part of the territory. How could he be calm when she stood so close that her breath mingled with his? There wasn't anything calm about the storm in her eyes, or the way her body trembled against his, sending a fever flood of heat streaming through him.

He fought through the desire swamping his senses. He had to. She mattered too much, and that was frightening.

"You weren't the only one to lose something here, lady. There's a piece of me—"

She slapped him and stunned him into silence.

It dawned on Ty what he said and how he said it. Fury stained her cheeks. Murder blazed from her eyes. But a sob escaped her lips and he found himself caging her within his arms, ignoring her struggles.

"Honesty, wildcat. Neither one of us can walk away from that now."

If Ty had hit her, Dixie couldn't have been more stunned. Her stricken gaze rose to meet his. "No. No," she repeated in disbelief. She had not thought, refused to think. "Please, if you have any mercy in you, let me go."

A rolling clap of thunder sounded, as if it made more of her demand. Ty looked up as the sun disappeared. Black clouds roiled, like the churning emotions seething inside him, warning of a storm's coming violence that more than matched the one between them.

"Get the horses saddled. We have to get out of here. I was wrong. Those clouds are piling up a granddaddy size gully washer."

He had to let her go. Snatching up his boots, he scooped up their gun belts, unconsciously not trusting her, and ran for the horses.

Dixie had to follow him. The deep-sided wash wasn't a place to get caught in a mountain rainstorm.

Slinging a blanket over her mare's back, she was glad of the work that forced her concentration away from Ty. And the reason for new fear.

A piece of him.... Her hand slid from adjusting the stirrup and came to rest on her belly. "Dear Lord, what have I done?"

Kah neighed, its sound almost mournful, and Dixie shook her head, before she resumed tying her gear onto the saddle. The coming storm made the horses restless and she took a few moments to soothe not only her own mare but the one that Greg and Livia had given to her.

Ty worked with silent efficiency. He heard the soft murmur of Dixie's voice calming the mares and wished she had tried a little of that on him. He wouldn't have minded feeling her hands petting him again, but as he turned to catch her eye, she ducked beneath the reins of both mares to keep distance between them.

With a curse and a scowl, he walked back to kick the fire out, scanning for anything left behind. He almost stepped on the forgotten hairbrush. She had her back to him, so Ty picked it up. He caught a few long strands of her hair and curled them over one finger, then tucked it in his shirt pocket.

Beyond the scattered ashes and the broken, crushed grass, there was no sign of their having been there.

With a shrug, Ty thought it just as well. He joined Dixie and took her gun belt from his saddle horn, then handed it over along with her hairbrush. For a long moment he met her bleak gaze, and then abruptly he turned away.

Trouble. The woman had been nothing but trouble from the moment he crossed trails with her and he would do himself a favor to remember it.

"Mount up. We've no time to lose."

Clipped and sharp, his order stung. She didn't argue with him. Ty knew this land, and she did not, but as she set her foot in the stirrup, she couldn't stop a sharp cry of pain. Ty was behind in seconds, lifting her up into Kah's saddle. He handed over the reins to the other mare, then mounted his own horse.

Just as Dixie reached the top of the slope to the wash, she gave in to the impulse to look back. There was no sign they had been there. Regret filled her. Perhaps it was just as well. The wind whipped her loose hair across her face, blinding her for a moment, until she gathered what hair she could with one hand.

She tensed the moment she felt Ty's hands cover her own as he drew close and leaned over from his saddle.

"What are you doing?" she snapped, for even the mere touch of his hand was more than she could bear right now.

"Tying this back. You can't ride if you can't see."

She knew instantly that he had done his share of hogtying. A quick slice of his knife freed one of the rawhide strings from his saddle. Within seconds a few half hitches had secured her hair at the back of her neck. She thought she felt the lightest brush of his knuckles at her nape, but he moved away too fast for her to be sure.

"Let's ride."

She stared at the rigid set of his features, at his most forbidding gaze and her thank-you died before she uttered the words. She had no one but herself to blame for his cold manner. Telling herself it was the best thing that could have happened, for he would surely cut loose of her now, didn't help ease the terrible empty ache she felt.

They rode on in silence for almost a quarter of a mile, beneath the ever-darkening sky and gusting wind. Dixie was deep in thought, her mind churning with regret and memories of her time spent with Ty. She tried to ignore the thought he had planted in her mind—that she carried his seed—and if she did, the child would be hers.

Alone. The regret she felt strengthened as she gazed ahead at Ty. He was a man who could easily kindle a love both gentle and strong, one that would shelter those he embraced from all of life's storms.

Once she could have been a woman with dreams of a man like him. Now she hunted a murderer, seeking justice in a land where there wasn't any. And she had a new worry to concern her.

What would she do if there was a child?

Because she was staring at Ty, she realized that he had slowed their pace. He leaned from his saddle as if studying the ground of the rough-cut path they were following.

"What's wrong?" she called out just as he drew rein. Greg's mare crowded close to Kah, forcing Dixie closer to the edge of the deep wash. Her mare responded instantly to the light tug on her neck rein and Dixie managed to get both horses away from the crumbling edge.

Instead of answering Dixie, Ty dismounted. He sent a searching gaze over the towering rocks ahead, scowling at the hiding places they could offer. He turned to study their back trail, too aware that Dixie watched his every move with growing alarm.

Dixie felt as if cold fingers were walking up her spine. She couldn't help but scan the trail ahead as far as she could see. She gave a quick look behind them and turned in time to see Ty clamber up the granite rocks for a better view.

The horses snorted and pranced restlessly as the lightning lit up the underside of the clouds above them. Seconds later thunder rumbled across the sky. Afraid that the horses would bolt, she gripped the reins tight and urged her mare forward to take hold of Ty's horse.

The move saved her life. Gunfire erupted. She screamed a warning for Ty. The mares started to rear. Dixie controlled Kah with a hard press of her knees, but the other mare jerked the reins from her hand. She called out to Ty again, keeping her body low over the horse's neck. She couldn't tell where the shots were coming from.

She heard Ty swearing as he slid and scrambled down to the path.

"Ride!" he ordered, swinging onto his horse.

A bullet creased the horse's flank and he reared, hooves pawing the air. Ty was thrown back and came down hard on his shoulder. He couldn't believe that Dixie was still there, trying to control her horse, calling out his name.

"Get the hell outta here!" he shouted at her, drawing and firing to give her cover. But even as the order hung in the air, Ty knew she couldn't ride ahead where someone—and he had determined it was a single shooter—waited, or ride back the way they had come, because she would be caught down in the wash when the storm broke.

Dragging in the thick, sultry air in an effort to help control the pain of his throbbing shoulder, Ty knew they didn't have much time before the rains began. He climbed a little higher, trying to give Dixie a chance to get away, wishing, not for the first time, that he had his Spencer repeater. The rifle's range would give him an edge that he needed badly. A handgun wasn't a match for their assailant's rifle.

He swore at seeing his horse take off down the path and disappear around the curve. The sudden pause in firing told Ty that the man was reloading. He took those few moments to find Dixie. There weren't enough swears or curses in his vocabulary when he spotted her in the rocks below him, crouched down, her own gun sighted toward the shooter. There was no sign of her mare.

"Damn you, Dixie!" His furious whisper was just loud enough to get her attention. She gazed up at him, and Ty felt fear like he had never known. "I told you to get away. The horses are gone and we're pinned down for as long as that bastard wants to keep us here. Can't you ever listen to me?"

"I couldn't leave you, Ty."

The softly spoken statement stole his fury. Honesty and courage—a damning and powerful combination in a woman. The realization distracted him. He couldn't figure out why he should think of it now, or what he was going to do about it. The resuming gunfire left him no time to mull it over.

"Keep your head down," Ty called out to her, "but get your tail up here with me."

He was reloading by the time she reached his side. All Dixie could make out was disjointed muttering, most of it directed at her lack of understanding how dangerous it was that she remained behind with him.

The first fat raindrops hit the back of her neck and the wind increased as the clouds opened up to release a solid wall of rain over them.

"If we can't see, it's kittens to cows that he won't be able to, either. Now's our chance, Angel. And this time, for both our sakes, follow my orders."

Already shaking from the chilling rain, Dixie merely nodded. If the thickheaded Ty Kincaid couldn't or wouldn't understand why she had stayed with him, she wasn't about to enlighten him.

Ty's lips against her ear sent a shiver of sensual awareness through her. She dropped the bullets she had pulled from her belt. Reaching for them before the torrent of rain washed them down the small gully, her fingers encountered Ty's.

"Let me do it. You're shaking." Self-directed anger sharpened his voice. If he hadn't suggested that it was safe to stay behind they wouldn't be facing an unknown shooter. But worry entered, too. Where were the other two men? Ty had no doubt that one of the three they were tracking had remained behind. But why?

He handed Dixie's reloaded gun to her, giving her hand a tight, quick squeeze. "We're going to try to go up and around him. All right?"

"I'll be right behind you all the way."

He came up out of his crouch, turned to find the easiest going for her, and when he mapped the path out in his mind, he turned around to face her.

"There's something I need first." He cupped the back of her head and drew her lips beneath his. This was the gentle, tender, cherishing kiss he had wanted to give her when passion's aftermath had left him shaken to his soul.

He eased his mouth away from hers, regret filling him. But he mustered a quick, wicked grin. "That was for luck. I'll claim the promise I just tasted when we get out of this mess."

"You do that, Kincaid," she whispered as he moved out. Dixie prayed that it would be true. There was a cold, hard knot of fear in her belly. She couldn't get rid of the thought that her luck, and Ty's, had just run out.

Chapter Fourteen

Ty tested his footing before he moved, conscious that he did it for Dixie and not himself. He had been in tight spots before this, too many times to recall now, but never had survival meant as much.

He told himself that she would be fine, that he didn't need to stop every few feet of the climb to see that she was right behind him as he had ordered.

Dixie had proven herself capable of holding her own with him. Yet he needed the visual reassurance that she was indeed keeping up with him.

Pain lanced him every time he had to use his arm to pull himself up over the slippery rocks. It was almost impossible to see more than a foot or two in front of him. The one thing he blessed the rain for was a lessening of the gunfire that had pinned them.

He couldn't stop himself from a mental tongue-lashing over the loss of his horse and his gear, especially the rope, water and a blanket. When they got clear—and he swore he'd made sure that they did—he'd need them. Ty knew his concentration should have been focused on finding safe hand- and footholds for Dixie to follow. But he kept thinking about the distraction that she presented to make him forget items needed for survival.

Ty paused to slick back his hair and with it the water that dripped into his eyes. His fingers were chilled and molded to his gun. The only good thing he felt was the icy water cooling the fire burning in his shoulder.

"Stay here." The words were whipped by the wind and he didn't know if Dixie heard him. He motioned with his gun for her to stay while he reconnoitered what lay in wait over the rim of rocks.

Dixie saw his lips move but didn't hear him. The motion he made with his gun let her know what he wanted. She knew he was in pain. By Ty would never have allowed her to go first. There wasn't a crevice big enough for her to huddle in, and the slashing rain began to sting.

"Be careful," she shouted just as he moved to go over the top and out of her sight. She rested against a long slab of granite, feeling her feet go numb as rain soaked her boots. She had to pry her fingers free from her gun. She recalled what Ty had done that night in the cave to warm them and put her hand to her mouth, but it only helped for a few seconds.

She couldn't stop worrying that Ty had been gone for a while. Dixie shifted, trying to flex muscles grown stiff, and felt herself slide down the slab. There was nothing to grab hold on, nothing to stop her as she tried to order her chilled body to respond. She tasted blood mixed with rain when she bit her lip and looked up to see her palm badly scraped as she fought to stop the slide.

Her boots hit a mud pocket. When she attempted to dig in, she slid farther down.

Ty crawled back over the rim and saw what was happening to Dixie. He holstered his gun, uncaring if a bullet waited for him, and went after her.

Scraped and bruised, he caught hold of her wrists, barely managing to wedge his boots between two rocks to give himself purchase. He saw the fear in her eyes, knew he had allowed her to glimpse the pain of his shoulder as he took her full weight.

The instant her slide stopped, Dixie demanded that he let her go. She saw the strain etched on his features, knew the pain in his shoulder had to be unbearable. And caught his quick denial with despair.

She struggled to find solid ground with her feet to ease the terrible strain on his arms. She closed her eyes briefly, offering up a prayer for help, then made the mistake of looking down behind her.

The path they had ridden on had disappeared beneath the water rushing down the rock face. Below them, in the wash, a rising level of rapidly moving current swept deadfall branches and small uprooted bushes within its swirling waters. If Ty let her go... if she couldn't hold on, Dixie knew it was her fate to be swept along in that killing current.

One look up at Ty's face and she knew he would never let her go. He had to understand the danger. He would go over with her.

"Don't even think about it!" he yelled to Dixie. He didn't need to read her mind. The direction of her gaze was not lost to him. He knew the danger, knew it even as he fought and was unable to stop her from sliding down another few inches. The footing was treacherous on the rain-slicked rocks. He demanded more of himself. He had to hold on to her.

Ty felt how cold her skin was becoming. Beneath his fingers he felt the fragile bones of her wrists. Dixie was strong. He repeated it to himself, but he knew how much her strength had been depleted. She was cold, and he was afraid she was already giving up.

"Hold on tight to me, Dixie." He could barely see the frantic moves she made with her legs as she tried to gain a solid foothold. He wanted to yell at her to stop, knew she was only trying to help him, but as he formed the order, she succeeded in jerking them both down another few inches.

For the first time, Ty had to admit to himself that this might be the one battle he was not going to win.

As if Dixie had the same thought, she called out to him. "Ty! Let me go!"

"Not on a bet, lady. I've got something precious to collect from you. Remember that, Dixie. Just think about how you're gonna sassy-mouth me."

He managed a firmer grip on her wrists, denying his own pain, feeling secure in his footing at last. As if to mock his efforts, the icy rain suddenly doubled in force. He was blinded by the new, harder torrent of water. His belly lurched with cold fear churning and his heart skipped a beat when lightning scored above them and he saw Dixie's terrified face. Her skin was blanched of color. Only her eyes held his as her lips soundlessly formed his name over and over.

He drew on strength he didn't know he had left. He wasn't about to let this damn mountain claim her. He swore nothing would ever take her from him.

She sensed, then felt his redoubled effort to pull her up. She prayed, begged and pleaded for the Lord's help. Dixie was terrified. But not for herself. She feared the ever-nearing lightning that could strike Ty.

Blood was still seeping from her palm and made his hold on her left wrist slip. She bit down hard on her lip not to cry out the fear that held her in its grip.

She kept her gaze on the fierce determination that marked his features until the rain so blinded her that she had to look away to clear her vision.

The sudden feel of her boot wedged into a solid crevice sent hope streaming through her. "I've a foot-hold, Ty!" she screamed above the rising wind.

Her left leg dangled uselessly, but she pushed hard with her right foot to take some of her weight and was rewarded with the gain of inches. She tried to find a tiny place with her left boot so that she could repeat the move, but her boot slid time and again. Dixie tried hard not to think of how long Ty had held on to her. Fear wasn't going to win. She was not going to fall. As she repeated this to herself, Ty jerked her up and she found purchase on the rocks.

"I can climb now. Let me go."

Ty ignored her demand. He'd let her go when he had her safe beside him.

"Once more, Dixie. I know you can do it. Together we can make it."

She felt as if a layer of ice covered her skin. Each muscle burned from the continued strain. Dixie closed her eyes, gathering whatever reserves of strength she had left. It was difficult to admit, as she looked up at Ty, that she only had one more try in her. If she didn't make it up beside him this time...

No! She couldn't think that way!

"Ready?" Ty called out.

Dixie saw him looming above her, dark, determined and defying the elements to make her safe. She tried to swallow and found she couldn't. She had thought of Ty in terms of a man she could learn to love. Meeting his gaze, seeing for herself the firm promise within that, no matter what happened, he was with her all the way, forced the realization that love for him was already curling its precious tendrils around her heart.

"Angel, it's got to be now."

"Yes. I'm ready."

She saw the delicate balance he was forced to maintain to keep his footing. Her own wasn't any better. Ty's knees bent, his back arched to give him leverage. The moment she felt him pull, she tried pushing off her toehold and this time she found an edge for both feet. He did not let go, not even when she was head high to his belly.

Dixie lay panting, on firmer footing now, Ty's hands holding her elbows, urging her the rest of the way up.

"A...min-ute," she pleaded, curling her fingers around his gun belt.

"I've got you, Dixie. You're safe now."

Threads of exhaustion were in his voice. She managed a nod, no longer caring about the stinging cold of the rain, or the ever-encroaching lightning strikes. She was going to be safe and warm the moment she wrapped her arms around Ty. The thought didn't surprise her; if anything, it gave her courage for the last effort.

Ty side-stepped to a small flat rock shelf and seconds later she was cradled in his arms.

"I thought I'd lost you."

She tried to smile, but Ty's lips were covering her mouth. She tasted his need and surrendered to it, for it was her own. Her arms were slow to obey her mind, as her need to hold him increased. Her body strained against his, seeking warmth, comfort and the heated kindling of desire. She felt possessed by him. In long strokes his hands ran from her shoulders to her hips and back again. Her mouth burned from the urgency of his hard, hot kiss, and all she wanted was more. Death had come too close. Ty was life.

When he lifted his head, she stared up at him, sipping the rain from his skin. At first she thought the shiver running up her spine was from the cold. But her belly clenched again with fear.

Dixie tilted her head back, looking up at the sky, blinking rapidly as the rain fell. She hugged Ty, unable to voice her fear, unable to determine what caused it.

"We need to get you and me out of this wet, Angel."

She jumped as thunder bellowed across the sky and a rapid fire of lightning flashes lit up the land around them. Ty slipped his arm around her waist, encouraging her to lean on him as he turned.

"It'll be sloppy going down, but you hold on tight, Dixie. I don't want to relive these minutes again."

She didn't need his urging to stay close to him. Fear churned in her belly. The rain had lessened, as if a curtain parted, for she could see how heavy it fell not more than a few feet in front of them.

"Ty, did you see who was shooting at us?"

"Not a hair. My God, but you're like ice."

"I'm afraid, Ty. Don't ask me—"

She gave no thought to their precarious footing on the rocks. Dixie stepped in front of him. She had to make him understand. Her fingers gripped the front of his sodden shirt.

"Ty, don't go ahead." Almost frantic now, she glanced around. They stood on the top of rocks, and before them waited another climb to avoid the churning water below.

Dixie didn't know what made her look around. Her scream was a silent one. There was a darker shadow up ahead, barely visible through the rain, which had increased.

The undersides of the clouds lit as if fireworks had gone off and her cry was torn on the rising wind. It was a man.

"Look! Ty, there he—"

Thunder crashed and Dixie jerked in his arms. Ty had drawn his gun, barely able to make out the form of a man up ahead. It wasn't until he heard the funny way she called his name that he realized she had been shot.

"No! Damn it, no!" He caught her with one arm, firing blindly. He knew how useless his gun was at this range, but that didn't stop him. Dixie sagged against him.

"Ty?"

Her voice was a murmur of pain, too low, confused, as if she didn't understand what had happened. He lowered her down to get her clear of the line of fire and crouched over her.

"Hang on, Dixie. I'll get that bastard if it's the last thing I do."

"No!" She clawed at his arm, trying to keep him down. "Don't leave me. Please, Ty, it hurts."

He scrubbed back her wet hair, cupping her cheek. Rock chips flew up close by. Too damn close. Ty was able to see that the man wasn't heavyset, which meant he wasn't Thorne, and he was too tall for the kid. But before he could go after him, he had to move Dixie. If there was a God listening, he hoped his prayers were heard, because this was one hell of a devil's pocket they were in.

Beneath them, the ground shook from rolling thunder. Off to the side, rocks tumbled free. Flattened over her body, the only protection he could offer her now, Ty found that he had a store of prayers to say.

The shots were fast and furious, keeping them pinned down. He knew his swearing was useless, but it held at bay his worry that he couldn't even find out where Dixie had been shot.

"Can you wrap your arms around me?" he whispered against her ear. "The lightning's getting worse, Angel. I don't relish being crisped up like a burned biscuit."

Ty knew the wound was bad by the length of time it took her to respond to his repeated plea that she hold on to him. He judged the strength of her right arm sliding over his shoulder and counted the ever-lengthening seconds until he felt her move her left one. He had a general location of a wound, but all he cared about was that she was alive.

"We're going for a ride. You just hang on as best as you can, Dixie. Let me do all the work." He rolled her over as gently as he could, afraid to look at her face. He tucked her head beneath his chin, wrapping his own arms around her waist. He felt warmth on his shirt-sleeves, seeping to his skin. In a moment of agony he closed his eyes. It was her blood he felt.

Digging in his boot heels, Ty ignored the pain of rocks slicing his shirt as he twisted with a rocking motion to bring them closer to the far edge. When he had scouted the way before the shooting started, there had been a V-shaped depression that would make a natural slide. The water, this time, would be the easement to take them down below.

"I don't want you to be scared, Dixie. We're gonna go over the edge. We won't fall. And I'm holding you. You know I won't let anything more happen to you." Even to his ears the words sounded so damn empty, but they were all he had.

Still he hesitated. No matter how careful, no matter how gentle he was, Dixie would get hurt. He wanted to spare her the pain, but like wanting to kill the man who had shot her, his wants and reality didn't match. Dixie first, he repeated.

Ty never knew what made him turn to look at the shooter. As if the rain were a curtain to be parted, he saw him clearly, a rifle raised to his shoulder, ready to fire at them.

As far as he could see, the heavens had opened up. Lightning sizzled the very air he breathed. He watched, and saw, as if time had somehow frozen the moments, the bright light gleaming along the rifle barrel. Jagged forks of lightning struck, repeatedly. An unholy cry was cut off.

Ty closed his eyes.

There was a God. His prayers were answered.

"Oh, my Lord . . . Ty? Did you—"

"Hush, love," he urged, cupping the back of Dixie's head and pushing it down to his chest. "Don't look. I wish to God I hadn't seen it happen. But it was justice, Angel. Don't ever, ever forget that."

There was no reason now for him to take a suicide slide off the rocks. He could take Dixie down slowly, safely.

And he knew where he would take her.

Home to the Rocking K, the one place he'd sworn he'd never return to, asking for help.

Chapter Fifteen

Ty used his shirt to bandage her wounds. It wasn't until he had her off the mountain that he discovered she'd been hit twice. One bullet had creased the fleshy part of her thigh, but it was the other one, the one that had hit her left side, that worried him.

When she couldn't drag herself another step, he carried her. He had no idea of time, or the distance he had traveled when the rain finally stopped. Dixie had passed out some time ago.

He knew she needed shelter and warmth. Traveling at this slow pace was going to see the two of them down before he could find help. He rested, lifted her up into his arms and began walking.

The rushing sound of the river led him to the cottonwoods. Ty didn't waste time agonizing over his decision.

He lay Dixie down, trying not to think about how cold she was. Searching the cottonwood trees, he found what he wanted. Two thick branches grew out head high from the trunk and formed a narrow V. It was high enough to protect Dixie, but not so high that he would find it impossible to get her up there.

Using his knife, he stripped off the small, thick-leaved limbs, weaving them with those growing on the tree. He thought of the hours spent on the ranch with Hazer Scofield teaching him how to braid his own ropes. Ty tested the cradle he made with his own weight, then filled it with leaves before he carried Dixie there.

Her small whimper of pain was her only sound as he lifted her up. He kissed her hand and knew she couldn't hear the promises he made. Words weren't what she needed from him.

For a moment he stood, head bowed, shoulders sagging, fighting off his own exhaustion. He had to cover her and leaves were all he had.

He looked back once, counting his steps from the tree to the riverbank, then he began to walk.

When he grew too tired to take another step, he thought of her smile. When he stumbled and fell, he remembered how much courage she had and found the strength to go on. And when there was nothing left to keep him going, he began a silent litany of prayer.

Dawn found him on his knees, trying to stand. The nicker of a horse, followed by another, forced his head up. The rising sun spread light on neatly planted rows and picked out the round huts thatched with arrowweed. Ty shook his head and struggled to his feet. He knew where he was—a Pima village.

If he judged correctly, he was close to the Hassa-yampa River, far downstream from the mining camp.

Rubbing the grit from his eyes, he blinked several times and studied the land around him. The peaks in the distance gave him his bearings. He was a grueling four-day ride from the Rocking K.

But his luck had changed, for he could approach the village openly. The Pimas had been scouts for the army long before the Civil War, some had served in the mostly Maricopa volunteer unit—one of the few Indian units to fight in the war. He was dredging up facts from memory, anything to keep him from thinking about Dixie and what he would find when he got back to her.

These Indians were farmers, and they had horses. Trade items were in short supply. He looked down at himself and without a moment of regret, knew what he was going to do.

Waiting outside the cluster of huts with their attached, open-sided sheds, Ty looked over the horses in the corral.

It was agony to wait when he wanted to shout his need for hurry, but to be refused a trade due to his poor behavior wasn't a risk he could take.

The blanket covering the opening of the far hut parted, and a man came forth. He would barely reach Ty's shoulder. His hair locks were braided, a wide-rimmed felt hat concealed the rest. Ty noted the cleanliness of his shirt and pants as he drew closer. The man's coarse, broad features and his moccasins told Ty he had guessed right, this was a Pima village.

"Ty Kincaid of the Rocking K," he called out, and to show that he meant no harm, he stripped off his gun belt, wrapping the belt around the holster and gun.

"I've come to trade. Need a horse. A good one. A blanket and food. Savvy?"

He itched with impatience while the man took his measure. Ty schooled his features not to reveal how desperate he was and had no idea if he was successful.

The moments stretched into minutes before the Pima nodded. "John Redbird. You come."

Ty traded his gun for the horse. Redbird merely nodded at his choice as Ty led out a piebald mare. He wanted the high-stepping sorrel, but the mare had a broad back that could easily accommodate both himself and Dixie. Her eyes were both gentle and intelligent, her black-and-white-spotted coat, gleaming. She was sound of limb, young enough to take the grueling ride, old enough to have some desert and mountain smarts.

Redbird had a little English, and Ty strained to remember some Papago as they dickered over his bullets for two blankets. Enticing smells rose from the camp fires. Ty fingered the gun belt. Conner had made it for him, and Logan had traded with a Navajo silversmith for the buckle with the initial K centered over a coil of rope. It had been his sixteenth birthday gift, one of the few things he had taken with him when he left home.

Ty handed it over in trade for food.

An abrupt angry spate made Ty turn around in time to see a woman. He knew it was rude to stare, but she stood poised to flee, breasts bare, her chest and her chin adorned with tattooed designs. That was the way of the Mohave women, not the Pimas. As he turned back, Ty saw the forbidding expression on Redbird's face and knew he wasn't going to be invited to return.

"You go now. Redbird bring food."

He held the hackamore rope bridle of the piebald and tossed the folded blankets across her back. The Pima returned with a basket. Ty took it from him, then looked back at the huts. Obviously Redbird had warned his woman, and the others, to stay out of sight. Holding the ends of the bitless bridle in one hand, Ty used his grip on the mare's thick mane to swing himself onto her back.

Redbird was already returning to his village as Ty rode out with the sun warming his back.

Less than a mile later, Ty realized he should have bargained harder for a shirt.

Dixie heard whispered rustlings. In her fevered state she thought it was voices she heard, voices that made her shake with chills. She couldn't open her eyes, the effort was beyond her. Her lips felt cracked and dry, like her throat. The rustlings grew louder, closer, and she fought to get away from them.

In seconds she felt as if she were being smothered. Heat baked her body. Pain lanced her when she tried to move. In her fever dream she saw herself stumbling into the desert, falling beneath a merciless sun that sucked the moisture from her. She tried to call out. No sound reached her ears.

She was dying. A throbbing began in her head, a quickening drumbeat that encompassed her in minutes and she thought her life's blood was seeping from her to its rhythm. But there was something... something she had to do.

Ty would help her. He'd promised. The thrashing noises increased in intensity, adding to the pain her overburdened body contended with and she knew she needed help.

Ty... his name became a short, panicked litany that brought no relief, no answer.

Terror squeezed Ty's belly like a cold, hard fist.

Even as he urged the mare to walk the few feet to the big cottonwood, he knew he wouldn't find Dixie where he had left her. The small branches that he had covered her with were scattered over the earth.

Still mounted, he reached up anyway, touching the woven cradle and testing the heat that remained. Since the sun was weak filtering through the thick boughs, he knew the warmth he felt was hers.

She hadn't been gone long.

But where? And how, wounded as she was, had she managed to climb down?

Maybe she didn't do it on her own.

The fist squeezed tighter until he shook.

She had the only gun between them, all he had was his knife. He slid from the piebald's back and set the basket down and saw the faint depressions in the earth. At a walk he headed for the riverbank, fighting not to run, needing to read every sign so he wouldn't make more mistakes.

Her footprints told their own story. And the cold, hard fist reached up and squeezed his heart in its grip. Here she had staggered, then fallen time and again, before she crawled and somehow stood up. The false start and stop where she had circled around in the brighter sunlight that was already drying the mud added to his pain.

A black rage against the Fates, the Lord and himself encompassed him.

He found where she had crawled, then dragged herself to a stand of cattails at the river's edge. And that's where she lay while he shook with fear that he was too late.

Ty was afraid to touch her. Guilt was overwhelming, swamping his senses, holding him prisoner before he broke free and fell to his knees in the mud beside her.

Angrily he brushed her hair from her cheek. Fever heat rose from her body to touch his own. Her skin was dry and hot. He stroked her cheek, praying silently, and was rewarded with her shallow breath caressing his fingertip.

Gently, very gently, he turned her over. The air he had been holding rushed out, and he had to drag in lungfuls, releasing them slowly as he fought to gain control of his fear.

When he stopped shaking, he kicked off his boots, then removed Dixie's. He couldn't stop the fine trembling of his hands as he unbuckled her gun belt and tossed it up onto the bank. Afraid of hurting her even more, he forced himself to be gentle stripping off her torn, mud-soaked shirt and pants. He made himself untie the makeshift bandages from her wounds.

Lifting her up into his arms, he rose and walked out into the shallows of the river to bathe the fever from her body. Her pitiful moans rid him of the foolish notion that he was going to ride toward home with her today.

But he welcomed the sounds of distress as he dipped her body over and over in the cold river. Every moan marked another minute that she lived.

All Ty had to do was make sure she kept on fighting.

He remembered his brother Logan taken with a fever, and the constant soft whispers of his mother's voice recalling stories of her past, of their births, and every incident, no matter how small, of their life on the ranch.

So he talked to her as he wrapped her in a blanket and got a fire started. The talk was a needed distraction for himself, as well. He had to heat his knife blade.

He didn't want to think about marring her skin, and he couldn't think of anything else.

Ty never knew what made him remember the scent of chia. He had ridden past the desert sage, its blue flowers weren't in bloom. The seeds...something about the seeds.

"Sweet Lord! I can't remember," he cried out, instantly narrowing his eyes as his gaze returned to the far hillside. He walked there, drawn by some unexplained force, only knowing that he had to gather as many of the plants' seeds as he could.

The scent drew him. The moment he held the seeds he remembered. He had hired on as an army scout, a job that lasted all of three days. His still-wet-behind-the-ears captain, who couldn't tell one Indian from another, believed the only good Indian was a dead one. He'd been incensed by the man's sheer stupidity, beat him to a pulp and quit. But he hadn't walked away. The captain got off one shot that creased his arm, and Ty remembered the Indian who found him used the crushed seeds of the desert sage to make a poultice.

He filled his pockets and hurried back to Dixie. "You're gonna live. No matter what promises I have to make and keep, you are not going to die."

It was pointless to count the trips he made to the river with her. He lost track of time as he held her in his arms, dribbling water over her lips, bathing her forehead. He rocked her, feeling how the fever had reduced her to a fragility she never projected in the time he had known her. No, that wasn't quite true.

Dixie had been fragile in his arms, coming apart for him. He banished the memory that rose to haunt him.

Only once did she open her eyes and look directly at him. The clawing motion of her hand on his bare chest lasted seconds before she let it fall to her lap.

Ty had to lean over and press his ear to her lips to hear what she struggled to say.

"He-lp...me. F-find—"

"Who, Dixie? Who is it that you want? Tell me, Angel. I'll hunt hell for you."

"Ty."

He jerked his head back. Within her glazed eyes the reflection of the fire danced. With a long drawn-out sigh she closed them as if the effort had been too much for her. Once again the fever rose in her body.

Ty knew he couldn't wait for morning to leave.

He blessed his choice of the piebald mare when he had to lift Dixie onto the horse's back. Dixie couldn't sit up alone, she fell forward against the mare's neck, her arms dangling off the sides until he could mount.

The mare stood placid, as if she knew how precious her burden was to him.

Night riding at its best—clear sky, full moon and stars so brilliant they sparkled like gold dust—was something Ty avoided if he could. He thought of other times he had ridden at night, nights when he used the stars to steer himself home. It was so long ago, but the memories came to him now of riding with Logan, their drunken voices blending together like two croaking frogs as they tried to get back to the ranch before morning service.

But never with Conner. Conner didn't hold with a man getting drunk. He thought less of his brothers for it. But he always paid for any damages done on those Saturday nights after their father had died. Conner had stepped into the old man's boots as if they had been made for him.

Ty regretted the memories that rushed at him with every foot that brought him nearer to home. Yet he could not help wish this was one of those times when he was the one who couldn't sit on a horse. He'd give anything to have Dixie be the one bringing him home instead.

Around and around his thoughts went as the night faded away and the sun rose like a brimming ball of fire. He knew he could cut a day's travel time if he headed for the desert, but Dixie needed water.

By the time the sun set, he was using water to cool his own burned skin. Which made the fire he had to build as chills racked her body so painful for him to be near.

He dozed and woke with a start. It wasn't a dream but his own guilty thoughts that surfaced as he checked Dixie. He thought her breathing seemed easier. Maybe he was wishing too hard.

He had called her trouble. He took it back. She began babbling of places and people he didn't know, but then he was doing too much praying to pay close attention.

Late the next night he crossed Queen's Creek. He was north of the Rocking K now. The willows' branches caressed by a breeze was a long familiar song that he had fallen asleep to when he camped up here. Ty was hoarse from whispering his memories to Dixie throughout the day.

The mare needed rest. Ty hoped she'd forgive him for asking for her heart as he pushed on. The way he made promises to Dixie, he made others to the mare. Her own stall. Corn and molasses grain. The sweetest hay this side of heaven and currying twice a day.

Ty scrubbed his eyes hours later. "Damn star fell," he mumbled. His arm stung from the thousand pinpricks as he shifted Dixie and shook it hard to get his blood moving.

The sound he heard had Ty shaking his head, as well. He was dreaming! Those were cows. He sat up a little straighter and peered through the dark. It wasn't a star but a small camp fire he saw.

"Help, Dixie. We've found help." But even as he whispered this reassurance to her, he kept the mare to a walk. The tingling had left his arm. He slid Dixie's gun from the holster and approached the camp cautiously.

Ty hailed the camp and was welcomed in. Three rifle barrels greeted him.

"I've a half-dead woman in my arms. We've been riding for near four days. Need some help getting to the Rocking K."

Silence. One man stepped out of the shadows, his face a war map of tanned creases. He swept back his battered hat as he lowered the rifle.

"Burn my britches! I'm blind as a stubbin' post! Set down yore iron, boys, Ty Kincaid's come home."

"Hazer? Sweet Lord, it's you." Ty tried to stop his fall, worried that he'd hurt Dixie. He was passing out, but other arms caught her, other voices promised help and he let go.

Chapter Sixteen

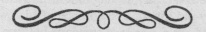

Ty awakened to soft, sweet-smelling linen sheets and cool adobe. He tried to turn but his body refused to respond. He kept his eyes closed, absorbing the well-remembered scents of home.

His pillow was stuffed with down, and the fragrant dried summer flowers. As a boy he had trailed along with his mother and Sofia through the mountain valleys gathering wild herbs, silk dalea, rock daisies, and the sweet sand verbena. He had run wild and free, exploring where he would.

He inhaled a deep breath and caught the faint trace of the cedar beams overhead blending with the lemon oil Sofia used to keep the furniture gleaming.

Enfolding him was the warmth brought by allowing himself to drift on the slow-moving current of memory's waterway. He could ride before he could run. For a brief, painful moment he recalled his father's hand on his shoulder, the pride in his eyes, and the praise he whispered for Ty's choice of his first horse.

The current quickened and flashes of rough-and-tumble play with his brothers gave way to the clashes that had followed their father's death. But there were images of happy times, laughter and fiestas to celebrate roundups, holidays, the acknowledgment of manhood.

He stirred restlessly, feeling that he had less strength than a day-old kitten. The absence of his own musty odor forced the memory of someone bathing him. He hadn't been able to lift his head, much less—

"Damn! Dixie!" He threw off the sheet and tried to sit up. The room tilted and swirled around him.

Cradling his head in his hands, Ty closed his eyes. He had to wait for the dizziness to pass. When he heard the door open, he couldn't even look up.

"You're awake. Good. But rest easy, little brother, you're in no shape to go anywhere."

"Conner."

"The same."

Ty heard the clink of spur rowels and knew that his brother had come closer to the bed.

"I've been on binges that didn't set the room twirling around like this."

"I remember," Conner answered. "Your back looks like someone worked a branding iron over it a time or two. Hazer said you rode in puny as a tick-fevered dogie and making about as much sense. But if you're moving at all, then Sofia worked her charms on you."

"Yeah." Despite his dizziness, Ty heard the underlying questions in his brother's voice and braced for what was sure to come—Conner playing ramrod of the

Rocking K, Conner acting the big brother, or Conner set on filling their daddy's boots. It was a toss-up for sure, because they all boiled down to one and the same.

"So, you had yourself some trouble. Hard, by the looks of—"

"The hell with me, Conner. Where's Dixie? How's she doing? I need to see—"

"Stay put." Conner used one large hand on his brother's shoulder to hold him down. He didn't miss Ty's wince of pain when his sunburned flesh was touched and instantly moved back.

"Both Ma and Sofia are with her. She's got a fever that won't quit, Ty, and her side wound festered. But you're not going to be any help as a nursemaid in your condition. 'Sides, you owe me a reason why you've come home looking like you fought with the devil and lost."

Relief flooded Ty at hearing that Dixie was alive and in the best hands that he could place her. She was a strong woman, he reminded himself. And much as he hated to admit it, Conner was right. He was in no shape to take care of her.

"Well?" Conner prompted, fighting to keep his voice level and his emotions under control.

"Shut the hell up, Conner. I'll talk when I'm ready."

"Guess all this time away from home didn't teach you any manners. Sure to hell didn't teach you to hang on to what you owned. Damn it, boy! You come—"

"Conner." Soft and quite deadly, Ty cut in and for the first time looked up at his brother. But Conner stood in front of the shuttered window with his back toward him.

"Listen, Conner. You want explanations. Fine. Toss me a pair of pants. After I see for myself how Dixie is, I'll tell you whatever you want."

Hearing the scratchiness of Ty's voice, Conner filled one of the beakers from the clay jug on the dresser and brought it to his brother. "Here, drink this before you croak like a frog."

The sunlight filtering through the wooden shutters hit Ty's eyes and he squinted as he took the beaker from Conner. He didn't really need to see his brother's face to know that a scowl likely masked his features. It was, he recalled, his brother's habitual facial expression whenever they went head to head.

Ty gulped down the cool, sweet lemonade. He wiped the back of his hand across his mouth and handed the beaker back to Conner.

"Sofia still makes the best I've ever tasted." Ty ran his hand over the clean sheets. "Soft beds, clean linen, good food, even a roof that doesn't leak over your head. Home."

"I'm surprised you notice or care, little brother. You've kept yourself scarce around these parts."

"And we both know why, don't we, Conner?"

It was a challenge that Conner refused to answer. Yet he couldn't resist a dig of his own. He lifted Ty's boots in one hand. "The boot size's bigger, sorta matches the size of your mouth, doesn't it?"

"Hard as it is for you to admit, and believe, Conner, I've grown some since I've been gone."

"Let Sofia fatten you up and I might believe it."

Ty grinned as he caught the pants that Conner tossed at him. It was as close as his brother would come to telling him that he was welcome to stay.

Not ready to try standing, Ty sat on the edge of the bed and struggled into the soft cotton denim. The fit was a mite on the tight side, and Ty realized that they were his own worn pants, left behind as most of his clothes had been. He eyed the boots that Conner set down before him, but wasn't about to attempt to put them on. He knew his own limitations. He wasn't going far today.

"Now, tell me where Ma put Dixie?"

"Right next door," Conner answered, stripping off his work gloves and tucking them into his belt. "We put her in Logan's old room."

"Logan's room?"

"That's what I said."

"And where the hell is he?"

Sorely tested, Conner strove for calm. "Logan made his own choice to bunk down with the hands about a year ago." He snapped his hat brim lower. The move helped him to conceal his concern as Ty rose from the bed and wavered on his bare feet. Any offer of help from him would be met with instant refusal, so he didn't even try. All he could do was stand aside and watch Ty make his way toward the door.

With his hand on the latch, Ty turned and looked at his brother. He gently shook his head. "So, you managed to push Logan out, too. I never understood that, Conner. Pa left you in charge of everything, the ranch, the mines, us. Guess he never knew what a greedy bastard you are."

"Damn you, Ty. I've had enough of your sass."

"Sass, Conner? That's for kids. Look again, big man. I'm not a boy anymore."

"Then stop acting like one. Pa left me in charge. I never asked for the job. I never wanted it. Not that he or anyone else around here ever cared what the hell I wanted."

Ty twisted around to face his brother, keeping both hands behind him on the door latch as he leaned back.

He eyed Conner's tall, rangy body. The man was corded and tough, straight as a branchless pine and as hard as ironwood. His boots and chaps were dusty, testament that Conner had been working for hours. Ty had never denied that his brother did more than his share to keep the ranch going and oversee the workings of the mines. And no one could tell that Conner was boss by his clothes.

But put him in a group of men, and the way he carried himself told everyone he was the man to reckon with. It wasn't jealousy that provided the conflict between them. Conner never bent, it was his way or no way.

When Conner claimed something, he valued it, and he rivaled the tenacity of the mesquite trees going after water, for the roots would go down to fifty feet or more in search of that life-giving essence. Conner would ride more than a hundred miles to reclaim anything that bore the Rocking K brand.

Damn trouble was, Conner had always thought that included his brothers.

As he looked up and met Conner's gaze, Ty noted the new lines that creased the skin around his eyes and his mouth. He'd put a few of the early ones there, fighting against Conner's belief that he was responsible for all of them.

And as he stared at Conner's blue-gray eyes the color of a winter's sky and about as friendly, Ty realized that Conner still believed it.

"Later, Conner."

"I'll hold you to that, little brother." But there was no heat in Conner's voice. He had stifled his impatience to demand that Ty tell him what kind of trouble he had brought home with him. He stifled the need to tell Ty that whatever the Kincaids owned was his if he wanted it.

He stared at the open doorway and thought of the young woman who fought for her life. Dixie. Now he had a name for part of whatever it was that forced his youngest brother to break his sworn oath that he'd never come asking for help from him again.

Conner closed his eyes and rubbed the bridge of his nose. He couldn't push. He'd have to wait. And he hoped that Ty wouldn't explode when he found out about Logan.

Ty held on to the cool, thick adobe wall, surprised that Conner had not followed him out of the room. It wasn't like his brother to linger while there was still a drop of daylight and work to be done. Maybe Conner had changed. Other than the one, brief outburst, he had roped his temper and Ty knew he had provoked it.

The moment he opened the door to what had been Logan's room, Ty dismissed Conner from his thoughts.

The familiar form of Sofia, their housekeeper, was bent over Dixie's naked body. She was mumbling to herself in Spanish, bathing Dixie. As in his room, the light was dim, due to the shutters being closed, but Ty saw that Dixie's color almost matched the sheet. Her long hair had been braided. If he knew his mother and Sofia, they had washed it, as well. But Dixie wasn't moving. He must have made a sound, for Sofia whirled around.

"Out! Shoo! Shoo!" She whipped up the sheet to cover Dixie and tossed the washcloth into the basin.

"Sofia, is this how you greet me?"

"Young stallions have no place near the fillies." She advanced on him, waving her apron in a shooing motion. "When I have made her respectable again you may come back."

Ty smiled at the small, plump woman who had ruled his home before his birth and caught her up against him in a hug.

"How is she?"

"*Dios* holds *la mujer* in his hands. I do what I can."

"Which is plenty." Ty's grip tightened around her. "She must live, Sofia."

"Ah, *corderito*, she means much to you?"

"*Sí.*" He knew he need say no more to her. He managed a smile at hearing Sofia repeat her childhood nickname for him. He released her and slowly shook his head. "No more lamb, Sofia."

"Always to me you are *corderito.*" She gazed at the bed. *Muy malo,* this fever. You do not worry. Your mama and Sofia take care."

Ty followed her gaze to the bed and the wooden crucifix adorning the wall above it. A bittersweet smile widened his mouth. Sofia's husband, Santo, had taken each of the boys to find the wood to make their crosses.

"Santo, he is well?"

"Santo is Santo," she answered with a shrug. "Like the mountains he is there."

"Rosanna must be a grown beauty now. And Rafael near a man."

"*Sí.* The little ones are no more. Rosanna will marry next year. Rafael does a man's work. Conner is proud of him."

She reached up with her plump hand and gently touched his brow. "It is good. No fever."

Ty caught hold of her hand and brought it to his lips. "A kiss for these hands that work magic to broken bodies." He held her gaze with his. "I need her well. Heal her for me, Sofia. She is a woman much deserving of life."

"And of love?"

"And of love," he softly repeated. He glanced at Dixie. "Most certainly of love."

"You will tell me of her when I have made her well."

Uncomfortable with Sofia's sharpened tone, for he wasn't ready to examine his feelings for Dixie, much less discuss them with anyone, Ty sought a distraction.

He pressed another kiss to the back of her hand. "What's this I smell? Lord, Sofia, your hand holds the scent of *capirotada.*" His loud sniffing as he turned her hand over and nuzzled her palm made her giggle like a young girl.

"Cinnamon, cloves, anise, brown sugar..." Ty stopped. He released her hand and frowned.

"Already you have forgotten? For shame, *corderito.*"

Knowing it would please her, he obediently hung his head as he had as a boy when he would beg her to make his favorite bread pudding.

"Tell me, Sofia, have you made *capirotada?*

"*Sí! Sí!* When your mama saw you slept in peace she came to me. Go, she says, I will watch over the young woman. All morning I am in the kitchen—"

"All morning?"

"*Sí.* It nears time for supper. You were meant to have a healing sleep. Then your mama, she comes to say we make this for my boy, we make that for him. He will be hungry when he wakes. I shoo her from my kitchen to come sit here. Sofia has no need to be told what to make for her *corderito.*"

Once more she raised her hand to his face, caressing his bearded cheek. "You go now. Make yourself handsome. I wash your lady. I will come for you to see her."

"Sofia, who do you think took care of her—"

"I do not wish to hear of this." She drew herself up to her full height, which brought her head level with Ty's chin. "You are home now. She is your woman. She is not your wife. You are *hombre* now, no more *muchacho.*"

"I'm glad someone around here realizes that I am a man and not a boy anymore."

"Ah, always it is you and that one. Conner was never *un niño.* That one was born a man. It is for shame that you fight."

"No. No fighting, Sofia. I'm not up to Conner's weight right now. I'm not up to much of anything but seeing that Dixie lives."

"I will do all I can." She started to block his way toward the bed, but one look at the agony in his eyes and she stepped aside. "A moment, no more."

Ty steadied himself with one hand on the headboard as he leaned over and kissed Dixie's forehead. Her skin burned his lips. He closed his eyes for a brief second, feeling despair. If Sofia, with her years of knowledge to heal, could not break Dixie's fever, no one could.

"Come. You go now."

Ty heaved a weary sigh and backed away from the bed. "All right. I'll go. But you call me the minute you're finished with her."

"We will pray and make her well again. You would do good to offer prayers as we all do."

"You use your prayers, Sofia. I used up my store just keeping her alive to get here."

"What is this store? No matter. We have many prayers. They have made your mama happy to have you home again."

Once more she was all bustling business, urging him out of the room. "Go. Go. Your mama waits for you."

Her sudden smile made Ty spin around. The move forced him to cling to the doorway a moment as he saw who waited.

"Ty." Macaria Kincaid whispered her son's name. She had taken her fill of watching over him during the night, her tears a blend of joy and regret. Only something desperate had finally returned her restless son to her. She believed she had shed all her tears, but her throat closed, and her eyes burned with the need to cry. All she could do was to open her arms in welcome to him.

He held his mother's graceful body, still as tough as hickory, as supple as a willow, and inhaled the special, familiar scent of sweet mountain lilacs.

Macaria pulled back and cradled his cheeks within her slender hands. "It is good to have you home again, Ty." She studied his eyes, smiling when his lips curved. "What is it? Have I changed so much?"

"Still the most beautiful woman in the territory. But there's more gray in your hair," he noted, reaching up to touch the neat crown of braids she had always worn. His thumb rubbed her forehead. "A few more worry lines. I hope they weren't over me. I know that things looked pretty bad last night, but I'm fine." Her quick, searching gaze made him add, "Well, I'm hungry and my back's a little sore, but there's nothing else wrong."

She linked her arm with his. "Then come. I will feed you food and tell you all that has happened since you've been gone. And you will tell me about the young woman you've brought home to us. But first, let me get you a shirt. I'm afraid that your old ones wouldn't fit."

"*Madre,* before you do, tell me where Logan is."

She averted her gaze, stopping by the hall table where a folded pile of shirts waited. "You've seen Conner, yes?" she asked, handing him one. "Of course you have. He was anxious to see how you and the young woman fared."

Ty eased his arms into a shirt so buttery soft it almost felt like silk against his skin. "Conner came to see me. No, we didn't fight. Yes, he told me that Logan had moved out of the house." He quickly buttoned up the shirt but didn't bother to tuck the tails into his pants.

"What Conner didn't say, and I didn't ask, was why Logan left."

"I was afraid of that. After you eat, I shall tell you. Rosanna helps me in the kitchen now. Did Sofia tell you she is to marry?"

Ty allowed that she had and knew when his mother wore that set, stubborn look, he would be foolish to push. She would tell him in her own way, in her own time. He followed her into the kitchen.

It wasn't the doe-eyed dark beauty who claimed Ty's attention but the tall, spare man who entered the room. The dark hair that Ty remembered was completely white, startling against the tanned webbing creasing his face.

"Santo."

"Have your eyes grown dim while you are away from us? Of course it is Santo." His gaze rested lovingly on Ty.

"He ran off a yearling colt and returns to us a fine young stallion. *El patrón* would be proud to see you, my son. Now, come greet an old man in the proper way."

"You old? Never." And as Ty hugged him for a long minute, he realized that Santo still had the strength of a young man in his body, despite the white hair.

Pulling back, Santo nodded. "It is good that you have come home to us. We will hear no more talk of leaving. You are needed here."

When Ty freed himself and didn't answer, his mother came to his side. "Ty? You have come home to stay?"

"You shall dance at my wedding fiesta," Rosanna said, adding platters of food to those already on the table.

"Answer *la patróna*," Santo ordered.

"There's a promise I have to keep. And I can't keep it if I stay."

"A promise?" Macaria asked.

"It is the young woman you brought home with you, yes?"

"Yes, Rosanna. I promised Dixie I would go after the man responsible for her father's death as well as for her wounds. And I made that promise," he added, turning to his mother, "to God if he would spare her life."

"*Por Dios!* You hunt an animal, my son. For one who would shoot a woman cannot be called a man," Santo exclaimed.

But Ty didn't look or answer him. He watched the color blanch from his mother's face. "First you, then Logan. Now you tell me you will go again."

"Logan's gone?"

The silence became tense as Ty looked from one to the other. Rosanna kept her back toward him.

"If someone doesn't answer me, I'll have to go and find Conner."

"You don't have to go far, little brother. I'm right here."

Chapter Seventeen

Ty spun around and swayed on his feet. He motioned Santo back as he moved to help him and kicked out the long bench beside the table. Much as he hated to reveal weakness in front of Conner and his mother, Ty had no choice but to sit down.

"Enough. All these questions will wait," Macaria stated. "Rosanna, fix a plate for my son. Santo, bring Ty wine." She turned to Conner, her voice instantly soft. "Will you break bread with your brother?"

"I'm not the one you should be asking."

"Oh, hell, Conner—"

"Ty!"

"Your pardon, *madre.*" Ty glanced at Conner. "Come sit with me. There's no way they're gonna shove all this in me."

Conner kicked out the bench on the other side of the table, murmuring his thanks to Rosanna when she set a plate in front of him. Santo poured the wine into their glasses and, at a nod from Macaria, left the kitchen with his daughter in tow.

"Now, you will drink together, eat together and then we will talk together. Agreed?"

It was an oft-repeated scene from their childhood, and Ty grinned at Conner, laughing when he saw his brother's face relax into a genuine smile of welcome.

"*Sí, madre,*" they said in unison, filling their plates under her watchful eye.

"Good. I will go relieve Sofia. When you are finished come to me."

Macaria looked back as she reached the doorway and caught Conner's eye. Their communication was silent, but then they had never needed many words between them. She left them knowing that Conner would hold his temper and tell Ty only what he must about Logan.

As her footsteps receded, Ty carefully set his fork down. "So tell me what happened to Logan."

"About six months ago we discovered that someone was rustling our cattle. Logan had a few ideas of where they were keeping them until they moved them out. He rode off and that's the last any of us have seen of him."

"That's it?"

"We haven't stopped searching for him, Ty. I've—"

"Hell, Conner, I know that."

The complete conviction behind those few simple words held Conner silent.

Ty leveled a hard look at his brother. "You didn't expect that, did you? Whatever our differences over the years, I know that you'd turn hell upside down, then go back and do it all over again if one of us was in trouble."

Feeling as if he were caught with his pants down, Conner shook his head. "Guess I can't call you little brother anymore."

"Oh, I wouldn't take bets on that. You've still got a good two inches on me." Ty sensed that Conner's emotions ran as deep as his own, emotions that neither had voiced to the other and weren't ready to say now. His thought was confirmed when Conner spoke.

"Yeah, I've got those inches and more than a few pounds on you. And when you see Logan—"

"Yes, when I see Logan," Ty repeated, exchanging a silent promise with Conner as their gazes met and held.

"Why, then you'll no longer be the runt of the litter. You've grown in more than height, Ty. But before we talk about ideas you might have about finding Logan, I want to hear about this promise you made to Dixie."

"You heard me." Ty toyed with the wineglass, his gaze roving around the kitchen. He saw without note the black iron pots hanging from their hooks, their sizes varied enough to make a meal for two or accommodate forty. Colorful pottery plates were arranged on the corner cupboard's shelves, herbs tied with string hung from the overhead rafters for drying. From where he sat, Ty could see partway into the pantry where crocks lined the floor and shelves along with sacks. He knew the pie press would be full, it always had been and was Sofia's pride. She alone held the key, given to her by his mother when she had married.

"Ty? Want to tell me about it?"

The fact that Conner was asking, not demanding, brought Ty to look at him. If Logan had been there, he would never have hesitated at all. Logan would not only listen but insist that he take part. But Logan wasn't here, and Conner was. He thought of what Sofia had said about his brother—he had never been a boy, but born a man. In a way, he knew that was true. By the time he had been old enough to understand, Conner, six years older, was already putting in a man's hours of work.

The thing was, he never knew how Conner would take what he had to say. Touch a grass blade of the Rocking K without his permission and there would be Conner's kind of hell to pay. But Dixie didn't belong to the Rocking K. She wasn't a Kincaid. And in view of Logan's disappearance, Conner wasn't going to like hearing that Ty had no intention of sticking around to take his place.

"Guess it was too much to hope that you'd trust me." Big as he was, Conner could move like the breeze so that only a whisper of sound was made when he stood up, snapped the brim of his hat forward and looked down at Ty.

"Tell *madre* I had to finish up. I'll see her after supper."

"Tell her yourself, after we talk." The words were impulsive, the result of the weariness in Conner's eyes, and perhaps, Ty thought, he had grown up enough to realize that Conner had shouldered too many burdens alone.

Conner sat.

Ty began talking.

And in the hallway, Macaria smiled at Santo, before they went their separate ways.

Macaria closed the door quietly behind her. "How is she, Sofia?" she asked in her native Spanish.

"She has taken a little lemonade. That is a good sign, *señora*. The fever does not end. She is young and she is strong," Sofia said, stroking Dixie's brow. "And she is very pretty."

"She is, indeed, and this young woman matters a great deal to my son." There was no hint of a question in Macaria's voice, nor was there rancor that Sofia was privileged to know while she was not. There had been many such conversations in the past concerning all three of her sons, where Sofia or Santo was the one chosen to be a confidant.

"It is as you say." Sofia made soft, comforting murmurs as Dixie stirred restlessly beneath her stroking hand. "Many times she has called out for him."

"Then we must see to it that she recovers quickly, for I will reward her with whatever it is that she desires for bringing my son home to me."

"She comes with trouble, *señora.*"

"Then I will put the Kincaid fortune at her disposal to help her out of her difficulties."

"And if the young woman wishes the *corazón* of your son, will you make this too available to her?"

There was a hard glitter in Macaria's eyes as she met Sofia's sharp gaze. "If my son has love for her, and she for him, then nothing must stand in their way. I will not have him leave us again. Ty's place is here, on the lands I brought into my marriage. Even now, as we speak, he conspires with Conner to keep me from knowing what this trouble is.''

"Then it is as it should be." Sofia nodded, once more turning to resume her bathing of Dixie's fevered body. "*Dios* has answered all your prayers, *señora*. Now your sons will learn to stand together. It is time."

"Not all, Sofia," she reminded her. "Logan must yet come home."

There was a softness to the night's dark that settled like a comfortable blanket over the land as Ty entered Dixie's room. He knew the slight easing of the tension within him came from the time shared with Conner. It was hard for him to take in the fact that they had talked, and he more than his brother.

He had Conner's assurances—never given lightly— that before morning, word would be out that the Kincaids wanted a man named Thorne.

Ty had added his own enticement to make sure that the man would be found. He offered his accumulated share from their mine holdings as a reward—twenty-five thousand dollars. It was the only protest that Conner made. When he saw that Ty was not going to be budged from his stand, he gave in.

Ty had never thought about the wealth that his brother had saved for him. And looking down at Dixie, he knew he would offer everything he had if her fever would break.

Rosanna was keeping vigil. Her back was as straight as the chair she sat in beside the bed. She smiled at him, then raised one finger to her lips as she stood and allowed him her place. The lamp was turned down low, shedding a dim glow that didn't reach the shadows in the corners.

Ty lifted Dixie's limp hand and brought it to his lips. He forgot that Rosanna was in the room, even as the creak of the rocker began. His whole being focused on Dixie.

Her hair seemed almost black against her pale skin. He skimmed a finger over the lace edge of the nightgown, finding the pulse he searched for, and for moments held his fingertip there, willing his life force to give needed strength to hers.

There was a salve on the lips he touched with his own, mixing his breaths with her ragged, shallow ones. The cold, hard, knotted fist that had been with him for days once again squeezed his insides as he leaned closer to whisper in her ear.

"Words have never really come hard for me, Dixie, but none that I know are right. I want you to fight, Angel. I want to make everything in your world right for you. I miss you...." His throat seemed to close up on him, and Ty leaned back.

Once more he took hold of her hand and gazed up at the wooden cross. Looking back at Dixie, seeing how still she was, he feared for her life. Ty slid from the chair to his knees by the bed. Lowering his head, he pressed her hot hand to his forehead.

He prayed.

He promised.

He rambled as the night wore on. He dreamed of her smile, and against the rhythmic creak of the rocking chair, he dozed.

It was hours later, in the deepest heart of the night that Ty stirred. He felt something wet on his cheek. Without opening his eyes, he reached up to brush it away and realized that they were his own tears. He moved to trace the small circle of wet on the sheet and found that it was not alone.

Understanding came slowly.

The sheet was soaked.

"Dixie. Dixie," he whispered. His hand trembled as he raised it toward her face.

Her cheek was wet, too. But not from tears. Her fever had broken and sweat soaked the sheets.

"Rosanna!" He roughly shook his head, clearing the sleep from his mind. "Where the hell—"

"Gently, my son. Gently, and quietly," Macaria admonished. "The crisis is over. Leave so I can change her and the bed." She accepted his brief hug and gave him a little push toward the door. "Sofia is waiting in the kitchen. Tell her our prayers have been answered."

Ty passed the rest of the night in his own fevered impatience to see Dixie. Sofia and his mother had set Santo to guard the room while they tended her. He clung to their promise that the moment she was able to speak, they would fetch him.

Conner found him in the small back parlor. He brought coffee and orders that Ty take a bath and shave.

"*¿Madre?*" Ty asked, accepting the steaming cup from his brother.

"*Madre* and Sofia," Conner returned, sipping his coffee.

"Conner, I don't want anyone to tell Dixie about the reward. There are a few things I left out about her. She can be stubborn—mule and mountain have nothing on her." He stared down at the dark liquid in his cup, mulling over what more he had to say.

"Still uneasy trusting me?"

Ty looked up. "No. I need your word that when Thorne is found you'll make sure Dixie stays here. I won't have his blood on her hands."

"Do you know what you're saying, Ty?"

"I know. A few days ago I thought about what I would do if she asked me to kill Thorne. I've never hired out my gun in the time I've been gone."

"But you've done your share of killing."

Their gazes met, and Ty found that he didn't need to offer explanations or words. Somehow Conner understood. He didn't question that Conner knew more about what he'd been doing than he had told him. It simply stood to reason that given Conner's nature, he would keep tabs on his brothers.

"I've survived. But you've got to understand that I want that bastard not just to give Dixie the peace she needs, to know that he paid for her father's death. I want him for what he did to her. Not just now, but before.''

''Will you let me go with you?''

''No. Don't ask that of me, Conner. This is my fight. Not yours. 'Sides, how would the Rocking K get along with you gone?''

That brought a laugh from Conner. ''You forget that our mother has most capable hands. And she has Santo.''

''What is this? You are talking of me?''

They both turned to see Santo at the door. Ty stepped forward, both hands gripping the cup.

''What's wrong?''

''I have come to see if you have made yourself presentable to see your woman.''

Ty rubbed one hand over his thickly stubbled face. A rueful grin creased his lips, and he turned to set the cup aside, missing the look exchanged between Conner and Santo.

''Guess I'd better get presentable.''

''Yeah. Go on, Ty. We'll talk again later.''

Santo stood aside to let Ty pass, then stepped into the room and closed the door behind him. ''It is better with you two?''

''It is much better,'' Conner answered, sitting on the arm of the hide-covered sofa. ''Has there been any word of Logan?''

''Would I stand here like a chair if there was? Rafael is worried.''

Conner looked down at his boots. ''And Enrique, is he worried, too?''

"Rosanna's intended, like my son, had become friends with your brother. He asks each day if we have news of him."

"Forgive me, Santo. Ty coming home now only presents new problems, when I thought I had all the trouble I could handle."

"Always this is the way for the strongest man. Come, we have work to do."

"Yeah. Let's go tree us a polecat for Ty."

Dixie whispered his name moments after Ty walked into the room. His gaze was on her, not his mother or Sofia as they backed away from the freshly made bed.

"Welcome to my home, Angel." He leaned close to murmur the words, unable to stop himself from caressing her cheek. Her skin was cool and he smiled as she turned slightly to bring her lips against his palm. He could feel her mouth move but couldn't hear what she was saying.

"Don't talk now. We'll have time. All the time we need." Her lashes fluttered, lifting and falling as if the effort to open her eyes exhausted her. He brushed his fingertip over her brows, gently skimming along the lines of her lashes.

"Rest. I'll be right here beside you when you wake." He thought his words had reassured her, for the line of her mouth became a gentle curve and she no longer struggled to look at him.

"Let me tell you again about the promises I made you. There's places on the ranch I want to share with you when you're well. Sofia will fatten you with her good cooking and Santo will find you the most spirited mare. They'll make Rosanna accompany us everywhere under orders from my mother. And you'll meet Conner, Dixie. He's a bit rough on the edges but he's a Kincaid, too. Just rest, love, and sleep.''

Ty wouldn't let her out of his sight, but as Dixie grew stronger and saw that her wounds began to heal after three weeks, she knew that Ty was beginning to chafe in the roles he had chosen.

He was her guide to the beauty of the Kincaid land. He would take her up before him on his horse, riding at an easy pace to some hidden valley where they would feast on Sofia's cooking and laze away a few hours.

He was her friend who listened to childhood memories, sharing many of his own, making her laugh at his droll antics.

He was her protector, gentle, tender, stopping her whenever she attempted to push herself to do more.

What Ty Kincaid refused to be was her lover again.

Beyond a chaste kiss good-night at her doorway each night, he kept his distance. True, they were rarely left alone. If Rosanna did not accompany them, one of the ranch hands did. When they walked in the garden that was Macaria's pride and joy in the evening after supper, Santo or Sofia was sure to be sitting close enough to keep them within sight.

Dixie tried to tell and show him that she was growing stronger every day. She had little resistance to the tempting array that Sofia coaxed her to eat, along with everyone else.

Ty ignored her.

Dixie knew it was wise advice that Macaria gave her to set aside her thought of revenge until she was completely healed. She accepted with secret joy the gowns that Rosanna and Macaria shared with her.

Ty didn't seem to notice.

She knew he cared about her. Hazy memories of his voice would come to her in odd moments, low, intense and husky, whispering promises. She couldn't remember the words.

When she asked him, Ty claimed she had been having fever dreams.

Dixie tried talking to him about her plans to leave. He said there was time yet before they had to talk about it.

Her temper came back. Frustration grew. And with it came need.

She desired him. She had come to trust him, but she could not find a way to break down the wall of reserve he had built between them.

Ty often caught Dixie looking at him with such intense longing that he felt as if he were being ripped apart to deny her, and himself. He was doing everything he could to protect Dixie's fragile health. She needed to be left alone to recoup her strength and that incredible spirit he had come to admire. She couldn't do it if he let her know how much he needed her.

He paid dearly. She flirted with him; he had to ignore her.

Seeing her every day was a personal torture he could easily have ended but not to see her was ten times worse. She and Rosanna were of a similar size, but he had never reacted to Rosanna's dark beauty dressed in her colorful gowns the way he did to Dixie. It was like watching a brilliant flower bloom in passionate color day by day.

He managed to ignore most of the remarks cast his way about his uncertain temper. Only when he was with Dixie did he retain his control. With her he could, because he must, stifle the desire that left him sleepless each night. And he never whispered of his growing frustration that no word of Thorne's whereabouts had reached him yet.

Ty cursed Conner, then accused him of withholding information from him. But when his brother asked him why he dared think that, Ty had no answer.

But Conner knew. They all knew. No one watching Ty and Dixie together could deny the passion that sparked to life the moment they were together.

Ty was frightened of how much she had come to mean to him. A black rage clouded his thoughts each time he remembered those moments on the ridge. Thorne would pay.

He didn't want to be tied down. Not that Dixie had hinted of marriage, but he caught the speculation in his mother's eyes. He evaded her query about his intentions toward Dixie.

The raw emotional edge he walked made him unsure and uneasy. Thinking about loving Dixie was such a deep complication when he needed to concentrate on finding Thorne and removing him as a threat to her.

Permanently.

And soon.

He was a man caught in a vise. He couldn't leave and he couldn't stay away from her.

Like a slow-building storm, something had to break.

Knowing it left Ty walking the razor's edge.

Watching it left those who loved him feeling helpless. Including Dixie.

Chapter Eighteen

Ty crashed off the razor's edge.

Thorne had been sighted. Conner brought the news to him in the cool predawn hours that Thorne had surfaced in Ajo, southwest of their ranch. The discussion that had followed with Conner was brief and ruthless. Ty was going after Thorne alone. He planned to leave tonight, once he was sure that Dixie was asleep. Nothing was going to stop him.

He never expected to have Dixie come upon him in the kitchen while the cool rage simmered so brightly within him. Ty could tell the moment she sensed it. He had no way to avoid her. Not without hurting her.

She had shadows beneath her eyes attesting to her lack of sleep. He had heard her open the shutters of her window, heard the soft sobs, since he, too, had stared out at the dark, unable to sleep for wanting her. He did not know where he had found the strength not to go to her.

But there was no doubt in his mind now, watching her as she entered the kitchen and saw him, that he had to do everything in his power to keep her from finding out about Thorne.

He didn't expect the longing in her eyes to mirror his own.

He hadn't counted on the passion flaring between them so quickly.

He never thought Dixie would act on it.

She came to him in a whisper of soft cotton, with desire for him shimmering within her eyes, his name a plea on her lips.

And there, in the cool morning before the sun painted the sky with pale shades of pink and lavender, Dixie cupped his cheeks to keep him from turning away.

"No more, Ty. I want to know why you deny these feelings between us. Are you afraid that I'll make claims on you? Don't be. I would never want to hold you that way. But I've needed you these last weeks. Needed you to hold me," she whispered, casting pride aside and praying that she could keep the love she felt hidden from him.

Her quest for the truth crumbled the wall he had built. There was no way to protect her or himself from the hunger that stirred from her light touch. He could not stand the thought of hearing another word from her lips without first tasting them.

One taste . . . one small kiss . . .

He remembered thinking that once before. It hadn't quite worked out that way. But he was stronger now. He intended to reassure her with a kiss that words just couldn't convey.

Memory had cheated him.

He had blocked out how very soft her mouth was against his. Blocked the way heat flared. Blocked the sweet taste of her, the giving, the absolute rightness of holding her in his arms.

He thought of leaving her with the belief that he didn't want her. He allowed the leash to slip a little to banish the idea.

Ty broke the kiss. Dixie's hands still rested on his cheeks. Her gaze was locked on his mouth. "Don't look at me like that," he warned.

She didn't blink, didn't move.

"I'm not made of stone, Angel."

"You could move, Ty. You could turn your back on me, on this." She raised up on tiptoe to brush her lips against his. Dixie knew the cost to herself to plead. His hesitation seemed to stretch out for an eternity before he made a hungry mating sound and lowered his lips once again to hers.

She tasted desperation. And hunger. She sensed he was holding back as he had been all these weeks. Despite his yearning sounds, his kiss was gentle. He rubbed his mouth over hers, almost a comfort-giving gesture. Dixie didn't want comfort. She didn't want gentleness.

Her hands slid down from his cheeks and caressed his shoulders. She slipped her fingertips inside the open collar of his shirt, pushing the soft cloth away. The need to touch and be touched, to hold and to be held after her brush with death made her bold.

His tongue shaped her mouth, pressing against the seam of her lips. Her lips parted, she wanted the taste of him. The intrusion of his tongue into her mouth was so tender, so sensual that she shivered despite the heat spreading between them.

The kiss lengthened. He used his tongue to stroke the roof of her mouth. He enticed her with this mock act of love until she was weakly clutching handfuls of his shirt. When he finally lifted his mouth from hers, she whimpered in protest. He buried his face in the soft hollow between her shoulder and her neck.

"Dixie, we can't," he groaned. "Don't, Angel," he added when she rubbed her mouth against his chest. "I shouldn't want you."

But she felt the evidence that he did.

Ty set her from him and walked to the open door, where he stood raking back his hair.

"Perhaps it's time for me to leave. I—"

"No!" He rounded on her but didn't make the mistake of crossing the room. Getting near her again would just about shatter the resolutions he was barely hanging on to.

"Look, Ty, nothing has changed. I still intend to find Thorne and make him pay for killing my father."

"Like hell you will! He almost killed you. Do you think I'll let you go?"

Anger had replaced the desire in his eyes and Dixie heaved a weary sigh. "You don't have a choice. I'm not something you own. I'd never be a possession to any man."

"Did I say I wanted you to be?"

No. You didn't say you wanted me at all. She kept her lips clamped tight lest she speak those words to him. Shaking her head, unable to discover what drove him, she tried one more time to reason with him.

"There's no reason for me to stay here, Ty. Despite your continued denial, I'm healed. I can't repay you or your family for—"

"Who the hell asked you to pay for anything? Who the hell—"

"Don't yell at me, Ty! I'm not—"

"This is my house! I'll yell at you—"

The coffee cup he'd left on the table shattered against the doorframe.

He stared at Dixie. "You threw that at me?"

She stared right back at him. "It seemed the only way to get your attention and shut you up."

"I suppose I should be grateful that you didn't have a gun in your hand."

She couldn't repress the shiver that crawled over her. "Don't make light of that, ever, Ty." Dixie's gaze locked with his. "I'm sorry I threw the cup."

"I'm sorry I yelled."

"I don't know what has me so edgy."

He flung back his head, staring up at the rafters. His hands curled into fists at his sides. Counting didn't help. Reminding himself of his need to stay away from her didn't work, either. He lowered his head, leveling a hard look at her.

She stood as if to flee, her hair entwined in a single, loose braid that curled over her shoulder and followed the curve of her breast. The ribbon ties of her nightgown were open, revealing skin that was the shade of pale honey. Sunlight streaked through the doorway at his back and bathed her in its glow. She had never looked more desirable to him.

"Ty?"

"You know what's wrong, Dixie," he began, advancing on her. "It's the same thing that's been eating at me. Get dressed," he ordered, stopping short of touching her. "We're going for a ride."

"But I thought—"

"Yeah. I've done a lot of thinking, too. Get dressed and I'll get the horses."

She searched his features, finding a residue of anger, but with it, in his eyes, was a blaze of desire so fierce she turned and ran.

There was no more doubt that he wanted her. It was the only thought that blinded Dixie as she rushed down the hall into her room.

At the far end of the hall, in the middle of her bedroom, Macaria placed her hand on Sofia's arm, stopping the woman from following Dixie. "No. This must be between my son and his woman. There is nothing more for us to say. It is for him to decide."

"You will speak with Ty?"

"No, Sofia. He would not listen to any words of mine. I am only his mother. She is his woman."

"That one will never have him dance to her tune, *señora.*"

"Perhaps not, but she is strong, and she loves my son. For me, this is enough."

"And for him, it, too, must be so."

* * *

Ty's black scowl warned everyone back and away from them as he and Dixie rode out. Only when he turned to look at her did his features soften. He had wanted to take her up before him on his horse, and ride as they had been doing for the past two weeks. He wouldn't have lasted longer than it took to ride past the fence line of the home corrals before he took her.

Dixie deserved better than another quick tumble. She had already had that and their recklessness nearly got her killed as a result. He owed her, and himself, something more.

Much as Ty wanted to, he couldn't shy away from the fact that he might not see her after tonight.

Dixie watched him. Tension rode his lean body. There was something different about Ty today. She wasn't sure what it was. She had a vague sense that he was worried. Every time he turned to look at her, she gazed at the firm set of his mouth. But she didn't ask. If she did, she would invite his questions. She didn't want to talk about the feelings that were coiled inside her, tighter than a tick and about as painful.

She knew she increased the ache every time she gazed at him. But telling herself to stop was as useless as whistling against the wind.

They crossed the creek where they had stopped several times before, but Ty kept riding, leading them through land covered with tall grasses. The sun made the day hot enough to pop corn and every insect seemed to want a bite of her. Ty, she noticed, didn't appear to be bothered by them. She thought of the way

Ty had raked his teeth down the side of her neck and a sensual shiver of awareness overcame her. She could almost feel the heat of his mouth and the sharp, pleasure-pain of his teeth nipping her earlobe.

He turned to look at her just at that moment, his gaze hot, his smile knowing.

She followed his lead as they neared a water hole and he circled wide to avoid disturbing the small herd of horses indulging in mud baths. Her mind conjured up the image of herself and Ty that day at the wash. It wouldn't leave her. She shifted restlessly in her saddle, feeling curls of arousal spread through her body.

Dixie let her chestnut have her head as they climbed grass-drenched hills, each one taking them farther and farther from the main house. She looked back once as they neared another plateau and couldn't see any sign of their passing. In the far distance, one of the herds of Rocking K cattle was spread out and she could barely make out the outline of a rider watching over them.

In the distance, a bright blue ribbon of water sparkled invitingly. As they rode closer, Dixie could hear the water tumbling over the rocks. Low-growing brush gave way to a stand of willows, but Ty rode a little ways beyond them to a lone, massive cottonwood.

He drew rein and dismounted beneath the tree's spreading branches. Before she could follow, he was at her side, lifting her out of her saddle.

Dixie placed her hands on his shoulders and, even through her riding gloves, and his thin shirt, she could feel the lean, sculptured muscles. Her eyes closed as Ty slid her down slowly along the length of his body. Her breasts felt heavy and she didn't think her legs would hold her.

"That," he murmured against her ear as he removed her hat and tossed it aside, "was to make sure that you understand how much I want you."

She looked into his eyes, eyes that reminded her of an unbroken night sky, glistening with the secrets of the dark. And she was distracted by the strange sensation that Ty was keeping secrets from her now.

"Ty, if something was troubling you, you would tell me? I mean—"

"I know what you mean," he answered, lowering his head to nuzzle her neck above the open collar of her shirt. "And sure, I'd tell you."

His voice was muffled, and the heat of his lips scattering light kisses over her skin made her push away the disturbing thought that he was withholding something from her. She shoved his hat off, leaning closer to him as she looped her arms around his neck and pulled off her gloves.

The moment he felt her bare hands slide into his hair, Ty brought his mouth to hers, caging her within his arms, and stripped off his own riding gloves. He stroked the length of her spine, pulling her tighter to his aroused body, leashing the force of his kiss.

He had made himself a promise to go slow, to woo and court her passion. Why didn't he remember that her need had been as great as his own? That she allowed him to take the lead only when it suited her stubbornness? He tried to temper his hunger, she unleashed hers, and he could feel the heat of desire trembling through her body.

Dixie tried to maintain a hold on her reeling senses. She felt the way her lips curved into his. The hard length of his thighs pressed hers and he lifted her up slightly to cradle himself against the already dampening heat of her.

She shuddered as he eased his tongue into her mouth slowly, deeply. He felt heavy and solid against her, in a way that was undeniably male, incredibly arousing. She could do nothing to stop herself from responding as he stroked and tasted her, for she had wanted this. Wanted him the same way she wanted air to breathe and water to drink.

Ty resented the strength of will he had to exert to ease his kiss to tender touches, before he lifted his head.

"Gently, Angel. Gently and slowly or you'll burn us up where we're standing."

Dixie forced open her eyes to see his serious regard. She tried to summon a smile. Her emotions were too raw, too heated and her lips refused to respond. She didn't want slow, she didn't want reason to intrude. She did want the fulfillment his kisses had promised. But she was very aware that Ty still thought she needed to be treated like fragile glass.

He pressed his lips to her forehead, stepped to the side and caught hold of her hand with his. "We need to talk and it won't happen if we stand here. Walk with me?"

A curt nod was all she managed. Instinct raised an alarm. Whatever it was that Ty had to say, she knew it wasn't what she wanted to hear. Somewhere in the time she had been sick, Dixie realized she had lost her ability to seal herself off. All the careful defenses she had built over the months she hunted her father's killer, seemed to have disappeared. And in their place had come the dreams she once had.

But Ty wasn't a man for tomorrow. If she had learned nothing else during this time at his home, Dixie had come to understand that he didn't want to be tied down. Shackled. That was the one word everyone used to describe Ty's thoughts about marriage, a home, a family.

He didn't want tomorrows. Now it was all she dreamed about.

She matched her pace to his, a slow, ambling walk toward the river. The breeze was cool, the sound of the water as it tumbled over the rocks in a shallow bed, a soothing song.

Even though he said he wanted to talk, Ty remained silent. Dixie looked up at him, her gaze following his as it roved over the land before them. Despite the growing dread that formed a knot in her stomach, she eased her hand free of his and turned to face him.

"Such serious regard means you have something on your mind, Ty. My father always said it was best to just say what was bothering you plain and simple. That way you didn't get sick worrying over how to say the words, and the one you had to talk to wouldn't get sick worrying what it was."

"Your daddy was a wise man, Angel. For some reason the words I need never come easy around you." He drew her close and turned her within his arms so that her back was cradled against his chest.

"Do you like this land, Dixie?"

"It's a good place for a homestead. Plenty of water, good grass—"

"Yeah, it's got that. This section of the Rocking K is mine." His voice was soft, he had made it so, but he could feel the tension that wrapped itself around her as surely as he had wrapped his arms to hold her close. It made no sense to him why she was tense. After all, he reasoned, he was the one who was about to make her an offer he'd never made to another woman.

"Would you be happy here, Dixie?"

The words were whispered in her ear and Dixie inhaled sharply, releasing the breath as a sigh and, with it, letting go of the tension that had held her. Ty's cheek nuzzled hers as he lowered his head and repeated the question.

"What are you asking me, Ty? Plain and simple, all right?"

"You don't have a home to go back to. I want to give you this land."

"Give me this land?" She spun around within the gentle cage of his arms to face him. "Why?"

He had hemmed and hawed all he was going to. Ty stepped back and rubbed his neck. "Plain and simple it is. I want you to give up this plan for revenge against Thorne. I want to know that you have a place of your own, where you will be safe. Conner likes you. He'll help you build a home here. The land is mine to do with whatever I want. I want to give it to you."

He reached for her, but she spun away from him and stared at the blue ribbon of water. "Is this why you brought me here, Ty? To make me a present?" The need to see him, to look into his eyes was overpowering. Dixie gave in and faced him. He hadn't moved, but his jaw had a stubborn set to it and his eyes were dark and narrowed.

"Is this the way you say goodbye? It must be expensive for your family if you offer land to every woman—"

"Don't say it, Dixie. Don't you dare cheapen what happened between us."

"I wasn't," she returned, then, in almost a whisper, she added, "I never did. I couldn't."

He closed the short distance between them. He knew his grip was hard as he caught her upper arms and hauled her against him. "Damn! I've made a mess of this. All I want from you is a promise that you'll forget about Thorne. It's not for a woman—"

"Ty, don't. Don't ask what I can't give you. This isn't your fight. I'd never ask you to make it yours."

"That bastard tried to kill you." He pressed two fingers against her lips to silence her. "Just listen to me. Please," he added at the mutinous look in her eyes.

"Just suppose you went after him and killed him. You think you have the stomach to live with that? I know what I'm talking about, Dixie. Killing a man is never easy. The memory always lives with you."

Ty slid his fingers down to cup her chin. "I've never told another woman I cared about her the way I do you. I've never needed a woman before. Can't you try to understand that I need to know that you're safe? That you have what you long for?"

"Ty." She closed her eyes against the need she could see for herself in his eyes.

"When you were ill you talked about home."

"Fever talk, Ty. That's all it was."

"No, I won't buy that. The words, the longings, those were from your heart, Dixie." With both hands he cradled her cheeks, gently, but forcing her nonetheless to look up at him. "Those words weren't lies. You have thought of what tomorrow will bring."

"And you? Do you ever dream of tomorrow, Ty? Do you long for a home of your own? A family?" The questions slipped out. She wished she could have stopped herself the moment he removed his hands from her face, his eyes briefly closed, his breath a sigh of regret. The realization of where this was all leading hit her with a sudden force. The dread that formed a knot in her stomach tightened to pain. *Ty was going to leave her.* All her hopes came crashing down. She had to face the questions he had asked her. Would she be able to live with herself after she killed Thorne? Was revenge worth the price to lose Ty?

She took that last as a given, for every instinct added reaffirmation that she would indeed lose him.

If she ever had him... and regardless of her decision about Thorne. After all, Ty was a maverick who wanted no shackles.

Chapter Nineteen

The first step away from Ty was the hardest one she had ever taken. The second, she found, was no easier, but definitely necessary for her own survival. When she had managed to put a few feet between them, Dixie turned and ran.

Ty didn't let her get far before he caught her up around the waist and stopped her cold. "Running isn't the right answer. It never was. I care about you." He allowed her to twist around and look at him, but he kept his arm about her waist.

"I care more for you than I have the words to say. I wasn't looking to get tangled up with any woman, Angel, but we both know how good intentions pave the road to hell. I couldn't live with myself if something happened to you." He searched her face, especially her eyes for some sign that he was making sense to her. But Dixie had learned to school her features into revealing only what she wanted. She'd learned how the hard way. He'd learned the same lessons, but he cursed them now.

He caught hold of her head, lowering his until his lips hovered above hers. "Don't shut me out, Dixie. Hear what I'm telling you."

Ty brushed his mouth over the tight line of hers, his chest burning, his throat constricted, but needing to say the words he'd never spoken to another woman.

"I love you."

The words were a whisper from dreams. He gave her no chance to answer, no chance to speak at all, for his lips closed over hers in a cherishing kiss that stole breath and reason with every second passing, until all she knew was Ty and the hunger he brought to life.

"Forget what I said," he murmured, his lips trailing kisses from her cheek to her jaw before tracing the curve of her ear. "All I want you to think about is us. No one else matters, Dixie."

For Ty the need to protect her was as strong as the need to have her admit she was his. He heard the underlying desperation in his voice as his murmurs drew dark, sensual images to life. But Dixie came to him like a desert bloom welcoming the rain as their lips met once more.

Dixie could taste the need in Ty from his kiss. There was desire, strong and hot, a burning flame that swept through her. But through passion's cloud, she still tasted Ty's need to protect her.

I love you. The most precious words she had ever longed to hear. Words that she never believed Ty would ever whisper to her. A small warning sounded in alarm, her own protective instincts trying once more to stop her from giving her heart to him.

It was too late. From the first, her heart had known what her head had refused to acknowledge—Ty was the man she could give her love to, he was the one who would cherish it and keep it safe.

Even as their kiss imitated the joining that would come, thoughts intruded. She fought them back. She didn't want to think of being forced to choose between Ty's love or her need for revenge against Thorne. She didn't want to think at all. Desire beckoned, offering her the chance to escape into the passion that rocked both their bodies, to a place where only feelings dwelled.

As if he had sensed her thoughts, Ty repeatedly whispered that she was to think only of them, nothing else and no one else mattered.

Only them. Only hunger.

She moved her hands to his chest, eager to slide open the buttons on his shirt, needing to touch his flesh.

Ty broke their kiss, pressing his forehead to hers, as if he understood her need, not only to touch, but to be in control. He was right to bring her here, to this place that was as free and untamed as her spirit, a spirit that had caught and held him from the first.

He felt the warm press of her lips against his chest as she spread open his shirt. He cradled her close and slowly rocked their bodies together as the desire heightened between them.

Guilt surfaced. He had told her he loved her, and to him, that meant sharing everything. He hadn't been able to tell her about Thorne, or what he planned to do.

As she lifted her head and her gaze locked with his, Ty knew he never could.

He freed her hair, spreading it over her shoulders. "I want to see you." He noted the fine trembling in his hands as he began to unbutton her shirt. "I want us to be together as if there were no place but here, no one in the world but us."

Lowering his head, he kissed the pulse in the hollow of her throat. "I want to love you as if it were the first time... the right time for us."

"Ty?"

With a kiss he stole the questing note in her voice, just as he stole her breath. His tongue teased the corner of her mouth, tantalizing her into wanting more, but his lips trailed fire down her throat.

She arched her back, feeling his tongue trace the lace edge of her chemise, his dark whispers of wanting her, only her, flooding her body and her mind.

His one arm caught her around the shoulders, supporting and half turning her as his other hand spanned her hip.

"You're strong and supple as a willow, Dixie. Wild and free as any spirit that roamed this land." Ty trailed his fingers up her side, teasing her and himself for long moments before he encircled her breast.

"Be wild for me, Angel. Just for me."

Through the thin cloth, Dixie could feel the heat of his hand. Gently, ever so gently and slowly, he began to brush his thumb over her nipple. She felt like a puppet whose strings had suddenly been pulled taut, every nerve demanding an end to the waiting.

Her legs threatened to give in to the fine trembling of her body and she clung to his strong shoulders. His ragged breaths heated already flushed, sensitive skin beneath the cotton.

"Ty, please . . ."

He lowered his head, his tongue flicking over the erect peak, fighting his own need to suckle her with the desire that turned his blood molten. He wanted to cherish her, cherish each moment of loving her, making it last and last as if this were the only time, a forever memory. Ty beat back the knowledge that it could be true. That he might never again hold her, kiss her, hear the soft sighs of pleasure and whispers of more that spilled from her lips to entice him to hurry.

He sank to his knees on a carpet of lush, thick grass, drawing her with him. The sweet, clean scent rose around them, but Ty drew in the heady fragrance of his woman's skin flushed with passion.

Dixie dug her hands into his hair and held his head against her. His lips sipped at her skin as he lowered the chemise and she shivered to feel the light rake of his teeth. His tongue moved gently to bathe her flesh, soft and wet and warm. And she knew he was holding back, trying to give her a gift of memory. It was all that held her silent when he drew her fully into his mouth.

Her knee was wedged between his powerful thighs and she moved as he coaxed her to straddle his leg. His dark murmuring voice between exquisite love bites tightened the coil of tension inside her until she bit her lip to still a cry.

"No. Don't hold back. I like hearing the sounds you make." Then in a softer, huskier whisper he added, "I want to hear you melt like sweet honey for me." Ty dragged one sleeve of her shirt off, then the other. "We don't need this between us." The shirt went sailing off to the side.

"And yours?" Dixie asked, already moving to discard his shirt. She couldn't stop herself from touching him. Her fingertips caressed him from wrists to shoulders, feeling the same fine sheen of sweat on his skin that covered her own, measuring the strength of his arms. She looked up at him, her head tilted to one side, her long hair falling across one shoulder, her eyes mirroring the desire that vibrated through her. She moistened her lips with the tip of her tongue, laughing softly when he bent to capture it.

Ty's mouth twisted in a cocky grin. He was held in the grip of a need so fierce he ached from its power. But he sensed her wish to slow things down. While half of him cursed himself for recognizing it, the other half was delighted to please her any way he could.

"A little hide-an'-seek?"

"Ty, it's just—"

"I know, Angel. Believe me, I know. You feel like you're dry timber and the fire's gonna consume you."

She held his gaze with hers for a long moment. "Yes. Like the fever's returned."

He leaned back a little and looked down at the thin chemise that still covered her. On one side the cloth was damp from his suckling, clinging to the hard tip. The sunlight filtering through the leaves of the cottonwood bathed her with a golden glow. He raised his hands to her waist, sliding the cloth of the chemise up very slowly.

"It's no fair for you to have this on. We'll never see how hot the fire can get." He scattered kisses over the skin he revealed, using his tongue to trace the undersides of her small, perfectly formed breasts. "An' my lady's a woman who wants things fair, doesn't she? Share and share alike? Both of us equal?"

"You're teasing me." The words ended on a moan. Dixie shivered to feel the edge of the cloth rub against the sensitive peaks of her breasts. Between them, his hair felt silky soft, another touch to tease and arouse her. She twisted to dislodge the cloth.

"Impatient, are we?"

"Yes. Damn you, yes."

"Then let's get rid of this." His hands slid up her rib cage, thumbs pressing against the sides of her breasts before he drew the chemise up and over her head. It too joined their shirts.

"Now for a little fairness." His husky laughter overrode hers when he bent her back over his arm and slowly lowered his head. His mouth fastened on her other breast and he wrung wild cries from her then, all he had wanted to hear, and more, for her cries became passionate demands.

Ty forced himself to ignore them for the moment. He raised his head a little, the subtle shift of their bodies bringing the feminine heat of her closer to his own violently aroused flesh. Brushing her hair back, he flicked his tongue against her ear, exploring the delicate curves as if for the first time. Knowing that she was as aroused as he was, he bit her lobe, instantly bathing it with the heat of his tongue.

Dixie slid her hands down his arms. Her fingertips made a gliding caress around his waist. With a sliding motion, accompanied by sounds of approval, she combed the damp, silky hair on his chest. She twisted her head to escape his marauding tongue, only to lean forward and use her own on the small brown nubs she discovered. His groan was her satisfaction.

"All's fair," she murmured, cupping his head to draw him down to meet her waiting lips. She held nothing back in her kiss, knowing how vulnerable it made her, knowing, too, that Ty had made himself just as vulnerable to her.

But she couldn't bring herself to whisper the precious words he had given to her. She couldn't tell him that she loved him. The belief was too strong within her that once those words fell from her lips, Ty would feel she was trying to shackle him into promises of tomorrow. She could show him that she loved him. Show him the force of the desire that swept through her as he lowered her to the grass and covered her with his body.

Ty braced himself on his hands, rising above her, his eyes studying her features. "I've never seen anything more lovely than you at this moment."

"Ty." His name was all she could manage.

"I want to capture this image forever and I want you so badly I'm shaking." He rocked back on his heels, his hands sliding down the length of her legs. With his gaze locked on hers, he eased her thighs apart, making a place for himself. He could feel the trembling that rippled over her body as he lowered his head and kissed first one thigh then the other.

"Mine," he whispered, his breath and kiss laying claim to the damp heat of her.

She wanted to touch him in return, but he forestalled her by moving down to take off her boots. His fingers tangled with hers as he opened the buttoned fly of her pants, paying homage with lips and tongue to each bit of flesh he revealed.

Her cry shattered the silence. Bathed in sunlight and shadows, Dixie held his head against her in the quaking aftermath. She had never dreamed of such intimacy with a man. Never knew that a man could love a woman without taking his own pleasure. She couldn't do more than murmur his name, even the effort of opening her eyes was beyond her. The moment Ty moved his head, she released him and heard the rustle of his own clothing being cast aside.

He came to her then, beneath the sky, all sleek heat and taut muscle, his voice whispering a litany of *I love you, I love you* until it was all she heard, and he was all she knew.

With his kiss she knew the tender lover was gone. There was urgency and desperation and possessiveness as he took her mouth with his. He drove into her with one powerful thrust and she held him tight, her fingertips digging into his shoulders.

Upon feeling the welcome her body offered him, the tight leash Ty had kept on his control snapped. She was sleek and tight, a fire burning bright. She wrapped her legs around him and he groaned, no longer able to separate sensations, no longer wanting to. Loving Dixie took him into uncharted territory. He had never felt as if his heart, mind, body and soul were joined so completely with another woman. The tiny ripples of release began for her all over again, drawing him deeper, until the world narrowed to a place where white-hot fire burned him to the marrow of his bones.

And she called to him with her woman's song, one older than time, a song filled with her joy and pleasure, and her unspoken love that entreated him to join her where she waited.

In the blinding moment before he spilled his seed into her, Ty knew he could never, ever let her go out of his life.

Awareness returned slowly to Dixie. Like gossamer veils, sensations and thoughts layered one upon the other.

The lightest of breezes came from the river, cooling heated skin and teased her with the scent of the sweet crushed grass beneath her body. Ty still lay upon her, his weight a warm heaviness she did not want disturbed. Each shaken breath she drew brought the dissipation of desire's mist that clouded her mind.

She refused the effort it took to open her eyes, content to remain still beneath him, measuring the slowing beat of their hearts. He lay with his face pressed against the side of her neck, his uneven breaths soothing to her ear.

My lady . . . I love you . . . think of you . . . only us . . .

The fragments rose from memory. There were no regrets mingled with repeating Ty's words to her. Dixie knew he had made a claim on her, there was no doubt that he loved her. No doubt at all that he had never said those words to another woman.

But why had he whispered those words to her without wanting something more? How could Ty tell her that he loved her and not want marriage? He had offered his land. It was almost as if he were leaving and not coming back.

She couldn't bear thinking about that. It brought pain and made her sigh a broken thread of sound.

A sound that roused Ty. Dixie used one hand to hold his head in place, unwilling to look into his eyes. And she was just as afraid to have him see what her own eyes might reveal.

She stroked his damp, silky hair, instantly noting the change in his breathing. He shifted his body, the move a subtle one, but expert enough to make her aware that they were still joined, still a part of each other.

Heat spread through her. His lips found all the small sensitive places on her ear and neck that brought shivers of sensual awareness. Dixie tightened her hold on him, her body eager to respond to the slow grinding move of his hips.

"Love me, Ty," she whispered, arching her neck and turning her head to an angle where their lips could meet. "Love me," she repeated, sealing her demand with a kiss.

If she loved him long enough, hard enough, she would have memories to last a lifetime.

"Anything, Angel. Everything you want." Ty could feel the tension that lay claim to her. There was a desperate, possessive neediness in her kiss that found its mate in him.

And he made a vow as he rolled onto his back and took her with him. He'd kill to keep her safe.

But now wasn't the time for thoughts of what he'd do to Thorne.

It was the time to show his woman that his words were not lies.

She straddled his hips, the sleek, damp heat of her thighs a flaming caress to his skin. "Share and share alike, Angel," he whispered. "Turnabout's fair play. Everything equal."

Dixie smiled at him. She felt no shame, no fear, for loving Ty was as natural as breathing, as if the Lord had created her for this one man. She tossed her hair back as Ty settled his hands on her hips. For the first time she felt the feminine power that was hers. She could bring him pleasure. She alone. The knowledge was there for her to see in his eyes.

Secrets. He could see them in the gleam of her eyes, the sweet curve of her mouth as she began to ride him.

"Glory, Angel. Sweet, wild glory is what we share. What we'll always share." Ty closed his eyes as she lowered her mouth to his. And he buried his lie of *always* a little deeper, until it joined his guilt about Thorne.

The day was branded with forever memories. Dixie cherished each moment. Sharing the bread and cheese he had thoughtfully brought along, drinking the cold, sweet mountain water, the teasing kisses that erupted into passion scorching enough to put a hot spring geyser to shame.

Ty was every dream she had ever had come to life. His tales of harrowing exploits to avoid Conner's belief that hard work and responsibility would be the making of him had her sides aching with laughter. In turn, she regaled him with adventurous stories of life with her father as they moved from place to place.

There were sober moments, too. The shared memories of childhood gave way to the awkward years. For Dixie, it was her need for a home, the longings that filled the dreams of her nights. For Ty, it was the need to find out who he was besides Conner's little brother and Logan's tag-along-for-trouble sidekick.

The heat of the sun rivaled the heat of the desire between them, and a shallow pool beckoned them for a swim. It was Dixie who began the childish play of splashing and ducking, and Ty whose challenge for a race ended in a kiss so cherishing she ached with the need to cry.

Later, wrapped in a blanket, Dixie rested her back against Ty's chest, her legs curled between the cradle of his. She told him of the night her father was killed, and the terror and guilt she had lived with ever since. And when she was done, he lowered her to the grass. With a tenderness that amazed him, as much as it demanded even more from him, Ty showered her with the most tender lovemaking until she cried from the exquisite beauty they could create together.

There was no past, no future, only the hours they spent together beneath the sky while a lone red-tailed hawk soared above them. Dixie chased the ghosts from his soul and he brought peace to hers.

Shame had no place here, and when she confessed her fear that her breasts were too small, Ty worshiped her with words, hands and mouth until she believed that perfection began and ended in her lover's eyes.

Dixie stopped counting the times he murmured that he loved her.

Ty was determined to wring those same words from her lips before he had to leave her.

She feared the growing tension in him came from his dread that she would demand marriage. She swallowed each *I love you* that rose to her lips.

A countdown of the hours he had left with Dixie added a dark and dangerous edge to his need for her. The more he attempted to bury his awareness of the lowering sun, the deeper the shadows played themselves over his lover's body.

Dusk laid its warning blanket over the land and, with reluctance, Ty urged her to dress. They made a last game of it—though neither one spoke of the need to go back—and shared last kisses, last touches before donned clothing brought the first separations to them.

"Ride with me," Ty whispered as they ended yet one more lingering kiss. "I want to hold you in my arms for every moment I can."

"Yes, I want that, too." Then, with an effort for a lighter note, Dixie added, "But there's tomorrow, cowboy. Did I ever tell you about this poker game I heard was played at the Queen Lily saloon?"

"Only heard about?" he teased, lifting her up onto his saddle and handing over the reins so she could lead her horse.

"'Fraid so." Her smile hinted of feminine secrets. She waited until Ty had swung himself up behind her, then settled back against his chest. "If you're nice to me I'll play poker with you where the stakes are ten times better than gold."

Ty ducked his head for a quick kiss. "Sounds risky."

"Could be," Dixie returned as he urged the horse into an easy canter. "You'll just have to wait until tomorrow to find out."

"Until tomorrow," he repeated, tasting the bitterness of the lie.

Chapter Twenty

It took every ounce of willpower that Conner possessed to turn away from Dixie's stricken expression. With one breath, he cursed Ty for leaving it to him to tell her that Ty was gone. With the other breath he damned himself for allowing his brother to ride off alone.

Not that Ty had offered him the choice. It was hard to admit that his little brother was a man. It was harder still to admit that his brother might not live to see the sun rise.

"Conner?"

He winced at the pleading tone of her voice. Schooling his features took a few seconds before he turned around to face Dixie.

"I know what you're gonna ask," he said in an effort to forestall her. "I don't know where he went. I don't know when he'll be back. And no, he didn't bother to ask what I thought of him going off without telling you." The lies tripped easily off his tongue, but then, he reminded himself, he'd been getting better and better at lying since Logan had left the ranch.

"I see." Dixie didn't think anything of the way his gaze cut off to the side of her. Impatience marked Conner, even standing still. She knew he wanted to get back to work, for she had stopped him when he rode in with a gather of culled cows. Two of his men would join with the three sent down by the Indian agent of the San Carlos Reservation to take the herd back.

Dixie spared a glance to where the cows milled in a close-packed sea of hides in the corral while the tally was made. She felt sorry for the animals that were cut from the herd simply because they could no longer bear calves, or never had. Pity for herself rose and she tamped it down with one ruthless thrust.

"Thank you, Conner. I'll let you get back to work. But I'd appreciate it if you have someone saddle that Indian pony. I can't pay you now but I will."

"Pay me? There's no need…" Conner's voice trailed off. "No. Forget leaving here. You're not well enough."

All she wanted to do was curl up somewhere and rid herself of the pain brought by Ty's abandonment. She did not want to argue with Conner. She did not want to stand there a moment more as an object of his pity.

Why? Why had Ty ridden off without a word? The oft-repeated question sent a fierce pounding beat in her temples.

Last night… Dixie wrapped her arms around her waist. Pain lanced her. She closed her eyes, seeing Ty as he had stood in the doorway of her room. He had lifted her hand and one by one kissed each of her fingers, then pressed her hand against her heart. *"Keep my love safe, Angel."*

She had thought he would kiss her once more, had even swayed toward him in invitation, but he merely grinned and teased her about giving him dreams enough for a lifetime. She had let him go then. The remembrance made her stifle a cry as tears burned her eyes.

"Hey, Conner, you gonna stand jawin' all day?"

"Keep your chaps on, Henley," Conner yelled back at the cowhand. "Dixie, go back up to the house. As soon as I finish up, I'll come by and we'll talk."

She nodded because it was what he expected. She even turned toward the house, but the sunlit adobe held no real welcome for her now that Ty was gone. She didn't belong here. No matter what Ty wanted. No matter what Ty said. She was not a Kincaid. She had no right to impose on them any longer.

But when she asked Santo to saddle a horse for her, she found out that Conner's word was law on the Rocking K. There would be no rides unless she asked for an escort. Her appealing to Macaria netted her the knowledge of where Conner and Ty got their steel core. Regal as any queen, Macaria was seated behind the massive desk in the study, calmly listening until Dixie was finished.

"My dear, you are our guest, not a prisoner. Conner only gave such orders for your protection."

"And Ty? What orders did he leave for me?"

"Only to keep you safe and to see that you had all you wanted." Shuffling the correspondence allowed Macaria to avoid Dixie's pain-filled eyes. As with Conner, Ty had given her no choice.

"And if I want my freedom?"

"Freedom?" Macaria's head jerked up, and her dark eyes pinned Dixie in place. "You want freedom to kill a man? Do not be shocked. Ty told me of your need to avenge your father's death. A most admirable desire, but have you ever thought that it is a woman who is given the gift to bring forth life? That a woman is the one who nurtures the children to grow straight and strong?

"She is the one who creates the civilized home, teaching those who grow within her care to live with a code of honor, to have beliefs that are fair for all. Without her, our lives are tainted by those who live without honor, without love. If you leave here now, you will risk losing Ty's love. Is that what you want with your demand of freedom?"

"No. I want to keep his love, but not at the price you believe."

"What I believed is that my son has misplaced his trust and love with a woman who cares nothing for his simple request that she remain where she would be cared for and safe." She forced herself to stand, bracing her hands on the desk as she leaned forward and met Dixie's stricken gaze.

"I am sorry if my truth has hurt you. Ty is my son, and you are the woman he loves. Remain with us until he returns. I promise you, it will not be too long."

"Why won't you tell me where he's gone?"

"Because he has asked me not to." Macaria, seated once more, lowered her head in dismissal.

She heard the sharp hiss of Dixie's breath, and without looking at the young woman whose fury was now turned upon her, Macaria added, "Stay with us, please."

Unwilling to be cowed, Dixie nodded, then said, "I will consider it. At least for today."

A grudging smile curved Macaria's lips. "By all means, take today to consider it." She was a strong woman, a fitting mate for her youngest son. If only...she banished the wish, for it was not her way and listened as Dixie closed the door behind her.

Ty felt as if a door had closed behind him once he crossed the Sand Tank Mountains. He blocked Dixie from his thoughts, not an easy chore, as he stayed north of the desert and found a dry ravine to camp in. He would be in Ajo by late afternoon.

He made his fire down the ravine a ways, dousing it once he'd made coffee. This was not a night when he could welcome a stranger to share his fire.

Settling himself to sleep, his gaze followed the dusting of clouds that trailed slowly across the quarter moon. He'd never set out deliberately to kill someone.

Time and circumstances made him react to the action at hand. But he had never hunted any man with murder on his mind. He wasn't a coward, had never been afraid of a fight, nor its outcome.

But he was afraid now. And the fear came from the insidious thought that he might not live to tell his woman she could have peace of mind and heart. That her father's killer had paid a just debt for the taking of another man's life.

There had been times in the past when he had lied to himself. This was not the night for lies. He faced his regrets as the hours slipped by, wishing for sleep, being denied that solace.

Against his will, he thought of Dixie. And he knew that no matter what tomorrow brought, he had made the right decision. The only decision. He couldn't have his woman tainted with the blood of any man on her hands. He loved her too much to let her ever live with the haunting ghosts that drifted through his nights.

As the stars began their retreat from the night's darkness, Ty once more built a fire. There was no hurry, only a deep calm as he sat cleaning his gun. When a gray dawn streaked the sky, he saddled up and rode for Ajo.

It was easy to detach himself from his intent. Emotions were wrapped as securely as the cinch belt around his horse's belly. He had left them behind, as he had left Dixie behind, and rode steadily through the morning's drizzle.

* * *

Ajo was a one-street town with hitching rails before most of the buildings. Ty was aware that he and his horse were being subjected to careful examination. He walked the stallion up the street heading for the livery stable. The blacksmith shop was conveniently across the street. The bank faced the mercantile, two saloons occupied opposite ends of the buildings. He noted the scattering of small houses beyond them, most of the yards bare, two fenced with the showings of gardens. Mud was already drying under the late afternoon sun as he stepped down and tossed the reins to the young boy who came forth from the stable.

The towheaded youngster stood calm, sizing Ty up, even as one hand was held flat out for the horse to lip. There was a world of knowledge in the washed-out blue eyes that met Ty's gaze with steady regard.

"There's an extra two bits for you to rub him down real good and grain him," Ty said. "An' another two for a little information."

A curt nod, and more quiet, patient acceptance from the boy. "Gonna be stayin' long, mister?"

"Not if I can help it." Ty snapped down the brim of his flat-crowned hat and slipped the rawhide thong off his holster. He slid his gun up and down a few times, satisfied with the smooth clearing of leather, then turned to look at the watchful boy once again.

"This the only livery?"

"Sure is, mister."

"Stranger ride in 'bout two, maybe three days ago?"

"Lots of strangers ride in, an' ride out again. Folks that ain't got business here tend to head down to Nogales."

With surprising directness the boy looked the man over. He appeared a cut above the usual drifter. It was a judgment he made based on the man's horse, whose sleek hide spoke of care and being grain fed.

"This man you're lookin' for, what's he look like?"

"Ugly as sin, 'bout twice as mean, with a heart so black the devil would have trouble welcoming him to hell."

A grin cracked the boy's thin lips. "Sounds like a lotta folks that pass through here."

"But this one has a scar," Ty noted softly. "Shaped just like a lightning bolt." It was only because he was watching the boy for a reaction that Ty caught the second's fear that appeared in the boy's eyes. It was gone in less time than it took for Ty to release his breath.

"Maybe I seen him. Then again, maybe I ain't."

Ty lifted a twenty-dollar gold piece from his shirt pocket. He held it high between his thumb and forefinger, angling it to catch the last dying rays of the sun.

"Now, boy, I've got a message to deliver to this man with the scar. But it's sort of a surprise. I'd be mighty grateful to know his whereabouts."

"He's an ornery son of a bitch," the boy announced in a matter-of-fact tone.

"That he is. The territory would be a safer place if his boots got planted somewhere. Here, catch."

The boy caught the coin and made it disappear into his pocket. "He's holed up at Nat Stargo's place." Stepping forward, he pointed to the saloon on the far side of the street. "Over there."

"Much obliged, boy." But Ty's thanks fell unheeded, the boy already having disappeared with his horse into the stable.

Ty walked diagonally across the street as if he had all the time in the world, as if murder weren't on his mind. Down the street a few hens cackled as they scattered to make way for a farm wagon rounding the end building. The wheels screamed for want of grease and the mules appeared in need of water. A scraggly group of children hung over the sides, staring at him with the same blank eyes as the man who drove them. Ty stood aside to let them pass, then made his way to the uneven wooden boards in front of the saloon.

If there was a sign, it was faded to the same weathered gray as the building. Slats were missing from the bat-wing doors. Ty peered in, noting the barkeep, who leaned against the far end of the bar reading a newspaper. Although the man hadn't moved, Ty sensed that he was aware that he stood outside, looking in.

In the corner near the stairs was a full table. Call it instinct, or lady luck, Ty knew Thorne was numbered among the men seated there.

Ty shoved open the bat wing and stepped inside. "Thorne."

One by one the men rose and backed away from the table. All but one. Ty said nothing. Nor did he move from where he stood. Thorne wasn't going anywhere.

As the men walked by Ty, he nodded to each of the Rocking K hands. There would be a bonus come payday for them.

"Barkeep," Ty called out, "this town got a preacher?"

"Ain't had a call for one," the man answered without looking up. "Appreciate you taking your business outside, mister. Glasses are hard to come by in these parts."

"Be glad to. Just waiting on the man there. Pity about the preacher. Man should have someone around to say a few words over him when he dies. Even for the likes of you, Thorne."

Thorne moved then. He fell to the side, taking the chair with him, firing and trying to scramble backward as he flipped over the table.

Ty made a diving roll that brought him around the far corner of the bar. Wood splintered off its edge as Thorne fired at him.

"That's two, Thorne." And to the barkeep, Ty yelled, "Any damages come out of his pocket. After his burying costs, of course."

The taunt had him duck low as three shots were fired in rapid order, punctuated by shattered glass and the fumes of rotgut whiskey. Ty had yet to draw his gun.

"Are your hands shaking, Thorne? It's time for you to ante up. Pity it wasn't you the lightning found on the mountain."

"Go to hell, Kincaid!"

"I've already been there. I watched Dixie battle death after you ordered Peel to shoot her. You're worthless scum, Thorne. Even hangin' you would be a waste of rope."

"You ain't the law, Kincaid. You'll hang if you shoot me. Those men'll be witness—"

"Those men work for the Rocking K," Ty announced in a cold, deadly voice. "And, Thorne, I'm all the law you're gonna get." Ty crouched down and slipped off his hat. He flicked the brim, then held it up and inched it over the top of the bar. He didn't believe that Thorne would fall for the old trick, but the second the hat cleared the bar top, the crown was decorated with a bullet hole dead center.

"I was right fond of this here hat, Thorne."

"You'll wear the next one to your grave."

Ty counted off the seconds, his muscles tense, a cold void filling him.

"But that was your sixth shot." It was all the warning Ty gave as he came up and out of his crouch to tear across the room to where Thorne cowered behind the overturned table.

With a vicious shove, Ty sent the table flying. His leap flattened Thorne beneath him, and the gun he'd been in the process of reloading went off. Ty knew he had only a few seconds while Thorne lay stunned from his fall. He clamped both his hands on Thorne's gun hand. He forced the barrel up against Thorne's head. Sweat dripped into his eyes, blinding him for a few moments as he strained to keep his grip.

"I want the name of the man who hired you to kill Dixie's father."

Thorne tried to buck him off, but Ty jammed his elbow into Thorne's throat.

"You can make your dying slow or fast if you give me the name, Thorne."

Once again Thorne tried to throw him off. Ty pressed harder with his elbow, cutting off his air.

"I gave you a choice. Now you and me are gonna play a little game I learned south of the border. I figure you managed to get two, maybe three bullets reloaded. What are the odds, Thorne, that if you pull the trigger you'll come up with an empty chamber?"

Ty knew he was squeezing the bastard's throat and chest so tight that the man could hardly draw a breath much less answer him. His only regret was that Dixie couldn't see the fear that gleamed in Thorne's eyes. The same fear of dying that she had known the night of Thorne's attack. But it was better this way. Better that it was just between him and Thorne. If Dixie was here, Ty wouldn't keep the calm edge he needed to finish this.

The fear that had sweat beading all over Thorne's face and body until the reek made Ty want to gag told Ty that he had guessed right. Thorne had reloaded at least two bullets into his gun before Ty had jumped him. If he hadn't the man would be spitting laughter at him.

"Blink your eyes if you wanna talk, Thorne. Like I said, fast or slow. But I'm gonna have the name." Ty wanted to taunt him, wanted to see terror in his face. He wanted payment for what Dixie had been through. He needed to know that Thorne faced the fact that he was going to die.

But Ty was no man's fool. He knew Thorne outweighed him and every moment's delay allowed Thorne to regroup his strength. Ty eased his elbow up from the man's throat.

"Chicken, Kincaid?" Thorne goaded, his voice reduced to a croaking sound. "Takes guts to pull the trigger when you're staring into a man's eyes."

"You wouldn't know. Back-shooting's more your style. Just like going after a woman earned your death." Ty's memory dragged up the sound of Dixie's voice recounting for him the pain and the terror this man had cold heartedly delivered. He fought the urge to pull the trigger himself and kill him. First, he had to have the man's name.

Ty moved then, removing one of his hands from Thorne's wrist to draw his own gun. He snagged the barrel under Thorne's quivering chin.

"I'm gonna let you have a choice, Thorne. That's more than you gave Dixie's father. More than you gave her and God knows how many others."

"An' I'm givin' you a choice, Kincaid."

Ty stilled as the chill metal of a gun barrel tickled the back of his neck. He knew the voice, even if now it sounded like sand was all the kid had had to drink for days.

"Cobie."

"You got that in one, Kincaid. Now, I got me a score to settle with Thorne—"

"No! He's mine." Ty couldn't swallow as Cobie pressed the gun barrel harder against the back of his neck.

"I ain't gonna jaw this over with you, Kincaid. That slimy bastard stole my horse an' left me to die up in 'em mountains. Ain't no man gonna get away with that. An' seein' as how I got the last gun in the line, I gets to go first."

Ty's body screamed with tension. He saw laughter in Thorne's eyes as Cobie ordered him to toss his gun across the floor. There was no way for him to get a shot off and disarm Cobie without risking getting shot by Thorne. His gun clattered against the planked floor.

"That's good, Kincaid. Now take hold of that army pistol this slime-bag here is so damn—"

"Now, boy—"

"Shut the hell up, Thorne! Ain't got no use for you. Worms ain't got use for the likes of you. I ain't no boy."

"Tell me the man's name, Thorne," Ty demanded. "Cobie isn't gonna let you live. No reason for you to keep protecting who hired you."

"Tell him, Thorne," Cobie ordered. "You're dead meat anyway you look at it. Maybe this hombre'll hire me in your place."

"Go to hell, boy." He looked back at Ty. "Kill him," he whispered. "Kill Cobie an' I'll tell you."

"I ain't got all day, Kincaid. Take his pistol an' toss it across the room."

Cobie prodded the barrel against Ty's neck twice before he forced himself to move. Hate consumed him as he wrenched the pistol away from Thorne and threw it out of reach. Cobie was going to cheat him of making Thorne pay. And he was as helpless as a babe in a cactus patch with that gun Cobie rubbed against his neck.

"Cobie, I'll make a deal with you. Let me have at him just long enough to get the name. It's all I want. You can have Thorne."

"Well, I already got him. You're a real accommodatin' fella, Kincaid. I'll remember that when it's your turn. Now, I don't wanna repeat myself, so listen good. You get yourself over to the other side of this bloated carcass. Do it nice an' easy, real slow like. That way I won't blow a hole clean through you, too."

"Cobie! It was rainin' so hard. I saw you go down. Can't blame me for thinkin' you was gone. I grabbed hold of that horse an ..."

Ty shut out the sound of Thorne's whining. He put no faith in Cobie stopping himself from shooting him, too.

He considered spinning around and taking the kid down by the knees. Ty lifted his leg to move. He looked down at Thorne, his gaze focusing on his lips. Ty thought of Dixie. He had come after Thorne because he didn't want her to have Thorne's blood on her hands. Would it be any better for Ty to go to her with the stench of Thorne on him?

He had told Thorne that he was the only law the man would know. But providence had sent Cobie here. What the hell difference did it make how justice was served?

"Kincaid?" Thorne mouthed. "Charles—" A shot splintered the planked flooring near Thorne's face.

"The only warning you get, Kincaid. Move off him."

Ty came down hard on his knee and rolled to the other side of Thorne. His move was fast. Cobie wouldn't fire at him when he had Thorne dead to rights. That was Ty's gamble.

As his dive took him within reach of his gun, Ty stretched his fingers out and touched his gun just as two shots and a thud sounded behind him. Another shot roared through the room, followed by another.

The smell of gunpowder filled every breath Ty inhaled. A bullet tore up the wood floor near his hand. He jerked the gun toward him, came up on his knees, spun and fired.

His shot was wasted. Cobie was already down, clutching his stomach. In Thorne's hand was a small over and under double-barrel derringer. It was only good at close range. God knew, Cobie had been close enough.

Ty came up out of his crouch carefully, keeping his gun aimed at Cobie. He walked the few steps to where the two bodies lay and stared down at them. The only regret he had was that he didn't get the man who hired Thorne. Charles was all he had for a name.

He holstered his gun and tossed a few gold pieces toward the barkeep who peered over the edge. "Make sure they get buried."

He was going home.

Home to Dixie.

Epilogue

Ty found Dixie right where Conner said she would be, right where she had been waiting each day for him to return. She sat beneath the shade of the lone, aged cottonwood tree, with her back toward him, the folds of a pale blue gown billowing around her. Sunlight threw glints of gold into her single long braid that fell dead center of her rigid back.

He could move with the same silence of a ripple of water when he wanted to, or had to, but he made no effort to hide his approach. Stepping down, he slapped the rump of his horse and left the reins to trail loose as a nickered greeting from hers beckoned.

Dixie didn't turn around, did not make any acknowledgment of his presence at all.

Ty had figured she would be angry with him, and when he stood in front of her and looked at the blaze of fury in her eyes, there was no doubt about her mood. The lady was in a tearing fury.

Ty wasn't about to apologize.

Dixie looked up at him. With the sun behind him, Ty was a tall, lithe shadow. Instinct warned her that he wasn't about to offer any reasons or explanations for his actions. He certainly wouldn't bother to apologize.

She wasn't about to let him even if he wanted to.

She pulled a gun from the billowing folds of her gown. "Sit down, Kincaid. I'm going to talk. You are going to listen."

"*A gun?* You're pulling a gun *on me?*"

Dixie didn't even blink. "Sure looks that way, doesn't it?"

"I'm unarmed. Haven't got a weapon on me."

"Pity. But we'll get to that later. Now, sit."

"Anything for the lady with the shootin' iron."

"Just remember that."

Ty noted the way she leveled the gun at him. He'd been the first to admit that Dixie knew which was the business end of a gun. He sat.

She raised her knees and wrapped her arms around them with the gun still pointed at him. It was the only way she could hide the fine trembling of her limbs as relief flooded her that he was unharmed.

"You had no right to go after Thorne by yourself."

"By your way of reckoning, I guess that's right. But he's dead, Dixie. Leave it be."

"You killed him?" She could barely get the words out.

"No. But I intended to. I went after him to kill him. Cobie beat me to it."

"Tell me."

Without embellishment, Ty told her what had happened. He left out his reasons for not telling her, just as he left out that he had learned the first name of the man who had hired Thorne to kill her father. She was silent as he spoke, so tensely silent, that he feared she was reliving every vile thing that had happened.

"Dixie?" Her eyes closed and he could have taken the gun away from her, but he had caught the glitter of tears. "Angel, it's all over. You'll never have to fear him again." Or anyone else, he silently vowed. If and when he found out who Charles was, Dixie wouldn't have to know anything about him.

"I know it's not the way you wanted or the way I intended to finish it, but Thorne's dead. Justice, or what passes for it out here, is served."

"I was so afraid that they would kill you."

Her whisper tore through him. Ty moved to take the gun from her, but she opened her eyes and motioned him back.

"Not so fast, Kincaid. You still have a lot to answer for."

"Yeah. I sure do. I tried to save your life. I tried to keep you from living with the nightmares that—"

"I know all that! For a man who didn't want any trouble, any complications in his life, you did foul things up. You had no right, none, Kincaid, to make decisions for me."

"I had no right?" Ty threw himself prone on the grass, locking his hands behind his head before he shook sense into her. "No rights, you say? The hell with that. I love you. That gives me one hell of a big right to do what I think best for you and for me. I offered you my land, along with giving you my love, and now I'm offering you marriage."

"Now?" Dixie nearly dropped the gun. "Now you offer... I can't believe I'm hearing this from you."

He rolled to his side and propped his head up with one hand. The other hand reached out toward her. "Are you gonna shoot me?"

"I'm still thinking about it."

Their gazes clashed. Ty felt as if his heart turned over. She was so proud, so hurt, that all he wanted to do was gather her up into his arms and keep her safe from the world. A foolish notion. Dixie wouldn't let him. But he had to try to make her understand.

"Angel, just listen to me with an open heart. I have never told another woman I loved her. I have never offered marriage to anyone. I never wanted to settle down and I—"

"Then why now? Why me, Ty?"

"I never met a woman who carried dreams in her eyes," he whispered softly, his voice husky with all the emotions churning inside him.

"I hated you for that. For making me remember what it was like to have dreams of love and a home."

"I know. It didn't sit easy with me to know that a woman could fill the empty places inside me that I didn't even know were there."

Dixie lowered the gun.

Ty moved closer.

"All I thought about these last four days away from you, Angel, was being able to hold you in my arms." He stared at her. There were no secrets in her eyes. He just longed to hear her speak the love that he saw within them.

"Your mother had quite a lot to say about a woman's place."

"Thank the Lord you are not my mother. I'm real good at avoiding shackles. I've had a marriage noose waiting—"

"I know. She told me. So did everyone else. Ty hates shackles. Now Ty wants marriage. Forgive me for finding it hard to believe."

"Let's get rid of this," he said, taking the gun and tossing it aside. "Believe me, you've got more powerful weapons to keep me in line." He came up to his knees and leaned forward to brush his lips against hers. "I'd kill for one of your kisses."

"Don't! Never say that, Ty. No more killing."

He leaned closer and nuzzled her cheek. He neither agreed nor disagreed with her. If the stranger whose camp fire he had shared on his way home was to be believed, he might not have a choice. Not if what the man said about Logan was true. But much as he loved his brother, and wanted answers about what had happened to him, he loved Dixie more. And he feared losing her.

The way she tilted her head invited his lips to trail kisses down her neck. The scooped, lace-edged neckline of her gown offered the enticement of more sun-warmed skin for him to taste.

Her voice stopped him. Her words made him back off.

"I want to believe you, Ty. With my heart I know that you love me. But I fear that marriage would only make you restless and one morning I'll wake to find you gone."

"Like I left you this time?" Regret laced his voice. "I don't know what to say to convince you. I've never wanted to watch a woman grow round with my child. But I've dreamed that about you. I've never thought about finding a woman with your spirit, strength and pride and wanting to have her beside me."

He used one hand to urge her knees down; with the other he caressed the curve of her belly. "You could already be carrying our child. I did nothing to prevent it."

"You could have—"

"Prevented it? Sure." His grin was pure devil. "I guess that even while I was fighting the rope that was wrapping itself around me, I knew I wasn't going to let you go out of my life."

"You are an arrogant, ordering kind of man, Kincaid." She slipped her hands around the back of his neck and barely touched his lips with hers. "I know you did what you thought was right about Thorne. I didn't want to have you carry the burden of his death—"

"It's over, done and gone. I'll give you so many happy thoughts you won't have room for him in your mind." He slid his hand around to the small of her back and stretched her out beneath him. "If loving you is what being shackled means, then lead me to the nearest blacksmith."

"You've got that mixed up, Kincaid. The preacher comes—"

"First," he finished for her. "But I'm a man who likes to stack the odds in his favor when he can. A pair of leg irons with you attached at the other end means you wouldn't be getting away anytime soon."

She cradled his cheeks and stared up into his dark blue eyes. Love waited there for her. "I don't know if I should throttle you or kiss you."

"Kiss me first. Then love me, Dixie. Love me an' I'll wear your brand for the rest of my life."

"High stakes, Ty."

"The highest. This man's heart," he murmured between ever-deepening kisses, "has been lost to the winner. And all the lady has to do is say three little words to collect her winnings."

"Just three?" she teased, holding his head for a soul-burning kiss.

When it ended, he braced himself above her. "Say the words. Say I love you, say you'll marry me, say you'll have my children and say you'll obey me."

Her eyes snapped open. "Obey you?"

"Aw hell, Dixie. You can't blame a man for trying."

"No, I won't do that. And I'll give you three of the four. I love you, Tyrel Kincaid. I will marry you and I will cherish bearing your children."

"Like I said, the lady holds the winning hand."

Held within his arms, dreamily feeding on cherishing kisses, Dixie felt she did indeed hold the winning hand. Her father's death had been avenged, peace would come. She had Ty's love and the home they would build and share. Her Kincaid had once been a maverick, but love, unconditional love, had placed a brand on him.

Her maverick, her love.

* * * * *

Harlequin® Historical

What do A.E. Maxwell, Miranda Jarrett, Merline Lovelace and Cassandra Austin have in common?

They are all part of Harlequin Historical's efforts to bring you longer books by some of your favorite authors. Pick up one of these upcoming titles today and see what a difference an historical from Harlequin can make!

REDWOOD EMPIRE—A.E. Maxwell Don't miss the reissue of this exciting saga from award-winning authors Ann and Evan Maxwell, coming in May 1995.

SPARHAWK'S LADY—Miranda Jarrett From this popular author comes another sweeping Sparhawk adventure full of passion and emotion in June 1995.

HIS LADY'S RANSOM—Merline Lovelace A gripping Medieval tale from the talented author of the Destiny's Women series that is sure to delight, coming in July 1995.

TRUSTING SARAH—Cassandra Austin And in August 1995, the long-awaited new Western by the author whose *Wait for the Sunrise* touched readers' hearts.

Watch for them this spring and summer wherever Harlequin Historicals are sold.

RUGGED. SEXY. HEROIC.

OUTLAWS and HEROES

Stony Carlton—A lone wolf determined never to be tied down.

Gabriel Taylor—Accused and found guilty by small-town gossip.

Clay Barker—At Revenge Unlimited, he *is* the law.

JOAN JOHNSTON, DALLAS SCHULZE and MALLORY RUSH, three of romance fiction's biggest names, have created three unforgettable men—modern heroes who have the courage to fight for what is right....

OUTLAWS AND HEROES—available in September wherever Harlequin books are sold.

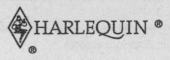

HARLEQUIN ®

Harlequin® Historical

WOMEN OF THE WEST

Exciting stories of the old West and the women whose dreams and passions shaped a new land!

Join Harlequin Historicals every month as we bring you these unforgettable tales.

May 1995 #270—**JUSTIN'S BRIDE**
Susan Macias w/a Susan Mallery

June 1995 #273—**SADDLE THE WIND**
Pat Tracy

July 1995 #277—**ADDIE'S LAMENT**
DeLoras Scott

August 1995 #279—**TRUSTING SARAH**
Cassandra Austin

September 1995 #286—**CECILIA AND THE STRANGER**
Liz Ireland

October 1995 #288—**SAINT OR SINNER**
Cheryl St.John

November 1995 #294—**LYDIA**
Elizabeth Lane

Don't miss any of our **Women of the West**!

HARLEQUIN®

Don't miss these Harlequin favorites by some of our most distinguished authors!
And now, you can receive a discount by ordering two or more titles!

HT #25559	JUST ANOTHER PRETTY FACE by Candace Schuler	$2.99	☐
HT #25616	THE BOUNTY HUNTER by Vicki Lewis Thompson	$2.99 U.S./$3.50 CAN.	☐
HP #11667	THE SPANISH CONNECTION by Kay Thorpe	$2.99 U.S./$3.50 CAN.	☐
HP #11701	PRACTISE TO DECEIVE by Sally Wentworth	$2.99 U.S./$3.50 CAN.	☐
HR #03268	THE BAD PENNY by Susan Fox	$2.99	☐
HR #03340	THE NUTCRACKER PRINCE by Rebecca Winters	$2.99 U.S./$3.50 CAN.	☐
HS #70540	FOR THE LOVE OF IVY by Barbara Kaye	$3.39	☐
HS #70596	DANCING IN THE DARK by Lynn Erickson	$3.50	☐
HI #22196	CHILD'S PLAY by Bethany Campbell	$2.89	☐
HI #22304	BEARING GIFTS by Aimée Thurlo	$2.99 U.S./$3.50 CAN.	☐
HAR #16538	KISSED BY THE SEA by Rebecca Flanders	$3.50 U.S./$3.99 CAN.	☐
HAR #16553	THE MARRYING TYPE by Judith Arnold	$3.50 U.S./$3.99 CAN.	☐
HH #28847	DESIRE MY LOVE by Miranda Jarrett	$3.99 U.S./$4.50 CAN	☐
HH #28848	VOWS by Margaret Moore	$3.99 U.S./$4.50 CAN.	☐

(limited quantities available on certain titles)

	AMOUNT	$
DEDUCT:	**10% DISCOUNT FOR 2+ BOOKS**	$
	POSTAGE & HANDLING ($1.00 for one book, 50¢ for each additional)	$
	APPLICABLE TAXES*	$ _____
	TOTAL PAYABLE	$ _____
	(check or money order—please do not send cash)	

To order, complete this form and send it, along with a check or money order for the total above, payable to Harlequin Books, to: **In the U.S.:** 3010 Walden Avenue, P.O. Box 9047, Buffalo, NY 14269-9047; **In Canada:** P.O. Box 613, Fort Erie, Ontario, L2A 5X3.

Name: _____

Address: _____ City: _____

State/Prov.: _____ Zip/Postal Code: _____

*New York residents remit applicable sales taxes.
Canadian residents remit applicable GST and provincial taxes.

HBACK-JS2

THREE BESTSELLING AUTHORS

HEATHER GRAHAM POZZESSERE
THERESA MICHAELS
MERLINE LOVELACE

bring you

THREE HEROES THAT DREAMS ARE MADE OF!

The Highwayman—He knew the honorable thing was to send his captive home, but how could he let the beautiful Lady Kate return to the arms of another man?

The Warrior—Raised to protect his tribe, the fierce Apache warrior had little room in his heart until the gentle Angie showed him the power and strength of love.

The Knight—His years as a mercenary had taught him many skills, but would winning the hand of a spirited young widow prove to be his greatest challenge?

Don't miss these **UNFORGETTABLE RENEGADES!**

Available in August wherever Harlequin books are sold.

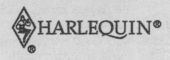

HARLEQUIN®

FLYAWAY VACATION SWEEPSTAKES!

This month's destination:

Glamorous LAS VEGAS!

Are you the lucky person who will win a free trip to Las Vegas? Think how much fun it would be to visit world-famous casinos... to see star-studded shows...to enjoy round-the-clock action in the city that never sleeps!

The facing page contains two Official Entry Coupons, as does each of the other books you received this shipment. Complete and return all the entry coupons—**the more times you enter, the better your chances of winning!**

Then keep your fingers crossed, because you'll find out by August 15, 1995 if you're the winner! If you are, here's what you'll get:

- Round-trip airfare for two to exciting Las Vegas!
- 4 days/3 nights at a fabulous first-class hotel!
- $500.00 pocket money for meals and entertainment!

Remember: The more times you enter, the better your chances of winning!*

*NO PURCHASE OR OBLIGATION TO CONTINUE BEING A SUBSCRIBER NECESSARY TO ENTER. SEE REVERSE SIDE OF ANY ENTRY COUPON FOR ALTERNATIVE MEANS OF ENTRY.